DIDN'T I WARN YOU

AMBER BARDAN

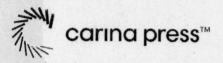

ISBN-13: 978-0-373-00394-5

DIDN'T I WARN YOU

www.CarinaPress.com

Printed in U.S.A.

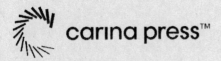
carina press™

Didn't I Warn You
By Amber Bardan

Not everything dangerous is bad.

From the moment Angelina laid eyes on him, she fell into a fantasy. Mysterious, foreign, gorgeous, Haithem offered her what she needed most—a chance to feel again.

But Haithem is much more than he appears to be. He lives in a world of danger where everything comes at a price.

For Angelina, that price is her future.

He's ensured the life she's left behind is in tatters. Made her family believe she's dead. He talks about protecting her, about keeping her safe, but she can't distinguish his truth from his lies. She can't separate her pleasure from his betrayal.

Haithem warned her. He told her he'd make her heart race, her body come alive, and her most primal needs rush to the surface. His for the taking.

He didn't say she'd come to love the devil who's destroying her, even as he keeps her prisoner.

Dear Reader,

Maybe the term *antihero* isn't a new one, but it does seem to be something that's been getting a lot of buzz in the past year or so in the romance world. But what is an antihero? In my mind, the antihero is one who has to be redeemed, providing a delicious platform for character growth and emotional conflict. But even though he's an antihero, perhaps doing morally questionable things we can't always approve of, he still proves his love and devotion to the heroine, providing us as readers with the opportunity to enjoy seeing a real bad boy get his happy ending.

I love a great antihero, and this April I'm pleased to introduce you to Haithem, from *Didn't I Warn You* by Amber Bardan. Mysterious, foreign, gorgeous, Haithem has a secret, and it's one he'll kill to protect until he accomplishes the goal he's set out to achieve. Lucky for Angelina, he chooses not to kill her...but he does kidnap her, holding her against her will, using her body against her. And when he ultimately becomes incredibly possessive of her... Haithem offers Angelina a chance to feel again. But can she love the devil who's destroying her, even as he keeps her prisoner?

Mr. Sexy *Bazillionaire* CEO Gregory Ryans might not be an antihero, but that doesn't make him any less compelling. The second installment of Laura Carter's darkly sexy Vengeful Love trilogy, *Vengeful Love: Deception*, is packed with tension. Adrift in the aftermath of a murder, each desperate to protect the other, Scarlett and Gregory are faced with a harsh truth: there are some things money can't buy.

Jen Doyle debuts with her contemporary romance, *Calling*

It. After a car accident nearly ends his career and with paparazzi surrounding his Chicago penthouse, professional baseball player Nate Hawkins can only think of one place to go: home. But when he finds his old apartment occupied by a half-naked woman wielding a baseball bat, he's not sure what to think…except that maybe his luck has finally changed for the better.

Also with a contemporary sports romance release this month is Elizabeth Harmon and *Getting It Back.* If you're a sucker for a second-chance romance, this one will be right up your alley with a former top men's figure-skating champion who's willing to risk everything for a comeback—except a new start with the only woman he's ever loved.

Mia Kay keeps things suspenseful. In her romantic suspense *Hard Silence,* an FBI profiler chasing an interstate serial killer never expects his love life and his professional life to collide. But he gets more than he bargained for when he falls for the lovely, secretive ranch owner—who just might hold the key to his investigation.

Move a little mystery into your life! In *Permanently Booked* by Lisa Q. Mathews, May-December sleuthing duo Summer Smythe and Dorothy Westin are back on the case after the murder of a dedicated librarian. To lure the killer out of hiding, they revamp the once-dull Hibiscus Pointe Book Club—and discover someone's added more than wine, cheese and book talk to the agenda.

If antiheroes are something you're looking for more of, we hope you'll check out *Didn't I Warn You.* And maybe take a peek back at Joely Sue Burkhart's *One Cut Deeper* and *Two Cuts Darker.* Coming in July, don't miss badass biker

Dare as he takes on his feisty heroine in Jade Chandler's new erotic motorcycle club series, The Jericho Brotherhood.

Coming next month: The fantastic conclusion to the Vengeful Love trilogy, male/male new-adult fare to make you happy, make you sigh and make you wish the authors would write faster, and an erotic new series from Anna del Mar.

As always, until next month here's wishing you a wonderful month of books you love, remember and recommend.

Happy reading!

~Angela James
Executive Editor, Carina Press

Dedication

Thanks for being my first fan.

PROLOGUE

LONG FINGERS CLOSE around my throat. Not squeezing, not hurting, but commanding. I look at him. This man I love. This devil I adore. He's gorgeous—dark hair, darker eyes, olive skin, body and features all chiseled hardness. But that's not what makes my veins jump under his hand. That's not what makes my skin slick with sweat.

There's more to this man than meets the eye.

His thumb strokes my pulse, gleaning secrets right out of my blood. His mouth curls to the side, forming a smile that reveals he knows exactly what I'm thinking.

"Didn't I warn you, Angel," he says, and his thumb moves up to my chin, "that it's not a good idea to love me?"

My pulse leaps from erratic to chaotic. I can't answer, only listen in horrified fascination to what I know will come next.

He traces the groove below my bottom lip. "Didn't I warn you my love would be bad?"

Shivers run hot then cold over my skin.

"Didn't I tell you, you'd pay for my heart?" He touches my mouth, dragging my bottom lip down.

My body sings, my blood hums right down to my womb. I can't resist him. He did warn me. He truly did. But I was greedy. I wanted him anyway.

I didn't understand how bad he could be.

He's the devil. Tempting me with what I desire most. Luring me to an irresistible destruction. A destruction I'm so close to I can smell it—taste it—touch it. Pain grips me, my insides bruise with it. My family believes I'm dead. The life I've left behind lies in tatters because of him. Because he keeps me.

He won't let me go.

He tilts my face, brushing his cheek against my ear. "I promise it will be worth it." His stubble chafes my earlobe, stinging and electrifying. I've felt those bristles scrape against my neck, my breasts, my thighs. There's not an inch of me that hasn't felt the sweet torture of their abrasion. "Can't you see it?" he asks. "The future where you're mine?"

My eyelids drift shut. I know it's only the hand cradling my face that's holding me up. I *can* see that future. I see it with fluorescent intensity. Life with the lights turned on. Life where living means more than existing. For everything he's taken from me, he's given me back more. He breathed a soul back into me. Without it, without him, I'd be a walking corpse.

I see our future. I ache for it, yearn for it, despise myself for it.

"Say it, Angel. Say, Haithem, I'm yours."

For all intents and purposes, I'm a prisoner—captive—perhaps even a slave. Because I have no choices but the ones he gives me. Yet, he gives me this choice— or at least the illusion of a choice—to choose him.

To love him.

As if making a choice had ever been an option. The moment I met him, I may as well have been branded.

ONE

One month earlier.

TROUBLE. NOPE, I DIDN'T love trouble, even if my foot did have a tendency to find its way into steaming piles of it. Like the time I failed my driving test, swerving for ducks only to plow right over a letter box. Yet, when trouble walked in—snug suit jacket clinging to too-broad shoulders, the sharpest gaze I've ever seen ripping through the café—my attention homed right in on trouble.

His chin jerked toward the person next to him. The other man slipped ahead, responding to the silent command by making his way to the back of the room.

I stared. *A little more.* He just needed to move about thirty degrees clockwise and—

He shifted, blasting me with the full impact of *him* front on. His gaze met mine the way lightning meets the sea. *Electric.* Black eyes burned a trail over me. The dark of his irises flicked between darker lashes, taking me in and peeling back the world.

No more café. No more dry Melbourne heat pushing sweat from my scalp into my hair. No more job interview in forty-five minutes. Only the sharp angles of a face that could have been cut from granite.

Oh, sweet god of chin dimples.

I swallowed, the bitter linger of coffee bouncing off

the back of my taste buds. Those eyes tracked the movement, almost as though he'd caught the secret slide of my tongue against my palate.

The table jerked. A cool spray splattered my neck.

The world burst back into focus—scraping chairs, humming voices, waitress walking right into my table...

"I'm so sorry." She slammed the tray down not two inches from my open laptop and set the empty glass of juice, the contents of which trickled down my chest, upright. "It's my first day."

I ran my hands down my throat, attempting to halt the slide of liquids to my brand new job-interview attire. "It's okay."

She tugged napkins from the dispenser. "I'm really sorry. There's orange juice on your shirt."

I scooped the napkins out of her hands and patted over my chest. Yep, of course she was right. A slash of orange streaked between my first and second buttons.

I took a breath. "It's okay. May I have a soda water?"

"Of course." She scooped up the empty coffee cups from my table and collected the tray.

I glanced at the laptop, blessedly spared a juicy coating. The cursor flashed at the top of the article I'd been working on.

"Aged Care Crisis—How everyday Australians are at risk of homelessness."

A laugh burst from my lips, and I clamped a fist to my mouth. The laugh turned to a nasal snort. Homelessness, not funny whatsoever. Yet the idea of turning up at *Poise* magazine, orange stain between my boobs, sweat I could literally feel spawning some kind of frizz demon in my hair, well, it would be no shock if they suggested I perform a little investigative journalism on the matter.

Like the deep-undercover, pushing-around-a-shopping-cart kind of investigative journalism.

"Here's your soda water."

"Thanks." I took the bottle and cracked the lid, then poured some out onto fresh napkins.

"Can I get you something else?"

My belly piped up like the over-excited child it tended to be. But I hadn't lost a dress size for nothing. "Just another coffee, please."

I wiped at my blouse, undoing the top button for maximum stain access. Dammit, juice managed to soak into my bra. My nice white one, too.

Excellent.

Tiny bumps rose where I wiped, a shiver rippling through my extremities. I looked up, dropping the napkins.

He stood right where my gaze had left him—facing me. As though he hadn't taken a breath since I'd stooped looking at him. His brows pushed together, as though maybe he were lost. I glanced behind us. People sat around tables. The man he'd been with earlier was nowhere to be seen.

I turned back to chin-dimple dude. His eyes moved just a fraction. It took a moment to realize where he'd stolen a peek.

I'd left my shirt open.

Heat flooded every limb, but something else, too. Something that made my spine go straighter and made my chest snap farther out. His gaze flew back to mine, and he smirked. An expression so close yet so far from a smile my chest hurt from it. Everything went liquid hot. My insides pounded warm and fluttery, yet also heavy.

There stood trouble all right. I experienced the full breadth of that trouble as a sucker punch to my vagina.

Did he want to see my boobs? That was a thing I could do. They'd have an "out the back" here, wouldn't they? Like an alley or something? I could handle soft-core flashing. Why not? No one else had seen them since—let's not even think about when.

Suddenly, he looked over me and strode through the café.

He walked right past me.

My arm almost shot out to stop him.

I forced my palm onto the table and let him go. My heart pitter-pattered around my rib cage. Air rushed from my lips. I knew this feeling...*excitement*. The real, actual kind. Not the supposed-to-be type. A slow smile widened until it stretched my cheeks to an ache. Well, that was nice. I could still feel that. It'd taken a while, but I was glad the feeling still lived in me. I'd almost given up.

Haithem

THE NAPKIN SCRAPED over the underside of my jaw before I scrunched it in my palm. She was a problem.

A problem that plowed through me like a train the instant I'd entered. Stealing the concentration from my mind.

Who the hell is she?

A billion possibilities swarmed. Had someone sent her to watch me? The waitress set a cup on her table. She smiled in thanks, cheeks dimpling. No, of course not.

Just a girl drinking coffee…

Yet, the thump under my ribs didn't slow. Now even sweetly smiling women sent suspicions coursing—this is what had become of me. The men at my table babbled nonsense that didn't bear listening to. I was about to educate them exactly how things would be.

But her.

She tossed her head again. A hand through her hair and chin to her shoulder. Did she think I wouldn't notice?

Or did she want me to?

If so, I should find out why. I dropped the napkin into an empty glass. How did things proceed like this? In the day. In public. I rubbed my fingers against my thumb. When was the last time I'd met a woman in daylight? Or one who wasn't ready, hand out, rules set?

From where we sat, I had the gift of her profile. It wasn't enough. Her bottom lip caught between her teeth, then popped back out.

My balls contracted. Went full and heavy. I might excuse myself for a moment, go over and—

No.

I expelled a breath. Whatever she was up to, she was too young for it. The girl was too young for me. Even if I couldn't remember the last time a woman had made me fidget. Or made me want to crawl out of my skin just to get to her.

"Haithem," Karim whispered.

This wasn't the time for distractions.

Today's company was a precious few that knew who I was and craved something from me other than spilling my blood. That didn't warrant complacency. I focused on the men across from me. They already knew I was the real deal. The sweat beading across Steve Parker's nose, and the way his tongue darted to the corner of his thin lips revealed negotiations would be wrapped up by the time I finished my tea. Steve's partner, Brad, was harder to read. He didn't sweat, didn't shift, but I didn't miss the tension corded in Brad's neck, either. They knew what was going to happen—that they were about to be the first people in the world to gain access to something that until now had only been dreamed about. I'd have them folding before they knew bargaining had begun.

"So, do we have a deal or not? We're losing patience."

My chin lowered at Brad's question. Direct. Good, things would move even quicker.

"There's no reason to lose patience. Considering the personal risk I'm taking just in being here, I'm sure you can appreciate my reluctance to commit until all my terms are met."

My gaze shifted over Brad's shoulder. *Dammit.* She baited me again, pale eyes boldly flirting in my direction. Her cheeks were flushed, and her lips parted as if she'd been running or was freshly fucked—or perhaps just wanted to be…

Karim cleared his throat. I presented Steve my final offer. Time to finish this. There'd be opportunity for play later. Five years of hell and we were about to make the deal that would change the world—yes, change the world—and cement the price on my head. Normally, this kind of business was done at night, in empty construction sites or parking lots. But I'd learned that sometimes the best place to hide is in plain sight. To anyone listening, this would sound like any average business lunch.

They'd be wrong.

I didn't need to look to sense her eyes on me once more. My muscles tightened, but I resisted the urge to give her a taste of my full attention. I studied her in my peripheral.

She rubbed the bare expanse of her arm below the sleeve of her blouse, and tilted her head slightly away from us.

She's listening.

The lust, only just acknowledged, morphed into something harder and meaner. Did she spy on me?

I responded to Brad's futile negotiations without narrowing my vision.

Who is she?

Brad and Steve caved at half a cup of coffee then took their leave through the rear entrance of the café. Karim and I had agreed we'd wait ten minutes before leaving for the next meeting in the building across from us. I'd have waited anyway.

Waited just to find out what she thought she was doing.

I'd have waited to see if her voice was as husky as I imagined it'd be. Or if it'd be light and musical.

Husky, I knew it'd be husky.

If it wasn't for today's business, I'd be right over there, offering what she clearly wanted. Maybe. If I wanted to break the rules.

"It's been too long since you enjoyed company, Haithem."

I drained the remainder of my tea and eyed my assistant over the lip of the cup. "We've been busy."

"Yes, and now you're getting distracted. Invite the girl to a hotel for an hour and clear your head."

I set down the cup with a clank. Too tempting, and a bad idea. She wasn't my type. Not my type at all. Plus I didn't like the way her attention fixed on me. "I'd need more than an hour."

"Then take it. There's a long trip ahead of us, there may not be a next time."

We didn't need to leave until morning.

I could take her now.

Just stride over there and tell her what I wanted, give her an offer she'd *never* refuse. My thigh brushed the table, and I glanced down. I'd stood without meaning to. A scowl twisted my lips. No, not what I needed. There was too much to be done.

Yet, it wasn't only the twenty-five minutes of silent flirtation making me want to finish the job. I'd wanted her from the moment our gazes locked. There was something there—in those pale eyes. Secrets I wanted to uncover.

All reasons why I had to leave her alone.

TWO

My entire midsection reached critical-point spasm. I'd heard his voice at least three times. Not close enough for words to actually be distinguishable but enough that the sound of him vibrated along my nerves. My fingertips shook while I pretended to use the laptop. I should've eaten. Would it have hurt to have one biscuit with those three coffees? I breathed in. The control-top panty hose beneath my skirt clutched my hips like the devil's tourniquet. My fingers splayed on my belly. That's right, no food babies allowed before interviews with trendy magazines.

But I hadn't eaten since breakfast, then there was this guy messing with my signals… Hunger and horniness all mixed together, encroaching on brain space, bringing about the legitimate possibility that I might go over there, eat that guy, then go hump the pastry counter.

Get. It. Together.

I shook my head and shoulders. Okay, commencing concentration. A voice, octaves lower than every other sound, filtered toward me. I brushed the hair back from my ear and tilted my head. Tried to get that sound as much *in* me as I could.

A scrape of chairs almost knocked my heart out of my chest.

Probably due to all the attempted eavesdropping. Not gonna lie—it wasn't an accident. Whatever he was talking about, I was 500 percent sure was way more interesting than anything I'd heard today. *Possibly ever.* I glanced at my phone, then picked it up and unlocked the screen. Freaking hell, any moment he'd leave and I wouldn't even have a photo of him to prove his existence to my best friend, Emma. Men like him didn't just wander into little Melbourne coffee shops—at least, not when we were around to enjoy looking at them.

Slow, swaggering footsteps padded behind me.

The phone clattered from my hand onto the table and my folder jumped like a cricket onto the floor. I reached for the folder.

My hand landed on another hand. A bigger, browner one, smooth and warm under my fingertips.

My breath froze. He crouched beside the table yet managed to still tower. He leaned on his heels and stretched an arm toward me. The folder lay in his grasp. I couldn't take it—no matter that's what you're supposed to do when someone hands you something. A smile twitched his cheek.

He looked up at me entirely too long before speaking. "You should be more careful, Angelina."

His voice wafted over me like an exotic breeze. Deep, warm and laced with something foreign, a subtle clip of accent. Then his words sank in.

Angelina...

The heartbeat fluttering away against my ribs stilled. How the hell did he know my name? I recoiled against my seat.

His eyes widened a fraction before his lips spread in a grin—a freaking sexy grin, revealing teeth that could sell the crap out of toothpaste. He tapped my folder, a long finger pointing to the name printed in bold font, directly above the contact details on the résumé in his hand.

Of course…

Just because I'd proved that hair color has no bearing on intelligence didn't mean he should enjoy watching me squirm.

Dammit, of course a guy that hot had to be a prick.

I reached out, half smiling, then tugged the folder from between his fingers. My face lingered inches from his, close enough to see the chocolate flecks in his dark eyes.

"Oh, I'm *always* careful…" I enunciated slowly. *But why stop there?* "Sir."

Those magnetic eyes intensified, and a look of something I didn't quite recognize flashed in their depths.

"Is that so, Angelina?" My name curled like smoke off his tongue, and I swear the sound of it reached out and licked me.

It took three long heartbeats for realization to click into place. The implication of what I'd said settled slowly between us. Heat prickled my neck and up to my face.

Careful girls don't *accidentally* stare at men. Careful girls don't *accidentally* let strange men see them wipe their breasts. Careful girls don't *accidentally* tip their folders at the feet of said strange men.

My stomach flipped over.

Oh no.

I clutched the presentation folder and turned away. He rose beside me. For a few pregnant moments, I sensed his stare boring into me. Whatever he waited for, I didn't give to him.

"Very well… Good luck at your interview."

His shoes clicked on the tiles. Some part of me wanted to look up, even call him back.

I breathed out and set the folder down and shut the laptop. *Maybe it's time to see the shrink again?*

I packed up my things, curled the cords, stashed everything in my handbag and went to the counter.

"It's all been taken care of."

I stared at the waitress. Poor girl, it wasn't her day. I hoped she didn't get fired. But then she kinda sucked at waitressing, so maybe it'd be for the best.

"No, I sat over there." I pointed at the booth. "Table five."

"Yes, that's the table. The guy you were speaking to took care of the bill."

"Oh." I blinked, then glanced between the booth to the front door. He'd paid my bill and left? "Um, thanks."

I slid my purse back into my bag and left the café. Why'd he do that? Maybe it was an apology for being a smart-ass?

A delicious smart-ass...

It wasn't as if he could get something out of the gesture. He must've done it because he liked me. Yeah, I'd leave it at that. He'd totally paid the bill because he was besotted with me. I snickered to myself. A girl's entitled to her fantasies. A horn beeped. The crossing signal flashed.

I crossed the street to the building opposite and pushed the bewilderment from my system. Spotting the elevators at the far end of the room, I raced in my heels toward them. A rush of people exited. I stepped back. More people pushed out of the elevator than stepped inside—not surprising, given my interview was the last of the day. Two women stood in front of me. Their perfume filled the space, thick enough to coat my tongue.

Geez, I'd forgotten to wear perfume. Was I supposed to? They weren't wearing shirts and skirts, either. They wore chic city dresses—the kind that made me choke when I looked at the price tag. My fifty-dollar shirt didn't feel quite as fancy.

The elevator glided up. My nerves seemed to be racing up faster than the elevator was hitting floors. I squeezed the leather strap of my bag. Maybe this wasn't the job of my dreams, it wasn't writing plays for Broadway, but it was a writing job.

I'd be happy with that. Any writing job would do.

Any job that got me out of my parents' house would be just fine.

TINA, CHIEF EDITOR for *Poise*, glanced up from my article. "Well, you can write. Very well, actually. And all this research, technically it's a great article." She looked at her colleague Fey. "It's just that—"

Fey dropped her paper. "—it's boring."

"Yep, boring." Tina nodded.

My chest, the great brick of tension that it was, bottomed out so hard I wondered that my blood still flowed. *I knew it.* I didn't let my shoulders roll, though. The interview wasn't over yet.

"Don't you have parents, grandparents? Elderly people that you like perhaps?" My gaze flicked between them. "I volunteer in a hostel—these are important issues…"

"Aww, honey." Fey leaned her elbows on the table separating us. "These are boring issues."

Tina's head bobbed again, her hair shuffling below her chin. "They really are."

"No one wants to buy a magazine to read about homeless old people—yuck." Fey's identical haircut shivered around her ears. "That's not sexy."

I kept the cringe on the inside. They wanted sexy. *Doomed.* My specialty. Just look at today's juice stain seduction model. You can't teach that kind of talent.

My teeth clicked.

Maybe I didn't want to work here. Tina and Fey had matching haircuts. It's weird for colleagues to have matching hair. They might've wanted me to be their third, and I had way too much volume for any style above the shoulder.

So what if I didn't get the job. Who needed to write for a syndicated magazine anyhow?

There were local gazettes I could try—so long as I didn't ever need to make a living. My fingers curled in my lap. "I could come up with something fresh?"

Fey's nose scrunched, but Tina leaned in. "What else do you have?"

"Something very…" I cleared my throat. "*Sexy.*"

"Oh?" Tina dropped her chin onto her palm. "Tell us about that one."

"Well, it's more of a concept." I tried not to look at the snark and skepticism in Fey's eyes. "There was this man in the coffee shop across the street from here."

"What kind of man?"

I turned to Fey, and for the first time since I'd walked in her eyelids had opened all the way. She looked better without the squint.

I smiled, and my heart rose back to its rightful place. There was one sure way I'd get to work for *Poise* magazine. I let my elbow join theirs on the table and planted my chin on my hand. "It's hard to say, really…he was pretty mysterious. Almost inexplicable…"

WHAT IN GOD'S name did I just agree to?

I stood in the elevator, blinking at the reflection in the mirrored wall. At the shirt now knotted at a belly button that had never before seen the light of the sun. The collar this time left purposefully gaping.

Thanks, Fey, for "fixing" me.

My hands flopped at my sides. This is what I needed to save *Poise* from—how to be told you're not good enough subject matter.

The elevator jolted then rose. *Crap.* I spun and hit the ground button, but too late.

I went up. Never mind, we'd go down eventually.

What I had to figure out was how to find my chin-dimple-heartthrob, and do one ridiculous exposé on his general mysterious gorgeousness. I just hoped he was actually as impressive as I recalled. My entire brain shrank around the memory of him that lit up the inside of my mind.

Blood pooled in all my sexy places.

Nope, we were good. Not exaggerated. But let's face it, if I saw him right now, it wasn't interviewing him I'd be interested in…

The lift stopped.

The doors slid open.

As if my wicked thoughts had tempted the universe, they revealed the man himself.

He stood in full, glorious person, suit jacket slung casually over one shoulder. His eyes flickered briefly before his face spread in a devastating smile.

His gaze drifted to my open button, and his smile turned voracious. In just a shirt, he was even more rugged than earlier. And damn, his shoulders were as muscular as I'd envisioned. Not muscleman muscles, just plain old I-am-a-strong-guy-with-lots-of-testosterone muscles.

I sagged against the wall. The magnetic pull of him went straight to my ovaries. If he touched me now, I'd probably have twins—or triplets.

He observed my changing expression and stepped through the doors to stand beside me. My skin tightened. Our arms brushed.

Make that quads.

He reached across me, all too close, and pushed the lower car park button. The side of his arm brushed my chest when he drew back. My mouth opened silently. The heat of his body next to me fried my brain. I almost forgot that I actually needed him. Not simply to fill my womb with his love goblins but as my highway to gainful employment. I turned and gave him a smile, complete with my own cheek dimples.

Our children will have all the aesthetic indentations.

"So, your interview went well, Angelina."

There he went, using my name again. Not fair, especially since his name would be a great place to begin my investigations. Yet he didn't look like the kind of man who knew the meaning of the word *fair.*

"Exceptionally well…sir," I responded then lowered my voice. "It hardly seems right, though…"

"What's not right?"

We were face-to-face. Or should I say, face to chest. I tipped my head back to look at him. The intensity of his gaze quickened my pulse, but I wouldn't be intimidated. Not this time, anyway. "Well, that you know my name but I don't know yours?" There were only three floors left before we reached the ground. "I think you just like hearing me call you *sir...*"

His eyes darkened, and a carnal flash crossed his face. I backed into the cool wall.

He watched me for the length of a breath before reaching across me again. *What is he doing?* His finger pressed the red button. The elevator shuddered, coming to a screeching standstill. I stumbled, foot twisting in my shoe. He grasped my arm before I could fall, and hauled me against him.

Holy crap, what have I done?

THREE

As MUCH AS I attempted to conceal my nervousness, air still rushed from my lips.

"My name is Haithem," he whispered. His beautiful accent thickened. "But of course you can call me sir." The look he gave me dripped with sin. I was in serious, serious trouble.

I swallowed hard. His hand rested on my arm. Its warmth seeped into my skin. The atmosphere charged, but I wasn't sure if it was with danger or something sweeter. His gaze devoured my eyes, my mouth, my lips, as if he memorized the angles of my face. I said nothing. I held his gaze, not able to—or wanting to—pull away. I'd never been looked at that way before.

Kiss me...

His lips met mine, spreading my mouth open. My heartbeat paused. His kiss consumed me. My pulse rushed back into a shuddering rhythm, thunking its way through my chest to send trembling blood through my body. He took possession. Of my mouth, my pulse, of the bend in my spine with the tilt of our heads. He opened his mouth over mine and pushed his tongue between my lips. My veins exploded with rushing blood. I pressed myself against him and kissed him back.

I melted—lost my bones. His jacket dropped to the floor, and he ran his hands down my shoulders. He surrounded me, pulling me closer to him, shutting out the world. A hungry touch glided over my backside, running down my leg and back up my thigh, then delving underneath my skirt. Shivers ran deep inside my core. His other hand slid into my hair, deepening our kiss, if such a kiss could get deeper. He filled me, his tongue, the masculine taste of him, the intoxicating tang of his cologne. He enveloped me. I could burst. He gripped my ass. Brutal hardness dug into my belly.

Icy realization hit. *What am I doing?* I pulled back, but the grip in my hair locked me in place. My limbs stiffened.

His hold on my hair loosened, and he leaned back, peering down at me through lowered lashes and warm, breathtaking eyes. His lips glistened softer and pinker. He rubbed his thumb lightly on my cheek.

Why was I panicking again?

"This is Building Management. Is everything all right in there? Emergency stop seems to have been activated." The voice echoed through the elevator from the speaker underneath the stop button.

Haithem's touch left my face, but the hold on my behind remained. A devilish smile played on his mouth. "My apologies. I seem to have accidentally knocked the button."

There was a pause. "Kindly depress the button, please, sir."

Haithem sighed, and he released my backside to reach for the button. The elevator sprang to life, dropping suddenly.

Within moments the doors opened, and without another thought I slipped under his arm and out of the lift. I rushed through the empty lobby, my heart screaming a warning siren in my ears, to where a security guard

waited at the doors. I glanced back. Haithem started
after me but stopped when the security guard moved
my way.

"Is everything okay?" he asked, gaze darting from
me to Haithem.

"Fine, I'm just leaving," I said.

He opened the door and I rushed into the crisp outside air and ran to the corner, then froze

Once again what was I doing? I needed him. Hadn't
even managed to get a last name from him. What was
wrong with me? I peered around the corner at the lobby
doors. Emma warned me about this. That there was a
chance my reproductive system would eventually turn
on me. Sex brain. Or as I fondly referred to it—horny-
stupid.

The door flew open.

The massive length of him emerged. I sank my back
to the wall. My heart hadn't slowed down, not for a
second. My lips were still bruised. Desire still rained a
plague of tingles in my fun area. I could fix this entire
issue. Take care of both sex-brain and exposé at once. I
just had to step out of hiding and call his name...

I looked around the corner. A black car pulled up at
the curb. My throat thickened.

Nope, couldn't. Duplicitous sex wasn't going to be
the thing to haul my ass out of celibacy. Haithem strode
to the car.

I held my breath.

He couldn't just get in the car and disappear. I'd
never get my story. *I'd never see him again.* Fate gave
me a last chance with Haithem in that elevator. There
wouldn't be another. As I knew so well, fate could be
cruel like that.

Haithem opened the rear passenger door. The ruthless beat in my ears turned pounding. I looked up at the orange-pink sky between office towers. I needed to get home. *Soon.* He slipped into the car. I raced to a cab at the corner.

Last chances were final.

Haithem

"YOU MUST SEE THIS," Karim called from the office next to my cabin. I joined him by the windows, took the binoculars he offered and peered outside. He indicated to the building across from us.

A flash of movement streaked beside the wall towards the corner.

The muscles in my arms coiled like a snake. My heart went hard. Head clear. Throat dry.

We'd been found.

Dread formed a crust around me. A crust of memories made up of blood and fear and loss.

Then I saw it—that same white blouse draping her lushness, the patch of sunlight turning a mass of hair from chestnut to red. The same hair I'd had my hands buried in not a half an hour ago.

Her.

Angelina was here. Why the hell was she here? My stomach clutched around a lump in my abdomen.

"It seems your chance meetings today were no coincidence."

I adjusted the focus and the sight of her sharpened. The burn deepened. "Perhaps she's desperate to see me again."

Angelina stepped out from the edge of the building

and her head dropped back. White fabric rippled at her sides and her breasts. Her hand moved to shield her eyes to the glare of dusk.

I didn't see her eyes, yet I saw them so clearly. The way her lashes had beat over captivating green irises. The way that beat quickened when her gaze set on mine.

Real.

She was real. What happened in the elevator was real. Her hair had been baby soft. The scent of shampoo clinging to her, clean and sweet. I tasted her breath in my mouth. The strain of need tightened my cock. How natural that was. For an instant I'd been myself.

When had I last?

"I've never known you to be naive."

The accusation barreled through my thoughts.

My chin snapped toward Karim. "Look at her. That is the single worst spying I've ever seen."

The one thing we could count on was that anyone sent for us would be the best. The best and the worst. Hair whipped across her face and she tore it from her mouth, spitting.

"That is not a professional." I handed Karim the binoculars.

We had intimate knowledge of professionals. If my past had taught me anything it was that you never see the devils until they're breathing down your neck, their gun wedged to your ribs.

"You remember the Russian girl?"

Or in the case of Natalya, until they were riding you like a carnival attraction, pulling a razor from beneath their underwire.

"She was different."

"I warned you off her too, but you wouldn't listen."

"You booked her."

Karim lifted the binoculars, but his neck flushed. "And I tried to send her away when my suspicions piqued."

He had indeed.

By that time I'd already seen her. The first chance I'd had for "recreation" in the longest months of my life, and she'd been five-eleven with legs for miles.

The rules should've protected us.

Escorts only.

Never the same agency.

Turned out there was no such thing as safe.

"Just like they pique now." He peered at the girl on the wharf.

"Maybe she's hunting adventure. You saw the way she watched me in the café. Then the way she kissed me in the elevator. She's probably spoiled and bored."

"She spies, Haithem." Karim stepped out from the window. "She followed us here."

I strode to the desk, opening my laptop. "There's one way to find out."

"What are you doing?"

I pounded the keys. Karim would resist my decision. He wasn't one for risks. Except, my life was already a gamble. If I had one bet to place, I'd place it on my own instincts. Right then that instinct bored deep, hooked an idea, wouldn't be shaken. "I'm going to find out who this girl is. Then we will make ourselves a new friend."

The binoculars in his hand fell to his side.

He spun around. "You can't intend—"

"I do. We have weeks of waiting ahead of us." Weeks where I'd lose my mind. Perhaps I already had. But something shifted under my skin—need—excitement.

"If I am right and all she wants is adventure, then she'll have her adventure." My lungs filled deeper than they had in years. "If you're right, if she's here to spy, I'll show her a wealthy brat. Prove there's nothing to see here."

Those ideas wrapped together nicely.

Win, win.

My favorite way for a thing to be.

Karim moved to stand on the other side of the desk. "If I'm right then you're inviting the snake into the nest."

"If you are right, then someone already knows we've been here. This would be the chance to extract information. You should be happy, Karim."

I belted out an email as we spoke. Usually, I preferred more information to feed my partner, Avner. But there was a lot he could do with only a name.

If Angelina Morrison is really her name.

"I'm not."

I hit Send. *Done.* Too late. A smile crept into the side of my cheek. Another new thing that seemed to be happening today. "You know what they say about where to keep enemies…"

"We bury them, don't we?"

I slammed the lid closed, but I couldn't slam shut my head. Or the images there. Nor the haze of terror and regret.

"What if I'm right and she finds something?"

I shoved away the laptop. Tried not to look outside. Not to think about the girl there. But mostly, I tried not to think about that sliver of glee that had nothing to do with danger and everything to do with desire.

I *wanted* this game.

"Then I'll do what has to be done."

FOUR

THE VERY LAST dying rays of a low-hanging sun cast a faint halo on the roof of Emma's Barina by the time I arrived in my driveway. With everything that happened this afternoon, I'd forgotten there was a party we'd committed to tonight. I bypassed the front door, going directly to the back entrance closest to my room. Even in the cab I barely made it back before zero hour—the time at which those who worry get shitty. The hum of voices filtered from the closed door across the hall. I groaned. My bag suddenly felt twice as heavy. I slipped it from my shoulder. Seriously, it was my own fault for being late.

And what had I achieved besides adding "he lives on a superyacht" to the list of reasons why today had to be a product of my fractured mental state.

I pushed open my bedroom door. "Hi, Mum."

My mother glanced up from my single bed, where she sat next to Emma.

"Nice of you to show up," Emma said, giving me a slow smile.

"How did the interview go?" Mum stood. "Did they love your article?"

"They said my writing was great." I tried to muster a smile and leaned against the door frame. "But they'd like me to try something more…commercial."

Definitely not entitled how-to-stalk-mysterious-hot-men.

Her hands dropped to her sides. "You're not going to write one of those trashy—"

"Mum."

Emma smirked, and pressed her fist to her mouth.

"Fine." My mother held up a palm. "But you know how your father feels about—"

"Mum."

"Fine, but next time, call us to pick you up if it's getting dark. You're lucky Dad's not here."

Heat spread across my neck into my cheeks.

Emma made a slight coughing sound. Oh, she no doubt found this hilarious. She'd call it adorable.

"I caught a cab." For the love of god, this would go on until I was thirty, possibly fifty.

"A cab?" Her jaw went slack. "Honey, for Pete's sake, don't tell your father."

I kept my eyes straight in my head. Managed to keep them from rolling back like the teenager they were determined to think of me as. It didn't matter. Soon I'd have my own job. My own place. My own life. "Don't worry. I won't."

"Sorry, love." She placed a hand on my arm. "You know how he feels about protecting you—after everything…"

Emma's hand slipped from her face, her complexion blanching.

A sharp drop slammed down my middle—cleaving me in two.

I'm never getting out of here.

"Dad and I thought it might be time for you to start driving the Mustang. It'd be safer for you to get around."

"Notachance," I said, so quickly that it came out as one word.

Her green eyes, so like my own, widened. I felt mine do the same. I might be the dutiful daughter my parents needed me to be, but it'd been a long time since they'd pushed me to do something I didn't want to. There were some things that duty and guilt wouldn't budge, and not wanting to drive *that* Mustang was one of them.

We stared at each other, both knowing the other's stubbornness, both knowing we could stand there all night. My heart raced. I'd spent my life longing to be seen by my parents, but now that I stood at the center of their goddamn universe, I just wanted to slip back into the shade of invisibility. I wanted to push back against their affection, tell them it wasn't fair. They should have given me their attention from the beginning. It shouldn't have taken disaster to make it happen. But it wasn't their fault, not really, and at some point, I'd have to forgive them... At some point, I'd need to find a way to forgive *myself.*

"Fair enough. You can speak about how you intend to get around, like an adult, with your father in the morning." Mum brushed past me, her perfume a pungent, musky bouquet, reminding me of when I was a child and used to sit on her knee. Reminding me that if I didn't find a way out, I'd always remain folded and squeezed into this place where I just didn't fit anymore.

She turned back to me. "Be home before midnight, girls."

I MAY HAVE lost the desire to party, but Emma's enthusiasm rubbed off onto me, and made trying on the outfits in my closet somewhat of an adventure. It made me forgive her for cozying up to my mother before the ambush. Not that I could begrudge Emma loving my mother when I was blessed enough to have one, and she wasn't.

We settled on a dark blue dress with pleating at the bust, and ruching at the waist. For herself, Emma pulled a tiny, floaty pink dress from her bag, which went beautifully with her platinum locks and baby blues.

"Guess what I did after work?" she whispered with a sly smile.

Emma worked at her favorite clothing store, the kind of store only genetically blessed people such as herself shopped at, while finishing university. She'd studied science, and as much as she hid her intelligence, her smarts were dazzling—just not quite as dazzling as her lack of inhibitions.

"What?"

"You remember Luke from the party last Saturday?"

I nodded and rummaged through my jewelry box for earrings.

"Well, he stopped by at work, and we went to his place for a bit…"

"And?" I asked. For a smart girl, her decisions regarding men were rarely sensible. Not that I could make much claim to sensible today, either.

"And—" she made a gesture with her fist toward her cheek "—it was fun."

"Oh, lovely visual—classy." I shook my head at her in the mirror and laughed. I knew why she did that. She wanted to get me talking about sex. Hopefully doing the sex. That would probably be healthier than what I had going on now.

She flopped down on my bed. "I was going to let him do me doggy, but I had to come here and get ready."

"Really?" I dropped my earring, shock not quite winning out over the morbid fascination that came with vicarious living.

Emma's tinkling laugh filled my room. "No, I'm messing with you. I promise I do have principles. Well, *some* principles." She grinned broadly. "I'd have totally made him buy me dinner before letting him give it to me doggy."

I tossed a pillow at her from my bed, hitting her square on. She dissolved into hysterics. I couldn't help joining in. This was why I loved Emma. She could make me feel the way we did when we were sixteen—before things changed. I finished with my earrings and tried on the shiny blue heels Emma insisted would make my vertically challenged legs look awesome.

They did.

"Thanks, Emma."

I caught her eye in the mirror, and my humor faded. A wash of concern filled me. I knew how it was with girls like us. Girls with a gaping emptiness inside that demanded to be filled. With food, drugs, or—as in Emma's case—cock.

Not me, though. I nursed my hollowness. I starved it, molded myself around the gnawing pain of it. Maybe I was just a nasty little masochist, or maybe I knew this emptiness was bottomless, and attempting to fill it would kill me.

"You know I love you?" I didn't say the rest.

Come to me, not them.

Emma's gaze dropped from the mirror. I watched the top of her blond head. "I know…"

I turned and placed my hands on her shoulders. We both knew what it meant to crave distraction. "I don't want you to get hurt… Is everything okay at home with your dad?"

Emma tossed back her head and blinked heavily, looking up at the ceiling. "We really need to get a place together. Now I'm finished Uni, I'll get a better job soon. It'd be good for both of us, you know." Emma looked back to me. "I need it, and you need to get out of your parents' house. You'll never be able to move on here."

"I want to." I swallowed, a thickness coating my tongue at the reminder of that-of-which-I-shall-not-speak. "I'm just not sure I'll actually be able to."

"Maybe it's time to start living your own life, and stop asking permission?"

I exhaled heavily, my cheeks puffing out. "Wait and see if I get this job, then we'll *talk* about it."

She gave me her every-tooth smile. "I'll hold you to that."

Emma stepped closer. We wrapped our arms around each other in a brief hug and then pulled apart.

"I love you, ho-bag," I said, then flinched at my choice of words, considering what I'd been up to.

"I saw that. What are you hiding?"

"Nothing." I spoke too fast.

"Quit holding out on me. I tell you everything—spill."

There was no negotiating with Emma when there was gossip to be had.

"I kind of met someone today—had an encounter—or something."

"I said *spill*, babe." She gave me her eager-and-undivided-attention face.

No use fighting it. I knew that look. So I told her the whole sordid story as we got ready. Most of it anyway.

THIS IS WHY I hate parties.

For one thing, they were generally populated with asshats and sleaze buckets. And hadn't I hit the jackpot with Chris, the guy who came up and draped his arm around me in a move that proved he was both asshat and sleaze bucket rolled into one. His arm clipped me to his side, and he used his superior height to look down the front of my dress.

The only thing stopping me from putting my elbow to his midsection was the group of people surrounding us. Watching eyes had power over me, made me feel kind of like a marionette—moving stiffly to choreographed movements, doing and saying what they thought I should do and say. Instead I shot him a look that should have had him backing away slowly.

How had I let Chris catch me alone?

We'd kissed once, two months earlier, and that one time had been enough for me. I couldn't have made myself clearer in that regard. "Stay the hell away from me" seemed pretty direct, to me—impossible to misconstrue. He'd called me "pretty for a chubby girl," and I just don't take my kisses served with a side of insults.

The fact I'd lost a few kilos might make me feel a little more confident, but if it made me more "palatable" to him, he could kiss my hot-then-still-hot-now ass. I pulled away and muttered something about going to the bathroom. Pushing through the throng of people, I searched for somewhere, anywhere to hide. I found sanctuary in the kitchen's walk-in pantry. I tugged at the hem of my dress and lowered myself onto a box of tinned tomatoes.

How long did Emma plan to stay? Luke had come, so she'd probably want to hang around longer than I could stomach. I leaned back and rested my head on the wall, then smiled. It didn't matter anymore what Chris or anyone else thought. I'd seen the way Haithem looked at me, I'd felt the way he touched me. A heavy sensation flowed down my chest. Why had I run? The most spectacular man I'd ever met wanted me, and I ran after he'd kissed me in a way that fried my panties right off. Just because he was a little, well—intense? I should've gone after him, article or no article. Should've taken the chance to take things further.

I wiggled on the box of tomatoes, and the rims of the tins dug into the backs of my thighs. So what if all he wanted was to get laid?

I knew what I wanted. I wanted to leap. Do the things I'd missed out on. I wanted to sleep with him. No— scratch that. I wanted to fuck Haithem. I wanted to get skin-to-skin sweaty and dirty with Haithem. I wanted to get on my knees for him, do everything I'd never done because I'd been too scared, or too sad, or just too damn uninterested.

But instead, I ran and hid. Both things I was good at. But what if I'd stayed?

My skin crawled with blossoming need. I could still go back to the dock. Who knew when he'd leave but he might still be there now...

It hardly mattered about the article anymore. I mean if I had to choose sex or article, then there were other jobs.

There was only one Haithem.

That didn't stop the excruciating curiosity to find out exactly who he was. Maybe I was cut out for the job after all. The door to the pantry flung open with a crash. I leaped to my feet. Chris stepped inside. I groaned. He was dressed in pale blue skinny jeans and a white T-shirt that showed off his slim build, but it was the smug expression he wore that made his twenty-one years seem more like twelve.

He ran his gaze over my face and smiled more deeply. I touched my cheek. It was hot—*I* was hot. But not for this boy.

"I knew you wanted to be alone."

He reached his hand into his back pocket and pulled out a foil packet.

Oh, for fuck's sake.

It took ten minutes to convince Chris I didn't want to "hook up." Ten minutes of my life I'd never, ever get back.

I searched for Emma, heading down the hallway to where a friend had seen her disappear into a bedroom. I raised my fist to knock on the closed door. A low, throaty moan reached my ears. I suppressed my own, different kind of moan and glanced back down the hall toward the front entrance.

I needed to get out of here. Pity Emma always had to be the driver. I pulled out my phone and texted her. She'd kill me for sneaking off, but I'd risk her wrath. I slipped out of the house and into the night.

FIVE

Stepping onto the porch, I sucked in a breath as the night air chilled the bare skin on my arms. It'd been more than warm when we arrived, but this was Melbourne. Emma's car nestled against the curb in front of the house. I rubbed my arms and walked over to peer in the driver's-side window.

Yep, there was my jacket. I wouldn't be interrupting Emma to get it. Didn't need any more mental scarring, thank you very much. My phone told me it was quarter to eleven. I knew what was supposed to happen now— me calling Daddy to ask him to come and rescue me from the big, bad, wild party. Me sitting in his car for twenty minutes, listening to commentary about how my dress might give men the wrong impression.

Because god forbid I give the wrong impression.

Mere weeks until I turned twenty-one, and in the past year, I'd regressed back to infancy as far as my family was concerned. Surprising how quickly dynamics can flip. I crossed my arms and walked onto the sidewalk toward the tram stop.

A car door thudded.

"Angelina?"

The sound of my name resonated in the night. I halted, spinning around to face the speaker. A figure strode toward me. I stepped back, stumbling into the fence behind me. My fingers curled into the heavy metal links.

Jesus, the first time I step outside at night by myself, and strangers approach me in the street.

"What do you want?"

The man stopped on the footpath. Like some kind of cat burglar, he wore all black. Black suit, black shirt, black shoes—even his hair and skin were dark.

Like night.

My chest squeezed. He seemed familiar. A beaky nose, a narrow forehead. But I didn't know him. He knew me.

The music from the party thudded dully in the distance.

"Don't be alarmed, Angelina. I have a message from a friend."

My name again.

From the lips of a stranger who'd somehow managed to find me—at night—in a street I never visited. I glanced down the footpath. The man stood between me and the party, between me and safety. My gaze flickered to his car. I'm no good at recognizing makes and models, but this oozed luxury.

He probably wasn't going to rob me, at least.

"A friend? I don't think you and I run in the same circles."

He smiled, teeth standing out against his skin in the darkness. "Oh, but we do. Someone you met today, in a coffee shop, perhaps? In fact, I was there also, but I don't think you had eyes for me." His accented voice spoke with familiar inflections. My hands dropped from the fence, and I studied him again. I *did* recognize him.

He'd been sitting next to Haithem, and he was right—
I'd only had eyes for one man.

"Haithem?"

The man closed the space between us. "Yes, he
would like to invite you to join him on his yacht tonight."

My mind almost melted, and I blinked slowly. Hadn't
I just been longing for another chance? Hadn't I just decided I wanted to do what I'd never done before?

I could go to him.

Have an experience I'd never forget. A distraction
that could occupy my mind not just for minutes, hours
or days—because something told me a taste of Haithem
would stay with me forever. And here it was, what I'd
yearned for, handed to me by fate.

"So, what do you say? Will you come with me to
Haithem?"

I looked at this stranger. Fate wasn't handing me anything. Even fate couldn't have placed him here, exactly
where I was. "How did you find me?"

He stared at me, not shifting, not giving away a thing.
No hint of guilt, no sign of discomfort or that he'd done
anything creepy. "I followed you here from your house
and waited."

"So, you're telling me that at some point this afternoon, Haithem decided he wanted to see me, had me
tracked down to my house, then followed to a party and
snuck up on when I was alone in the street?" I shook my
head, the absurdity only beginning to settle in.

"Your address is public record. I only followed you
because you had company. Discretion is absolutely essential."

So says a serial killer.

I brushed my hair back from my face. "Dude, you know this is all kinds of creepy, right?"

His eyes widened. Probably because I'd just called him dude. Most likely, he didn't get that too often. Either that or he took offense at me calling his actions creepy...

"It's all kinds of necessary."

The comeback, spoken in his formal tone, was all-kinds-of-hilarious. A soft laugh escaped me.

He gave me a tight-lipped smile.

"Okay, that's a little creepy too, though. That *discretion is essential*, I mean." Exposé-wise, it could be excellent... Questions already rushed through my brain. Who was he, and what was he up to? He was probably a diplomat, most likely secret prince. That would work for me. I could run with that angle. Just maybe in daylight. "I'd love to see Haithem again. But it's late, and this is all too much." I gestured around us to the dark street. "Why don't you give him my number, and if he really wants to see me, he can call me like a *normal* person?"

He shook his head. "This is a onetime invitation. Haithem leaves the city in the morning. If you want to see him, now is your chance."

Haithem leaves in the morning?

A deep and bitter disappointment washed through me. I shouldn't feel that way, but I did. The memory of his kiss tingled on my lips.

Didn't I owe it to myself to at least try to get his story?

Or something.

I already had far more regrets than I could live with.

I looked the man in the eye. "Take me to him."

MY FRIENDLY STALKER had a name. Karim. He held my hand as he escorted me on board the yacht, helped me, because I couldn't have done it myself. My legs moved as if they'd gone hollow. A dream-like quality settled over me, convincing me that at any moment I'd wake up and not be there at all.

Hiding on the dock hadn't prepared me for walking onto his yacht at night. Three floors high and big enough to host a town. A floating castle, pale against black waves and white moonlight.

Definitely running with the secret prince angle.

Karim ushered me across the deck and up a narrow flight of stairs to the top. A stiff breeze whipped my hair around my face and my dress around my knees. But I wasn't cold anymore.

"Wait here," he said, and he strode across the deck alone.

I nodded, but I couldn't help drifting to the railing and wrapping my fingers around the cool white steel. My god, I'd never seen Melbourne from this vantage. It *glowed*. So warm and vibrant. Hard to believe I'd lived here all my life and never seen it this way.

Footsteps padded behind me, but I couldn't turn around. I gripped the railing tighter, as if I might blow away. Hands clutched my waist, and a hard body made contact with mine, heating me from my calves to the back of my skull.

Haithem—I knew the scent of him already. Amber with something else, something intoxicating. He leaned over me, and his rough cheek brushed my ear, prickling in a way that made my skin shiver, made me want to feel that delicious friction all over.

"You've been bad, Angelina." He growled the words into my ear, but the growl contained a hint of purr.

Apparently, I was in trouble. The kind of trouble I had a feeling would end with my own purrs. His hands slid from my sides to wrap around my middle. He pulled me tighter against him. I opened my lips but couldn't form words. The movement of my blood had gone from rapid dance to outright chaos.

"You ran from me today. Tormented me with a taste and ran before I'd had my fill." His teeth caught my earlobe, nipping it gently.

I made a sound, a tiny squeak that was lost on the breeze. Pleasure shot from my ear through my body, sensitizing my skin, hardening my nipples, sending blood coursing between my legs.

"For that, you'll beg before you come."

Moisture flooded the fabric of my panties, as if his voice alone could compel my body to do just that.

Beg.

I should've been offended, but there was no pretense. No pretty words to sugarcoat what he wanted from me, just raw honesty.

I licked my lips. I would—I'd beg. Did he want me to beg now? I didn't care, I'd do whatever he said if he'd just save me from this feeling. There'd be time for sleuthing later. My head lolled against his shoulder, and his teeth moved to my neck, scraping skin before branding me with his mouth, sucking hard enough to let me know he intended on marking me.

I'd *never* been so excited, so expectant, so goddamn terrified.

He shifted, and I felt it—what I'd done to him. The hardness at my back rivaled the steel under my fingers.

My hands slipped from the railing, and I lifted my arms above my head to find the soft hair at the back of his neck and grip it.

"Please," I whispered.

Haithem tensed, then rocked his hips against my backside. "You're begging already? I haven't even started." He grasped my breast through the fabric of my dress and plucked my nipple. It hardened at his command, tightening painfully.

Holy shit, he was going to fuck me now.

Not make love—fuck. I could feel it coming. One movement and he'd raise my dress, and I'd be nailed up against the railing. My first time on the deck of a yacht...

Just like that.

I lowered my hands. He stilled then released my breast and took my hand.

"Come," he said, and led me across the furnished deck, through double doors and into a large cabin. His cabin—his room, I knew, because the first thing I saw when I stepped inside was a bed. The biggest bed I'd ever seen, with three rows of pillows across the top. A square of lights, inlaid in the sleek veneer roof, illuminated bed linens I guessed were higher in threads per square inch than anyone could count.

A beep accompanied by a flickering red light emanated from a phone attached to the wall. He released my hand. "Excuse me, this is urgent, but help yourself to something."

I tore my gaze from the bed to the small table laden with cheeses and wine. Haithem walked to the console and answered the phone.

Wine, now that's what I needed.

I took a glass and filled it to the brim. Bubbles foamed at the top, and I sipped them off. I turned the bottle and read the label—champagne, not wine. Not that I knew the difference, really. I only cared if it gave me courage. I gulped and coughed. Bubbles fizzed down my throat.

Haithem rested a hand against the wall and spoke. His words weren't English. They were harder sounding, more clipped. There was something about seeing him standing there in his pants and shirt, bare feet, dark hair slightly tousled, speaking in a foreign tongue, on a goddamn yacht, that made me feel as if I'd just stepped into another world.

A world that was about to get a whole heap more fun.

SIX

Haithem

THE SIGHT OF her pink tongue sneaking out to lick the foam off her lips was enough to make me want to take her right where she stood. I restrained myself. She'd already tensed on deck. I had to be sure why she'd followed me.

I know.

Her pulse had raced against my mouth. Her breath had rushed beneath her breast. She wanted this. She wanted me.

Was desperate for the chemistry the two of us concocted in that one kiss. Something had held her back. Made her run away. But then she'd come after me.

And by the time we were done, I'd know the secrets she didn't even know she kept.

A smile built on my lips.

"—graduated with a Bachelor of Arts with honors."

The smile broadened.

I listened on the intercom to Karim reveal every detail of her sweet, exquisitely boring little life. *Perfect.* Everything about her was so perfectly normal. Her father was mayor of their suburban municipality. Probably impressive to neighbors.

"Are you ready to admit I was right?" I whispered in Arabic.

"Just because we didn't find anything doesn't mean there isn't anything."

I snorted. "She still lives with her parents."

"Exactly why she'd be such a perfect plant."

I shoved back the black ball of suspicion. Wouldn't succumb to that today. There hadn't been a time since this began where I hadn't balanced on edge—all that I thought I knew slaughtered by what I might not. Yet, right then the air was breathable. Fertile and hopeful. There was more than *this*.

There might even be an after. If I survived.

I breathed that suddenly lush air. *After*. Why had the concept not occurred until now?

Angelina finished her champagne and poured another. Usually I didn't mix sex and drink, but in this case the alcohol would help. She'd be more receptive if she relaxed. I'd have a better chance of convincing her to give me what I needed. She wouldn't like my plans— pretty young women like her rarely did. They were too romantic, their expectations too high.

"You are a sore loser and we didn't even bet for money," I said. Either way, I had her now. There were just a few boxes to tick. A couple of edges to smooth, to make this all neat and tidy.

She caught my gaze on her and tucked a lock of her rich, not-quite-brown, not-quite-red hair behind her ear.

Fuck me, she's lovely.

Big dimple in one cheek, smaller one in the other. Huge green eyes and curves I could drown in. I wasn't sure what was riskier—letting her come along or letting myself taste something that could become an addiction.

I hung up the intercom and faced her. She clutched her glass to her chest and gazed at me. Caution was required. She was young, maybe twenty-three or twenty-four, maybe intimidated by an older man. Might run, after all.

I had to be patient. But patience had never been one of my virtues—not that this life had left me with many virtues.

I took the glass from her hands and filled it with more champagne. No, I wasn't above being a bastard to get what I wanted. I handed the flute to her and led her with a gentle touch on the small of her back to the couch. I didn't sit next to her—that wouldn't work. I took the armchair opposite and pushed it closer. She set down her glass.

Her gaze fixed on me, shining. She licked her lips. My hands curled. I fought the compulsion to leap up and show her exactly how I'd like her to use that tongue. Her eyes glittered, her color was high—she was ready.

She'd do as I wanted.

"Angelina, I'm glad you came." I leaned closer. Tried to keep my tone light. "But we need to talk."

She shifted, tugging her dress down. Her gaze fell to her knees. "Talk?"

I touched her thigh. She needed to look at me. "Yes, I'd like to invite you to spend some time with me."

Her gaze snapped up. "What do you mean?"

I peered directly into the green of her eyes. "I want you to sail with me up the coast. Two weeks of sea and sun, on my yacht. You'd have everything and anything you desire…"

EVERYTHING AND ANYTHING *I desire.*

His gaze bored into mine—dark and hypnotic. My ears buzzed. The champagne had gone to my head. I'd thought I'd known my deepest desires. But now, sitting across from him, I realized I'd always denied myself the things I wanted most.

Like the warmth of getting close to someone. Really close. Close enough that it would break me again to lose them. Close like this, where there didn't seem to be air between us. I could touch him, and I'd be swept away.

But go away with him?

I'd never been *away* with someone. I'd never been with anyone, period. It was easy to get lost in the magic, but this was real life. One that came with responsibility...

I studied the hand on my thigh. Huge compared to mine. Could swallow mine completely. Yet his thick fingers were still long enough to look nimble.

How was this even happening?

Me on his yacht, him touching me... I knew why I'd come. Sitting across from him, my hand in his, I wasn't there for an article. But, why'd he go so out of his way to find me?

He could have anyone. Why hunt me down?

"I can't just leave for two weeks."

He touched my chin and lifted, until once again, I was cornered by his gaze. The look he gave me was one I doubted anyone ever resisted.

"You can. You're just afraid to take the risk."

I breathed deeply, getting a little high on his delicious cologne. Maybe I could. Maybe I could say to hell with everyone else. Say the hell to *no*. Say the hell to caution. Do one thing, just one thing for me. For two weeks, leave absolutely everything behind and *escape*. But reality intruded, snapping at my conscience.

"You don't understand—I have responsibilities."

His touch moved to my cheek, stroking my skin. I couldn't resist leaning my face into his warmth.

"I can take care of your responsibilities. Tell me what you need and I'll make it happen. Someone to fill in at your workplace? Your dry cleaning collected, appointments rescheduled? Write me a list, and it will all be done."

Warmth spread from where his fingers touched my cheek to deep in my chest. All my life—for so many reasons—I'd always faded into the background. Never felt as if I was a star in my own show. But in that moment, there was no denying I was front *and* center.

"You'd do all that for me? Just so I'd come with you?"

His hand slid to the base of my skull and tugged me forward. His lips hovered over mine. "You have no idea what I'd do to have you, Angelina."

My skin prickled, the hairs on my body stood erect and my stomach flipped over. How could he say those things to me? I'd never been wanted like this.

And by a stranger.

Why?

I eased away from his lips, and his fingers trailed away.

"It's complicated, Haithem."

"Let me make it uncomplicated." He looked me in the eye, so directly, so purposefully. "Do you want to come with me?"

I rubbed my palms on my thighs. A yes-or-no question. The air in the cabin seemed to grow thinner.

"Yes." The word breathed out of me.

Yes.

A simple yes. He smiled. The kind of smile that made my head spin. A satisfied smile, yes, but so warm and beautiful I had to grip my legs to keep from touching him.

"Good," he said. "Then there's just one other thing we need to talk about." He reached for my hand, held it in his. The heat from his fingers enveloped mine, warmed me to the bone. "I've been in Melbourne on business."

I watched his lips move, watched the way he pronounced every word so artfully. My attention pricked. He was going to tell me things.

"It's very, very important business, Angelina."

I nodded. Probably not as important as this, though. Probably not as important as what was happening right here. I could feel my cells vibrating in anticipation. Not of the impending revelations, not even of the mad-awesome sex I knew was coming, but in anticipation of doing this one wrong thing, this one selfish thing.

Of being a little bad and loving it.

"It's important, *secret* business." The hand on mine squeezed gently. "Do you understand?"

I slammed down from euphoria. The place in my head that had flicked back and forth between coming *for* him, and coming here *because* of him, switched gears.

He had secrets—*I knew it.*

"Sure, you have important, secret business." I leaned forward, attempting to sound uninterested, and put my lips closer to his.

He made a gruff sound in his throat and grabbed my chin as though stopping himself from kissing me. "It needs to stay secret."

My heart sped up. *Ha.* Let's not mention articles or exposés.

"Okay," I whispered.

His thumb slid up and swiped across my lips. My mouth opened, and I tasted him. Tasted the salty clean taste of his thumb.

He dropped his hand and looked down at me through lowered lashes. "That means you can't tell anyone about me."

Well, that ruled out my editor and the wider public. That also ruled the whimsy out of his mysteriousness.

"You can't tell anyone where you are going or how you are going."

My head spun, and I snapped back against the couch. I glanced at the table with the champagne. I wouldn't touch it again. The cabin seemed more real. I could smell the wood, the sea, the scent of *him*. I could see the shadows against the walls and dents in the carpet where someone had moved furniture.

This was real, and suddenly it felt dangerous.

Haithem didn't waver, didn't back down. He leaned in after me, and this time his eyes were deadly serious. "I'd need you to sign a confidentiality agreement."

This wasn't good. Not for an ulterior motive and most particularly not for me.

If he hadn't been so close, if his voice didn't crack with tension, if he didn't make my heart race in a different, dangerous kind of way, I might have laughed.

Because this was crazy, so crazy. At most, the piece I'd planned to write on him would have been fun and frivolous. About a playboy. A teasing look at the unattainable and why that makes smart girls go crazy. But, who asks for a confidentiality agreement before hooking up with someone?

Whatever he was involved in, it wasn't good. Things you need to hide rarely are.

I looked at the handbag I'd let fall to the floor, leaned forward slowly, then dragged it into my lap. "I'm not much of a liar, Haithem."

That wasn't even said for misdirection. If our conversation had gone any other way, I'd have come right out and told him why else I was there and hoped he'd help me out with it.

I stood.

He stood with me.

I slipped my handbag over my shoulder and glanced at the door.

"I'd pay you," he said.

My gaze flew back to him. "What?"

"I'd pay you to sign it." He slunk forward, somehow closing the gap I'd created before I could move any farther away. "I'd pay for you to keep my secrets. I'd pay for you to tell whatever lies you need to tell to satisfy whoever it is you're afraid of lying to."

Cold snapped the heat still zinging along my skin clear out of my system. I hadn't heard him right. Surely he hadn't just offered to pay me?

"I'm not taking money." I scooted around him, sliding myself closer to the exit. "And honestly, it's pretty offensive that you think I would."

"Everything has a price, Angelina—everything."

A chill crept up my neck, and I took another step.

His gaze tracked my movements. If I'd thought I could sneak toward the door all inconspicuously, I was wrong. He knew what I was doing, and damn him, he looked disappointed.

His mouth turned down at the corners. "I've never taken anything I wasn't prepared to pay for."

I flinched. What was I, then, something to be acquired? So much for romantic fantasy. But then that whole idea had died right about the same time he'd asked for an agreement.

"Well, you can't pay for something that isn't for sale." I stepped again and swayed. Dammit, too much champagne. "I'm going."

His expression hardened. He looked intimidating as hell, and I just bet that icy glare of his usually made everyone around him cave in to his demands. Arrogant jackass.

"Don't run from me again, Angelina."

The warning in his voice froze me. I shook my head. It was probably a good thing I'd found out he was a bossy, cold-and-dead-on-the-inside asshole now. Especially since he looked, smelled and tasted anything but cold.

He really shouldn't have let me think there was more to this, that he felt anything special for me. Clearly, he saw this—saw *me*—as some kind of transaction.

I could think of fifty-one articles I could write about this the instant I left. Unfortunately none of those could be published under the umbrella of "sexiness."

Disgruntled with malekind, ready to form my own all-female commune—those were not *Poise* magazine angles.

"I'll do what I like." I raised my chin and gave him a glare that dared to be challenged. "Next time you're trying to get into a girl's pants, maybe try not treating her like a whore."

I didn't wait to gauge his reaction, just turned to the door.

A touch on my arm stopped me. "Don't run because I hurt your pride. There's something between us bigger than pettiness."

I looked at him. His lips pressed tightly. A squint fanned his eyes, almost as though he had emotions. *There's something between us bigger than pettiness...*

I don't know where my fight went, but it ran out on me. Left me alone with Haithem to overtake my senses and do as he pleased.

He kissed me—seared me from the outside to my insides. Brutal, ruthless, possessive. His tongue invaded the cavity of my mouth, took everything I had. Stroked me, inflamed me until I held his shirt just to remain on my feet.

He tasted like life, made me want to dive right in. He seized me up in his arms and surrounded me. My breasts ground against his chest. I wanted more, more friction, more of his tongue in my mouth, more of his hands on me, more of *him*. I gripped him by the shoulders, tugged the cotton covering him.

Haithem jerked back and stared down at me. We panted. That kiss proved why he really wanted to pay me—he wanted to own me.

"You want this. Behave and we can both have what we want."

Behave.

I shivered. I had images of doing just that. Behaving for Haithem. Being his paid pet. But the thought spiked a pain deep in my chest.

I had to get away from him.

I pulled back and fled the cabin.

His footsteps thundered behind me. "Stop, Angelina."

"Just stay away from me." I turned and faced him, my anger finally catching up with me. "You want to know the truth?" I took a deep breath and let it all rush out. "Yeah, I'm attracted to you, but you're a massive prick. I've got no desire to *behave* or do anything else for you."

His jaw hardened.

For an instant a shard of true fear spiked me. Would he possibly stop me from leaving?

No.

That would be crazy. Criminal. Evil. He couldn't—wouldn't.

But… The way his eyes narrowed. The way he assessed me. How could that be? Hot one moment, cold the next?

Cold. Suspicious.

Agreements and secret business. There was worse, and more sinister things to him than I'd first seen.

What was he hiding?

Why did Haithem, beautiful, rich, sexy, smooth Haithem, look at me as though I might be something to be studied and broken, shaken until my secrets spilled free?

His posture shifted as if he'd shrugged on a coat of formality. "Fine, if that's how you feel, I'll walk you to the dock and have Karim drive you home."

I backed up, placing my hand on the railing. "You just don't get it, do you? I don't want *anything* from you. I have a phone, and believe it or not, I have access to money. I'll walk myself out and take a cab."

He just stared at me, his body so tight my own stiffened at the idea of what he might do. Insist I follow orders, most likely.

"Suit yourself. Goodbye, Angelina."

He turned and stormed back into the cabin. The door crashed behind him. The vibration shuddered under my feet.

As quickly as they'd formed the ridiculous suspicions I'd had melted on the salty breeze.

He'd given up. Haithem had given up.

I'd have bet he was incapable of such a thing.

A shameful longing in the area of my rib cage mourned the fact that he wasn't immune to defeat. I'd let myself fantasize that I was invaluable to him, that he'd fight to have me. That his macho bullshit was a facade. I just didn't realize how much I'd believed in that fantasy until he walked away.

Now I felt the disappointment to my toes. The wind blew gusts, and air whipped around me, flapping my dress around my thighs and sinking a chill into my skin. I crossed my arms, then shuffled to the stairs and grasped the railing. I shot one last look over my shoulder. Light filled the cabin. He'd closed the curtains, but the silhouette of his shadow stalked back and forth.

I'd agitated him. Gotten under his skin. I let that brazen satisfaction take hold. Haithem was *different*— larger than life—and *I* affected him. He tempted me with things I didn't dare dream of doing. He'd drawn a picture of a seductive fantasy where I did everything I'd never allow myself.

Wrong or right, I wanted to live that fantasy.

I closed my eyes briefly. A blast of wind hit me from behind like a giant hand. I tripped and grasped for the railing, but the yacht dipped suddenly, and I fell forward, propelled across the rails. My body hurtled over the edge. The wind stole the breathless scream from my lips as I plunged through a wave of lights.

Then fell into darkness.

Pain.

Pain then heat. I twitched my fingers. My body ached, throbbed from my ankles all the way up to my cheeks. Not to mention the bitch of a headache murdering my temples with invisible ice picks.

Hangover—a hangover from the fiery pit of hell.

I tried to sit, but something smothered me. I rolled onto my back and fumbled with the covering. I broke free and—dear god, the light.

Blazing light almost took out my eyeballs. I covered my face, then shielded my eyes. A blue glare pierced my vision. I blinked. The blue divided into a pale sky above and glittering water below.

What the actual fuck?

The world slowed, and I dropped back onto my elbows. I didn't remember getting home. All I remembered was realizing Haithem was the devil—and apparently I had an appetite for destruction—right before heading to the stairs.

I clutched my head. The freaking stairs… Wind… Dipping bloody boat.

I glanced around, my stomach dropping. The ocean spread on my left, and the white expanse of a superyacht towered over me on the right. I moved around a bit, my feet tangled under a tarp. *A lifeboat.* I'd fallen through a tarp and into a goddamn lifeboat on the lower deck.

My heart seized, and I looked all the way up to the railing on the narrower top deck. I patted myself down with trembling hands. Somehow I'd landed in one piece, in spite of my splitting headache and aching limbs.

Faaark.

My parents were going to kill me, or, at the very least, ensure I wished for death by the time they finished with me. It was daylight, and I wasn't home, and I hadn't called them. All hell would have broken loose, and I would soon be trussed up and ready to be roasted. I disentangled my legs and threw one over the side of the lifeboat, then shimmied onto the floor.

My heels touched the floor, but the world swayed. A shout boomed across the deck. I turned in time to see a figure rush toward me, yelling indecipherable words. The man came into focus, then another emerged.

The silver barrel of a handgun flashed. It was trained on me.

My vision narrowed until the gun was all I could see—and instinct kicked in.

I ran, adrenaline spiking through my veins. I fled in the opposite direction, down a hallway. Footsteps closed in behind me. Light broke at the corner, and I strained to reach it. Darkness flashed across the light, and my face slammed into something solid.

Hands clamped over my arms, and I did the only thing I could think to do.

I screamed.

I filled my lungs and let sound boom out of my chest like a siren.

"Angelina?"

The sound of my name wrapped around me like an embrace. I looked up at Haithem, taking in his magnificent features drawn tight and fierce. My blood pounded manically, thudding in my eardrums. I clung to him, buried my hands into his shirt and held on.

"There are men with guns." I glanced over my shoulder.

The men slowed. The one with the gun held it loosely at his side.

Haithem wound an arm around my waist and pressed my face against his chest. I breathed in the subtle strength of his scent.

He spoke quiet, foreign words, and the men fell back.

"Come with me," he said, and grasped my arm, leading me around the corner and upstairs.

We glided across the deck, then into his cabin. The walls swam around me. I still felt hot, as if I'd been baked alive under that tarp. Haithem lowered me into a chair. I sank down, then gripped the arms. Things had gone blurry again. I needed water. There were cracks on my tongue. He dragged another chair across the carpet and positioned it in front of me.

Haithem flicked the button of his right shirt sleeve, rolled the material and pushed it above his elbow, then did the same to the other side. His bulky forearms flexed. The raw masculinity of those meaty arms hit me even through the madness flooding my system.

All I could think was *Man. Man. Man. Man.* My upper lip twitched where moisture cooled the skin. Finally, it made sense. The weirdness. The fogginess.

I must be dreaming.

That seductive nightmare where I wanted those arms to crush me. Where I could do all the things I longed for and be absolved of guilt for choosing to do them. Hadn't I longed for this? To escape with him?

But I couldn't make that decision. Not without facing an ocean of guilt. So now dreams took over and let me have my fantasy.

Nicely done, imagination. In that case, I'd bloody well enjoy it.

I reached for that warm olive skin, but his roughened voice stopped me.

"Why are you still on my yacht?"

He wasn't acting like he should be in my dreams. He wasn't revealing the rest of that magnificent skin. Wasn't touching me. He was acting serious—being *real*.

My fingers flew to my temples, where pain radiated and scattered the flood of thoughts. "I fell into the lifeboat."

He leaned forward, rested those forearms on his knees and studied me. Studied me as if he just might open his mouth and swallow me whole.

"We departed Melbourne over twelve hours ago. You expect me to believe you only just scrambled out?"

Twelve hours...

I couldn't have been on the boat that long. I ran my hands over my crumpled dress, and smelled the slightly sweet scent of sweat clinging to me like film. "I think I knocked my head..."

His jaw flexed, and his words took on lethal sharpness. "I'm going to give you this one chance, and I hope you are smart enough to take it..." He scanned my eyes. "Who do you work for?"

I straightened up. The absurdity of it all, of being on a yacht with armed men, of his questioning, sank in. I laughed. Laughed until the sound snorted out of my nose, and tears leaked out my eyes.

Haithem wasn't laughing. He scowled, and that

look—my god, it made me laugh harder. It was entirely too fierce for one man's face—it probably made people piss themselves, but I could only piss myself laughing.

He stared at me until my laughter wafted into giggles.

"Who do you work for?"

I'd lost it. Maybe it was the hit to the head, the fact that I couldn't see straight, or maybe I was drunk on his nearness. Or maybe it was the part of me that still didn't believe this was real.

"Are you supposed to be some kind of James Bond?" I lowered my voice and put on the world's worst English-stroke-Scottish-stroke-who-the-fuck-knows-what accent. "Who do you work for?" I laughed again at my own hilarity. Certainly not a magazine—they hadn't hired me yet. "I'm more of a Jack Reacher girl, myself. Although, I have to admit, they both have nothing on you in a suit."

He rubbed the underside of his jaw with his knuckles. "I will find out, Angelina. Don't say I didn't warn you. It's up to you whether we do this the hard way."

The hard way...

My skin overheated, and moisture itched along my hairline. I tasted salt and leaned back into the chair. I stroked the hair back from my face. My temple throbbed where my fingers brushed, but then again I could feel *everything* more. My skin felt overly sensitized. I looked at Haithem, my eyelids half-closed, and let one hand trail down the side of my neck.

"You promise?"

His stare followed my hand. "Promise what?"

"That we can do it the *hard* way."

His gaze snapped to mine. I tried to hold it, but my

eyelids fluttered. Ringing chimed in my ears, and I could only watch him from hooded lids. He stood, reached for my hands and pulled me to my feet.

"Take off the dress."

I felt stripped by his words. Naked already. I'd never have the nerve in real life, but this couldn't be real. My limbs were so light I could've floated away. I fished behind me for my zipper and stumbled. Screw that—this was my fantasy. *He* could undress *me*. I swept my hair over my shoulder and presented him with my back. His rush of breath whispered across my neck. A gentle tug pulled between my shoulders, then fabric parted down my back with a gentle swoosh of the zipper.

Salt coated my lips. I was hot, so hot, yet the fingers that touched my skin burned. They traveled over my shoulders and down my arms, pushing my dress away. My senses homed in on the stroke of his fingers. The dress pooled at my waist, caught at the flare of my hips. His hands moved from my arms to grip my waist. A hum vibrated through my lips. I gazed down at myself, naked to the waist but for my bra. Large tan fingers pressed into my flesh, making my skin seem paler, softer than I'd ever seen it look.

His fingers flexed, and he tugged me back, cradled me against his hardness. I needed the support to remain standing. He splayed his hands at my sides and moved them to my belly, sliding his open fingers down, down, down to the place that throbbed and ached to be touched. But he didn't touch me where I wanted him to. He stroked down my thighs, and pushed my dress to the floor.

I leaned into him and closed my eyes. His body changed, and a thick thigh wedged between mine, opening me to him, holding me up. He stroked the insides of my thighs, burning a path of pleasure toward my core. Finally, he closed his hands over me, and I made a sound, half moan, half plea. He rubbed over my panties with firm, determined strokes. I arched into his touch. Blood plunged though my veins, erratic and uncontrolled. His thumbs hooked under the elastic of my panties and slid up and down the sides. I could only watch his hands move, watch the white lace flow through his fingers. He moved to the waistband, performing the same little ritual.

Not the touching I expected, not the kind I craved, but he was close, so close. He teased me with the nearness. I waited for my panties to follow the dress to the ground. Instead, his hands traveled over my skin again. The muscles in my belly contracted under his touch.

I raised my arms and gripped his shirt collar. He wedged his thumbs under the middle of my bra, the small stretch of material nestled under my cleavage. My breasts pulled forward with the tug, straining higher, hungrier. He brushed against the inside of my breasts. My nipples tightened. His thumbs ran beneath the underwire, tracing the curve as high as they could toward my armpits, then his hands pushed inside, stroked their way over my sensitive skin.

I shivered, and gasped for air. Lace dragged over my nipples with just enough friction to be exquisite. Just enough friction to frustrate the hell out of me. He pulled his hands free, and my breasts fell heavily back into my bra. I bit back a groan and tugged his collar. Fast breaths against my hair warmed the top of my head. He slid his palms over my breasts, finally squeezed them the way they begged to be squeezed. My head tossed against his shoulder. He plucked my nipples through the bra, flicked them gently then stroked over them.

"Haithem…" I moaned.

His hands left my breasts, and he turned me sharply. I caught the briefest glance at his face before he held me to him. His expression, dark and ravenous, burned into the back of my eyelids. An unforgiving hardness pushed against my abdomen. I rocked my hips against it and wished I were taller, so it could rub between my thighs. He gripped my bottom, holding me still and tight. I wound my arms around his neck, trying to draw him down for a kiss. He resisted but buried his lips in my hair.

He explored my ass through my panties, running over the curve, skimming under the elastic, even for a moment running his fingers down my crease. I shook against him and stretched up, seeking his warm skin with my lips. The movement brought that hardness closer to the place that craved it. My mouth found the base of his neck, the soft skin just below the start of his bristles. I filled my mouth with that skin, tasted its tang, tasted the subtle bouquet of cologne.

His touch traveled over my back, up to the clasp of my bra, yet again, he only ran his hands under it, didn't tear it off. I clamped my teeth on his flesh, not hard enough to break skin but enough to show him my impatience. He jerked and made an animalistic sound against my hair. He grasped my ass again and dragged me higher. I wrapped my legs around his waist and hitched myself up with my arms around his neck.

He moved, and a part of me knew it was toward the bed, toward the place I knew he would make me a woman in the way I wanted to be one. My sweat-slicked skin burned. I *needed* him. Needed him with every cell. The bristles on his neck prickled my cheek, and I turned into it, ran my tongue over the sharpness like the wild feline thing I'd become.

My back lowered into divine softness, then he traveled down my body. I arched into the scrape of his face. He nipped my ribs with his teeth then descended, stopping to run his tongue just under my belly, where the waistband of my panties rested.

The wetness between my legs flowed, and the entire area pulsed. He knelt between my knees, ran both hands down one of my thighs then gently bent my leg at the knee and kissed me on the kneecap. I felt his lips against me as if he'd kissed the place between my legs. My core tightened. His fingers smoothed over my calf then tugged off my shoe. He held it in one hand and slid his other hand down to remove my remaining shoe.

He sat back, holding my shoes. His gaze flowed over me, over my knees, which had fallen open, to the place between my legs that I knew had soaked through its covering, then up to where my chest heaved and my breasts strained.

His nostrils flared, his jaw ticked, and he met my eyes. Every trembling part of me seized. His gaze was voracious, rapacious and shaking with fury.

"I'll give you one thing. You're a fine little actress."

He scooted off the bed, my shoes in his hands. Confusion blazed through my overloaded senses. Haithem stalked to the door. Some of the fog cleared, and alarm rose in my belly. I rolled off the bed, an odd emptiness and nausea turning my stomach. I followed him out the door. He strode across the deck to the back railing, and I ran after him. He stopped at the rail, grasped one of my shoes, and tugged out the insole, then tossed it over the rail and looked inside my shoe as if it contained some sort of mystery.

"What are you doing?" I called, my sweaty skin chilling.

He paused and looked at me. His features had evened, smoothed into the shell I'd already come to know. "You said you wanted to do it the hard way. I'm obliging. Let me know when you've had it hard enough—and maybe then I'll play nice." He snapped the heel off my shoe and peered inside, then tossed it over. I grasped the railing and watched my shoe and heel fall into the water.

My head seemed to crash with each wave. "I liked that shoe."

I looked at him, only to see my other shoe receive the same treatment. He turned to me, and my skin flushed again. *Too much—way too much.* This was one screwed-up fantasy. The edges of my vision clouded. At least it looked as if I might be waking up.

"Do you have anything to say to me now, Angelina?"

I stared at him and nodded—then emptied my stomach onto his polished black shoes.

Haithem

MAYBE THE FIRST honest thing I ever experienced from her was the moment she vomited on me. That wasn't faked. She was sick. Most likely from spending the night in a freezing lifeboat in nothing but a dress.

I ran my gaze over her shuddering sweat-coated form. Her skin glistened with moisture in a way that sank my attention into every section of her exposed flesh. Some of her hair clung to the smooth rounded curves of her face, the rest was wild in a rolling-in-bed kind of way. Her hips and tits still screamed for me, even after I'd forced her back into that dirty dress.

They chose well.

My enemies chose so well it made it hard to swallow. I hadn't realized I had a type. When you're living in obscurity, on the move, there's no time for types of girls. There's only available ones. There's only easy ones.

I wouldn't have guessed this pretty, girl-I-could-know kind would make me want to throw caution to the soulless sea. Because I could know her. She had lips for kissing but eyes for talking to.

A soft throaty voice that begged to be listened to.

She moaned.

I shut my eyes. Stopped myself from going over to the bed and shaking her awake and demanding answers. Because I'd sedated her.

I linked my fingers together and watched again.

Her head tossed against my pillows.

Maybe they thought I was weak. That I missed my family and having a life. Maybe they thought I'd look at her and remember what those things were like. That I'd get fuzzy ideas and bare my soul to a spy.

Another low keening sound tore between her teeth. I sprang out of my seat—even though if it weren't for the fact her temperature was so high I'd be tempted to doubt even that sound from her lying duplicitous lips.

She'd find I wouldn't be easily overcome. There wasn't that much hope left in me.

They destroyed my life.

They murdered my family.

They killed my optimism.

I crossed to the bed, and stared down at my pretty little prisoner.

Hope couldn't be used against me. For the briefest moment, it almost had. Not anymore.

Her hands curled in the sheets. My fists curled at my sides. I'd read her university transcripts. She'd completed a dual major in journalism and theater studies. She was literally an actress.

A very, very good one.

She tossed again, her face turning towards me. Her lips parted with a throaty moan that sent a wave of need slamming into me.

Fuck. Swamping lust gave my heart a deeper rhythm in my veins.

I shouldn't touch her.

Shouldn't.

I couldn't look away. Sweat beaded her upper lip, clinging to fine invisible hairs as innocently as a milk-mustache. My hand parted ways with my will, reaching for that mouth.

What a perfect weapon.

I brushed her top lip. *Shouldn't be touching.* The heat of her skin branded my thumb. Jesus, her skin was warm.

So fucking warm.

A dark blend of shame and desire had me hard and desperate, even if unwilling. Her heat should've been a giveaway. My palms prickled with the memory of her fevered skin flowing slick and quivering under my touch. I sank to my knees beside the bed. Perhaps, I should've known she was unwell.

But I hadn't wanted to notice—I'd wanted to *touch*.

Just like I had to touch now.

I rubbed my thumb back and forth over the irresistible petals of her lips. Over the tiny split on her bottom lip that broke the silky smoothness. Why not touch—she was mine. Everything in me shook with the compulsion to sink my thumb into her hot mouth.

Whoever recruited her knew what they were doing. Kept her life squeaky clean. Perfectly mundane.

I'd found their one mistake.

Six weeks.

Her nose scrunched. I moved my touch over her cheekbone, where light freckles fanned out and faded. *So deceptively wholesome.* There were six weeks missing from her life where she'd vanished from the face of the planet. Six weeks where even though her absence was noted on her academic record, it was forgiven without reason. Six weeks long enough for an intensive training program with the right people.

My fingertip found the groove in her cheek, where even resting her dimple creased skin.

Yes, Angelina was the ultimate angelic weapon,

Karim had been right. I'd been naive. I wanted to believe in her and I wanted to believe in what we'd shared. But one coincidence is a coincidence too many. Now there were four. The coffee shop. The elevator. The spying on the dock. Stowing away on a lifeboat.

I'd be a fool to believe any of it, no matter how tempting it was.

I tore myself free of the thrall of touching her, and stood.

She'd been there on my bed. Thighs apart. Panties damp enough to see pussy-soaked fabric. Wet enough the musk of her lust reached me. That was believable. I could have fucked her. Clamped a hand around her throat and fucked her hard and rough the way the look in her eyes demanded.

But she wanted that.

She'd enticed me to take her. Is that how she'd get to me? Did she plan to seize me by the cock?

Never.

I scrubbed the side of my face with my palm. I still felt the lick she dragged over my jaw. The way she'd run her tongue over me like an animal—she took no prisoners.

Neither would I.

She had no idea who she was dealing with. If she thought she did, she was about to find out how wrong she could be.

I'd be the one to take her. Push her. Exploit her weaknesses. Use her lust against her the way she'd intended to use mine against me.

By the time I was done, I'd know her to her deceitful core.

EIGHT

THERE'S SOMETHING ABOUT puking up your guts that makes everything very real. You just don't dream that shit—the heaving, the muscle contractions, the burning and definitely not the vile, acidic stench. I curled onto my side and retched foam into a bucket. When I fell back onto the pillow, a cool cloth pressed over my forehead.

"The medication will work soon, and you'll feel better." The familiar voice was soft, and smothered my burning system with another layer of heat.

Haithem, whoever and whatever he was.

I draped my arm over my eyes and groaned. The cool cloth stung my skin. If I'd still believed I'd dreamed up the whole experience, this would be the part where it turned into a nightmare. This would be the part where smart girls ran. But my body groaned with heaviness, immobilized by fever, the roiling in my belly and pain in my joints—and something else, too. The tiny focused place inside me that was having a meltdown of its own.

"Your temperature was extremely high, but it's coming down. You'll be all right."

I resisted the urge to rub my rump, where a stranger had jabbed a needle while speaking gibberish to Haithem. I let one eye slip free from the cover of my forearm and glanced at him. Bright red lines marred the skin on his neck, but the look on his face was even more haggard than the rest of him. *Holy shitballs.* I covered my eyes again. I'd scratched him like a crazy person. I'm not sure what I'd been thinking. Things got a little hazy after I puked on him. I only remembered the stranger, the flash of a needle, and fighting like a demon. Because that's what you do, obviously, when you're delirious, and spies are trying to administer medical treatment to you.

"What's wrong with me?" Bitterness burned the back of my throat, and my tongue felt twice its normal size. "Did you drug me?"

Haithem tugged the arm off my face. "You were ill. I took care of you." The way he'd said that. Slowly. Purposefully. My temperature leaped back up a few notches. I stared at him. The way he *looked* at me when he'd said that. Intimate—possessive. *He took care of me.* As though I was *his* to take care of.

I went hotter still—hot yet shivery.

An image struck me of being his. Being his pet. Taken care of. More shivers swept me.

He released my arm and leaned back. Bristles coated the wide angles of his jaw. Somehow making him hotter. Somehow making him more rugged, a little dirty, yet more touchable. His eyes glowed black in the dim cabin.

The sheets clung to me—his sheets, the sheets on his giant sex bed.

"You made yourself sick from hiding in the lifeboat overnight."

My mouth opened. "From falling into the lifeboat, you mean."

He didn't blink, just watched me—read me, I'm sure. If he could really read me, then he should've known the truth.

"I need to go home now."

His jaw pulsed. A rap sounded on the door, then Karim burst in. My little black bag swung from his hand, and the last dying note of my cell phone ringtone trickled from inside it. He rushed to Haithem and held out the bag.

"We found this in the lifeboat."

Haithem took my bag and yanked out my phone. His finger swiped across the screen, and I sat up, seeing the flashing missed calls notification before the screen faded. He drew back, eyes trained on the screen, fingers tapping. His expression hardened, turned cold and empty.

He turned to Karim. "How long have we been in range?"

"About half an hour."

Haithem flashed a look at me then handed the cell to Karim. "We'll detour. Dispose of this immediately."

"No, it's mine." I lunged for the phone, and my head spun.

Haithem grabbed my wrist and urged me back against the mountain of pillows. "You need to rest."

"I don't know who you think I am, but I'm no spy—give me my fucking phone." I shoved his hand away, panic spurting through me with enough force to subdue the hot, sick feeling clinging to me. "I need to go home."

Haithem switched languages, speaking softly to the man behind him without taking his gaze off me. Karim nodded and left the room. I pushed off the blankets, scrambling after him. Haithem dropped my bag and seized my arms.

"Calm down. Everything will be fine." He spoke

in soothing tones, and despite myself, it calmed me. "You'll be home before you know it."

His touch gentled. His fingers on my skin were light, his hold on me ludicrously comforting.

I relaxed against the pillows and smoothed a hand over the dirty dress that somehow had magically materialized back over my body while I was passed out. "So you believe me?"

He said nothing but reached down for the handbag on the floor. The mattress rose and fell under his weight. I held out my hand for my bag, but he flipped open the top and rummaged inside. He placed my lip gloss and compact on the side table, then fished inside and pulled out my emergency tampons.

My cheeks burned. "May I have my bag, please?"

"Soon," he said, and drew out my wallet.

"There is absolutely nothing in there that could possibly interest you."

He flicked through the pockets of my wallet, pulling out old receipts and movie ticket stubs and placing them beside the other items. He moved to the inside pocket, and I sat up quickly. He tugged out a worn photograph.

"Don't touch that." I reached for it.

He held the photo higher, rising off the bed and examining it. His lips thinned, and he looked at me. "What's this?"

I knew what he saw, and my heart rushed, my chest squeezed and pain echoed through my limbs. *Me and a boy.* Me and a boy, embracing inside a blue Mustang. My hair wild from a ride with the top down. Joy in my eyes and in my heart.

"None of your fucking business."

He sank to his knee beside me. "You have a boy-

friend, Angel?" Under other circumstances, the nick-
name might have been an endearment, but he spoke it
now as though it were a curse. "You have a boyfriend
yet kiss men in elevators, meet them on yachts?" He
leaned down. "Is this the responsibility you were talking about?"

My pain exploded into rage, and I snatched the photo
from his hand. He let me take it.

"Shut up. You don't know what you're talking about."
My eyes burned, my lungs burned, my skin burned. I
could have caught fire, but the scariest part was the
sobs building behind my ribs. Sobs I could never let out.
Sobs I'd held back a year. I pressed the photo against
my collarbone and rolled away from him. "I don't have
a boyfriend."

I felt him watching me. Felt him staring, judging,
weighing my truthfulness. He moved, and the slap of
cards against wood sounded next to my head. *Bank
card, library card...* I listed them in my head.

The sounds stopped. His movements stopped. He
muttered something foreign.

I rolled onto my back. He held my driver's license
in his hand, staring at it as though it had singed his
fingers. He glanced from it to me. His expression flattened. "You're only twenty?"

I frowned and nodded. "Yes."

He stood, dropping the card, and stared at me so long
I became painfully aware of my entire external self.
Aware of every hair on my head, of my eyelashes, of the
split that had developed in the middle of my bottom lip.

I ran my tongue along the crack. "May I call my
parents, please?"

He continued looking at me, staring. "No."

No?

The skip, skip, skip of my heart became a bang, bang, bang.

"I need to let them know I'm okay. They'll be freaking out." I sat, leaning up on one hand. I needed to get home. Needed to get as far away from him as possible. "I won't mention you...if that's what you're worried about."

"You're learning," he said, and sat next to me. "I'm glad you understand you can never, ever speak about me." He placed a hand on my arm, his grip firm and inescapable. "Tell me you understand, Angelina?" He tugged me closer and looked into my face. "For your own good, agree that I don't exist."

I didn't try to pull away from him. Not that he'd have let me. There was zero give in his grip. I panted. It was almost as if the lining on my lungs had thickened. Thank fuck he didn't know the other reason I'd come here. I wiped words like article and magazine from my mind. No matter what happened, I could never tell him now. I'd say whatever I needed to say, whatever he wanted me to say to get him to let me go. "You. Don't. Exist."

He smiled, but it was cold and jagged. Then he reached out and smudged the sweat above my mouth with his thumb.

My lips parted.

He watched my lips too long. "Good girl." His hand stayed on me, moving to my cheek. "Where are you then, Angel? If I don't exist?"

I blinked. What was he doing? Goose bumps managed to spring along my arms despite my internal furnace. This was a game. A game with rules I had to learn or I'd lose before it even started. I couldn't lose this game.

"I ran off with a boy from the party."

He traced the outside of my jaw, but his fingertips curled, and his knuckles bumped my chin.

"We're staying in a caravan park," I whispered. My gaze traveled to his mouth. He had such a compelling mouth. Pink smooth lips, but the stubble around them was hard and sharp. His teeth were large and white and straight. He tapped my chin with his thumb, bringing my focus to his eyes.

"Why would you run off with a boy from a party without telling anyone?" he said, studying every flick of my eyes. "That's not very nice."

The heat in my cheeks cooled. His words were a kick to my chest. He was toying with me. Showing me a way home but making me pay for it. My teeth clamped together.

The muscles around my nose scrunched, then I let the truth bleed into our contest of lies. "I'm tired of being nice. I'm tired of doing the right thing. I wanted to get away."

"You wanted to get away?" he asked. "That's a good enough reason to hurt the people you care about? That's enough reason to make your mother cry, your father sick?"

My gaze snapped up, and my lips shook. "It's not like that. I'm smothered. I can't breathe. I can't move." My lungs burned like I'd inhaled smoke. "But nobody even sees me. No one hears me at all."

My shoulders twitched. I clamped my arms around myself. Somehow everything I'd been tying down came springing free.

He gripped the back of my neck and pulled me close, planting his lips on my forehead. "Good girl."

His kiss was electric cool.

I grabbed his shirt and tipped my head back to see him. "Let me speak to them now, please."

He pried my hands from his shirt and leaned forward, opening the drawer in the side table, and pulled out a notepad and pen.

"I assume your family members have email addresses?"

He held out the pen. I took it. He opened the notepad. I scribbled Dad's email.

"I'll make sure they know you're okay, and that you'll be home safe with them in three weeks."

The pen slipped from my fingers. "Three weeks? You said two."

My heart ping-ponged from hope to horror. An email might keep my parents under control for a weekend— but not for *weeks*.

I couldn't be stuck with him for weeks. A day couldn't end soon enough.

He scooped up the pen and handed it back, not looking me in the face.

"That was before. Things have changed." He held the notepad out again and seized my gaze. "Before, with your agreement, I could've trusted you. Now I need to be sure when you leave, I'll be a ghost…"

NINE

I SHUDDERED WITH a ripple of fear and dread. Fear over what staying here one more moment would cost me, and dread over the idea that one day soon, I'd wake up and Haithem would indeed be a ghost—yet another one to haunt me.

"You can trust me," I whispered. "You want me to sign something? I'll sign it."

He looked just as hard and unreasonable as before. I reached out and placed my fingertips on his hand.

"I swear—you never existed. I never met you at all."

His gaze flicked to my touch, and stuck there as though the touching of *him* was not something that was usually done. His expression shivered and whatever I thought I saw vanished. He rose to his feet. "I'm afraid a promise made under duress is no promise at all."

"What do you mean, duress?" I leaped off the bed.

He strode for the door. Apparently, he thought our conversation was over. Pity—I wasn't done. I followed him onto the deck.

Salty air swept hair across my face.

"It's not as if you've threatened me, so I'm not under duress."

He paused, pushed the notepad into his pocket and turned. "You think someone has to hold a gun to your head for you to be helpless?" His movements changed, went sharp yet somehow also slinky. He walked—not to me but around me. "I have all the power, all the say. And you—" he pointed his finger directly at me "—you, Angel, are a scared girl who wants to go home."

His words whipped me like lashings from the wind. Painful, cutting lashes that made me want to cry. He stalked me, closing his circle just as surely as a shark. My veins spurted adrenaline, instinct compelling me to *run*.

But I didn't run. That would break the dubious politeness he'd affected, and this small glimpse at what lay underneath was enough to shake the skin around me.

There was nowhere to run. He'd catch me, and—god help me—I might even enjoy it.

I might enjoy something so real and so raw as being caught, even if it hurt. No polite control. Nothing proper or respectable. Just *real*.

He walked and walked, round and around. My neck strained to keep up with him. I couldn't drop my gaze, couldn't let him out of my peripheral vision.

"You owe me nothing. I expect nothing from you. I trust no promises from you." His voice softened, whispered around me from what felt like all directions. He stopped directly behind me, his hands coming down on my shoulders so I couldn't turn. "But this doesn't have to be a nightmare. It doesn't have to be a trap or a prison." He pulled me back against him, and suddenly his arms were around me and the beast was gone, replaced instead by a comforting protector.

My pulse jumped. How quickly he could change.

"This isn't fair. For that, *I* owe *you*, and I always honor my debts."

I'd slipped into hyperawareness—of the arm around my waist, the body at my back, the voice in my ear. I could almost see myself in his arms, standing like a waxwork, so still and glassy-eyed. *Mesmerized.*

"I saw your face when you told me you're smothered so tightly you can't breathe," he whispered. "You could be free..." He brushed his cheek against my temple. "No one around. You could be yourself."

He rocked me, so softly I almost missed the shift of my weight from one side to the other. I no longer knew if I was holding myself up.

"I can give you sunsets on the ocean. I can show you space so endless you'll lose yourself."

My hair caught on his bristles.

"Have you ever run down a deserted beach, Angel?" His hand moved on my belly. "Have you ever swum naked in salt water?" His voice penetrated my head, my blood, sinking down somewhere even deeper.

"Imagine three weeks where anything you ask will be indulged. All your demands met. Ask me for something—ask me for anything."

My eyes closed.

"Do you need someone to hear you?" His word curled into my ear so gently, I felt the heat of his body in his breath. "I'll listen to you talk for days."

He touched my chest, pressed his palm flat against me.

I twitched.

"You can tell me what it is you keep buried in here. What you're holding on to so tightly that you can't let go. You can give it all to me, Angel. Just hand it all over to me..."

Air flooded my lungs, and I lunged out of his grasp. My heart beat so fast, I could imagine coronary damage taking place. I turned and faced him, backing out of reach.

Had I let him read me so thoroughly? Had I laid out my weakness so well that he could drive himself into my head and fuck me there?

Because that's what he was doing—he was fucking my mind. I knew it. He knew it.

It was working.

But he didn't know me yet—not really. No one did. Not even Emma. My heart squeezed just thinking about her, about my parents, too. How things must be while I stood here and let him toy with me.

"Ask you for anything?" I said. "I want to go home right now."

He lowered his chin. "You know that's not possible, and that's not what I meant. Ask me for something else—something just for you."

I swallowed. Of course, he wouldn't give in. "All right, I want to be draped in diamonds." I pulled back my shoulders and watched him.

Go find that in the middle of the ocean, asshole.

He just smiled. "I'm disappointed in you."

"Too much to ask?"

"Not hardly," he said. He nodded then walked toward the stairs, toward the lower deck. The lower deck where there were men with guns.

"Wait, where are you going?" I called. "What am I supposed to do up here?"

He didn't look back. "Just stay put."

As if there was another option.

TEN

I DID WHAT any reasonable prisoner would do—I tore apart the cabin. Not in the way a toddler would, not dumping clothes onto the floor, although the thought appealed—but sneakily. I rummaged through every drawer, searching for some clue I could use. Some scrap of something that could give me leverage...that could give me an advantage.

All I found were socks, handkerchiefs and a wardrobe full of clothes that only made me picture the man who owned them. My hands stilled on a leather jacket. I pulled it closer and ran my fingers over the collar. I hadn't seen him in anything like this.

Casual.

Relaxed.

The thought of Haithem's big shoulders filling black leather—oh god.

I let the jacket drop and shut the wardrobe. I needed to get off this yacht before I started rolling around on the enemy's sheets just to catch a whiff of his scent. Already, the walls seemed to be closing. Small spaces didn't suit me. Free time suited me even less.

There'd be nothing but time here. Nothing but hours and hours on the damn boat.

Wondering, thinking, remembering.

My shoulders tensed up. Some girls dreamed of days

spent lying in the sun. But not me. The mere thought of being still for so long made me twitchy.

I walked to one of the two doors on either side of bed. The handle stuck at half a turn.

Locked.

I stared at the doorknob, my thoughts slowing. The other side of this door would be where I'd find what I wanted. Locks are for secrets. And I'd discover every secret I could. I went around the bed and tried the other side. It opened into a cavernous bathroom. White marble, a deep tub, shower, toilet, a double vanity. I raided the vanity cupboards, coming up with nothing more exciting than toothpaste, razors and aftershave. I tugged the lid off a bottle and sniffed. The smooth, musky scent went straight through my nose and into my blood.

Wood, amber, a hint of something like rum. Haithem. Rich, deep and all male. I jammed the lid back on the bottle, tucked it back where I found it, then stood. The reflection that greeted me in the mirror made me flinch.

Oh, damn.

I leaned in and pressed my hands to my tangled hair. This level of dishevelment created a whole new category of unkempt. I picked up a lock, somehow at once both frizzy and lank, an achievement in itself. I brought the hair to my face and sniffed. The odor of puke and sweat permeated the chestnut strands. I let go and groaned.

Had Haithem actually rubbed his face in my hair?

My cheeks went warm then hot. Either he was taken enough by me not to care about the stink, or he was an incredible player.

I'd bet player.

This was not okay. Not just for vanity's sake, but hygiene-wise. I groaned again then glanced at the shower.

I wanted to run to it, bury myself in the hottest stream I could manage. But something stopped me. Something made me not want to remove a single piece of clothing, not remove the smell of vomit, or sweat, or mess. It was as if stripping and washing it all away was some kind of acceptance. Getting comfortable. Making everything better.

It wouldn't be better until I went home.

I turned back to the mirror. Shadows ringed my eyes. I looked like hell. Whether here or at home, no one needed to see me like this. Not even me. I closed the bathroom door and slowly flicked the lock. Then I took off my clothes and set the shower to scorching.

I'D WASHED QUICKLY. Something about being naked for any length of time on the yacht, locked door or not, seemed like wearing a bright red hood in the forest on the way to Grandma's. I'd managed to shampoo my hair, turning it into one large mat without conditioner to tame it. I dried myself briskly. My limbs loosened, and my body felt warm and human again—relaxed, even. I wrapped a towel around myself and another around my hair.

I shouldn't have showered.

Exactly as I'd feared, the comfort of such a small luxury—washing away the dirt and grime of the past couple of days—had mitigated some of the worry, some of the anxiety clinging to me.

I could almost hear Haithem placating me now. Telling me it was only three weeks—no big deal. I should relax, enjoy myself.

Enjoy myself right around his cock, most likely.

I snorted and walked to the wardrobe to pull out one

of his shirts. He'd gone and screwed that possibility up for both of us. Friday night, I might've been willing to take a risk, plunge myself into the sensory kaleidoscope of Haithem's arms, find out what all the fuss was about fucking, but in the cold, hard light of—what was it now, Saturday, Sunday?—and this clearly not being a dream, I'd had just about as much risk and consequence as I could handle. I let the towel drop and pulled the shirt on over my arms.

Being held prisoner didn't exactly turn me on, either, no matter how many lush red bows Haithem tied on the situation. I shook my head. I'd brought this on myself. What man looked like him, talked like him, acted like him, without there being some deep, dark catch? Maybe I'd wanted a little trouble.

Served me right.

But my family were innocent. My poor, suffering family. I slipped the top button through the hole then stiffened.

He stood behind me.

Had he made a sound? Had the door clicked?

I didn't think so, but I knew as surely as if he'd been announced over a loudspeaker that he was back there. The remaining buttons seemed to do themselves up. Every inch of my skin bristled, painfully aware of how nude I was under the shirt. I tugged the hem, thinking of the underwear I'd washed and laid out to dry over the towel rail in the bathroom.

I turned on the ball of my foot.

He stood by the bed and scanned me from my bare toes to the top of his shirt. The slow movement of his eyes warmed my skin more than the shower stream could have hoped to do.

And I was naked under the shirt.

Maybe he suspected, but I knew the thrill of that secret nudity. The knowledge made me hotter, wetter. But let's face it—I'd been wet since the moment I slipped something of his over my head.

He scowled. "What are you wearing?"

Well, damn, you'd think he didn't like seeing a half-naked woman in his shirt. Shouldn't such a sight give him a hard-on or something?

"Something that doesn't have puke on it," I said, and smiled. It probably wasn't the most innocent smile of my life, but then I hadn't really intended it to be.

His brows rose just slightly, as if it'd only just occurred to him I hadn't exactly packed for my surprise trip.

"Come here," he said.

God, the way he said that. As if I could have stopped my feet. His voice made every single female cell in me roll over. *Come here.* Spoken the same way he'd say "Come to me" or "Come to bed"—or "Come for me, Angel." Husky and deep and sensual.

I walked to him. Knew my hips swayed more than necessary, but I hadn't told them to do that. He looked at me, watched me move toward him. And when Haithem looked at me, he *really* looked at me. He narrowed the world and put me in a tunnel somewhere between where I was standing and his eyes.

I stopped in front of him, my heart playing a fast little number against my ribs.

"Turn around."

I shuddered as if he'd touched me somewhere private. Was this dirty? Had he asked me to do something dirty?

Turn around, bend over, good girl.

I'd read romance books. All kinds. I turned, some little nagging part of me reminding me that I didn't actually have to do what he said.

He shifted, and I stared at the cabin wall, listening to the sound of my own breaths. He stepped close to me, and his trousers brushed the backs of my naked thighs.

Brushed my panty-less backside.

I gasped, and his arms came around me, reaching past my shoulders, and laying something cool on my neck. My hands flew to my throat, and I looked down.

He fastened a clasp at my nape.

A string of clear stones circled the base of my throat. Not diamonds, obviously. Because you couldn't get a necklace with this many diamonds. Could you? I touched them. Small, hard, shiny, but not real. Most likely not real.

"What's this?" I asked.

He turned me around then rested a hand on my shoulder. "You asked to be draped in diamonds." He touched the center stone on my throat. "I always deliver on promises."

"You expect me to believe these are real?" I pulled my chin back, trying to see the necklace better.

He grinned. Grinned so full of confidence there could be no doubting him. "Would you like to see the certificate?"

If this were a movie, this would be the part where I swooned, or where he pretended to snap my fingers in a jewelry box, and I threw my head back for a giant, toothy superlaugh. I wasn't swooning. And I wasn't laughing.

"But this must be…" I looked at the stones again,

trying to remember how much fine jewelry cost these days. "Worth as much as a car."

Haithem laughed, and the sound seeped into me and made my chest shake. His face transformed. White teeth flashed, hardness giving way to pure beauty. I didn't think I'd heard him laugh before. I'd never thought a person's laugh could be so dangerous. But a laugh like his? It would compel a person to do almost anything to hear it again.

"It'd have to be one incredible car."

I tried not to be impressed. Tried not to like the absurd reality that Haithem would really give me things, out-of-this-world things. But his actions meant something to me. It meant something to have someone do stuff for me, give to me. Because I'd spent my life giving and giving until I thought it might kill me to give any more.

Now I stood in front of the most insanely attractive man I'd ever laid eyes on, and he'd manifested diamonds out of the ocean because I'd asked for them.

I blinked and looked at the necklace again. "So, you just plucked these from thin air?"

"No, I had them in my safe."

I studied him, but his expression didn't flicker.

Why did he carry diamond necklaces in his safe?

A man traveling alone…what need did he have for such a valuable commodity if there was no one to give it to…

A wave of something I'd never felt before washed over me. It took me a moment to realize what it might be.

Jealousy.

I gaped and stepped back. "Did you have these for someone else?"

Oh, hell no, could he be? The possibility ticked through my head, and things made sense.

"Are you *married?*" I sank my hands into my hair and turned around, my heart dropping hard. "Oh my god. That's why all the secrecy?"

He stayed quiet, each moment of silence confirming my suspicions. I turned back around and faced him. The asshole didn't even have the decency to look guilty.

"You're screwing with my entire life...because, why?" My muscles shook with energy. I shoved him in the stomach. "Because you don't want your wife to know you're a cheating, lying, philandering fuck-hole?"

He didn't move, didn't react. Made me feel a bit like a toddler trying to push over their parent. He placed his hands over mine, and that's when I saw it—what I hadn't seen before because he was so good at keeping it all below the surface.

My own rage reflected back at me.

"I'm not married, Angelina." He let my hand go and stepped into me, so close that I would have fallen back if he hadn't caught my hip. "I told you my policy on promises, and that extends to vows, but believe me—" he tugged me forward, so I could taste his breath when he spoke "—this would be so much easier on both of us if that were all this was."

I stared into his eyes—angry eyes that burned with such conviction I couldn't deny the truth of his words. I couldn't deny my relief, either.

Relief that Haithem wasn't taken. Wasn't married. That he was *available*.

That he hadn't planned on making me a seedy in-discretion.

At this point, I shouldn't have cared if he was taken or not. I wouldn't be doing anything with him in any case. Yet it would've hurt.

I'd nail this down to my pride taking a hit and leave it at that. Nothing deeper than that.

I breathed in, then out, and my energy scattered. The necklace shifted on my neck, reminding me that he still hadn't provided a reasonable explanation for why he had it.

"So, what...? You're a pirate then? You plucked this out of your treasure chest?"

Haithem smiled, but the smile held the same dark-ness as his eyes. "Have I ravaged you yet, wench?"

I rubbed my tongue on the roof of my mouth, looking for some moisture. *Yet*. As in, still to come... I couldn't answer, afraid of what I might say.

He released my hip, and I stepped back.

"It's currency."

"Currency?"

"Sometimes, in business, it helps to have something other than cash on hand."

What kind of business was that? The kind of busi-ness that is better conducted without paper trails. The bad kind.

I touched the necklace again. "So, this really is very valuable then?"

"You have no idea."

I glanced around him to the door, an idea flickering to life. I'd never make it past him without him stop-ping me.

I rubbed my throat. "Do you have anything to drink?"

His eyes narrowed a moment, but then he nodded and crossed the room as if it wasn't the first time I'd casually asked him for something. He crouched in front of a cupboard and popped open the hidden bar fridge I'd found earlier.

I inched toward the door.

He glanced up, and I froze.

"Cola, juice or water?"

"Juice," I said.

He leaned into the fridge, and I ran. Out the door and over the deck. His steps thundered behind me, but it didn't matter. I didn't need to make it far. I yanked the chain at my neck hard, snapping the clasp.

I reached the railing and flung my arm out over it, the necklace dangling from my hand. The footsteps slowed. He crept toward me like a predator. My fingers shook. *This better freaking work...* If it didn't, I had a feeling I'd come to regret it.

"What are you doing?"

"Give-me-a-phone-now." The sentence rushed out as a single word.

He came closer.

"Stop," I said, holding out my free hand. "Go get me a phone, or I drop this in the ocean."

Haithem stopped moving and held up both his palms. "Angelina, we are miles away from any mobile phone towers. Do you really think a phone would work out here?"

"I think there's no way you'd be out here without some way to reach the outside world. I think you most definitely have a satellite phone or something capable of making a call."

I breathed heavily.

Haithem watched me and smiled a smile so cold it almost gave me frostbite. "Clever girl. I didn't expect you to be so sneaky. I'm surprised."

"Good," I said.

He took a step, and I raised my hand further over the railing.

Haithem paused. "I won't be next time, though. You only get to fool me once."

"Shut up and get me a phone."

"No," he said.

My heart beat as if I'd swallowed a mouthful of speed. So fast it hurt. "I swear I'll drop it."

He moved closer.

"I won't say anything about you—I'll just put my family at ease."

He smiled wider but just as coldly.

Fuck, he knew he had me.

Haithem closed in.

I couldn't let him win.

I could drop his necklace in the ocean. I could test him and see what he was really made of. What he'd do to me. Find out who I was really trapped with. Put my infatuation with him to the test when I suffered whatever punishment doing something so reckless would get me.

But I'd never been brave. When I was little, I was the first to cry at the mention of a blood test. God, how I hated needles. Dad used to call me a wuss.

Now I wanted to push, to see how mortal this peril I was in might be.

I, more than most people, understood the full significance of my own mortality. I might be flirting with danger, but these days I wanted to *live*.

The only question remaining was how I now defined being alive.

Haithem reached my side, his fingers moving toward the wrist I held over the railing.

Don't be such a wuss, Angelina. I flinched, hearing my father's words in the back of my brain.

I opened my hand and let go.

ELEVEN

THE NECKLACE FELL straight as an arrow—from my hand into the dark gray water lapping against the side of the yacht. Haithem didn't watch the necklace fall, didn't lean over the railing and yell like a person who'd just lost something valuable. He kept his gaze on me, his lips tightening over his teeth the instant my fingers opened.

Silence extended between us. The only sounds were the ocean and the roar of blood in my ears. White clouds blanketed the sky. They must have moved, because it grew darker on deck. I stared at Haithem, unblinking. My heart didn't seem to want to stay in my chest—it rattled my rib cage.

I wanted to hit Rewind, reverse time by a few moments and take back my actions. I'd always known Haithem was dangerous. Looking at him now, his features tight and cold, bristling with fury, I knew again for sure. He wasn't a man you'd want to cross.

But I had.

I'd messed up. I just prayed I had it in me to survive the penalty.

Yet I'd wanted this. Wanted to watch him explode. I guess I could call this buyer's remorse. I fell against the railing. He still gripped my wrist. My throat tightened, but I needed to speak, needed to be the one to crack through the silence.

"What are you going to do to me now?" My voice didn't shake, but my body did.

Haithem raised his brow. "Do to you?" His voice dripped with honey, laced thick with a false sweetness that was perhaps more terrifying than if he'd yelled at me.

Not that I wanted to hear him yell.

Not at all.

"I'll pay for this, won't I? You'll punish me some way… I know you will."

He turned closer to me, trapped me between his body and the railing. He didn't let go of my wrist, nor did he hurt me. He could've. He could've squeezed, exerted just enough pressure to make me a little more afraid.

He didn't.

Maybe that counted for something.

"Because you know me so well?" He finally dropped my wrist. He didn't need to hold me anymore. He had me right where he wanted me. "Who am I, then?"

Who is he?

I stared at the stubble on his neck, black spikes that ran toward his chin. His skin didn't move, didn't jump at the base of his throat the way he must've seen mine flickering like crazy. I gripped the railing.

I had no idea who Haithem was.

Someone up to no good, sneaking around in secret, afraid to let me go. I could only speculate. Spy, secret agent, mobster, criminal? Who knew… Maybe he was even a pirate, after all?

But the one thing I did know was that at that exact moment, I was no one to him. Not a lover, not a friend, not an ally—just a sexual conquest gone wrong.

A problem.

Something told me I wouldn't like the way Haithem dealt with problems.

He touched my face. I flinched, but he just guided my chin up, forced me to look at him. "I'm not going to punish you."

I swallowed. "You're not?"

He brushed his thumb against my chin as though he was wiping a smudge. "No, you did me a favor."

"A favor?"

"Yes, a very big favor."

His words didn't relax me, didn't reassure me. If anything, my skin pulled tighter around me as all my hairs stood on end.

"Don't you want to know what that necklace was worth?"

I shook my head, and his hand stayed on my chin throughout the movement.

"It was worth a million dollars." He leaned in and whispered. "It was worth a million dollars, and I let you drop it into the ocean."

My heart had never beat that fast. Through all the shock of the past few days, that moment was the worst. I couldn't get in enough air; I gasped as though I were breathing at an ultrahigh altitude.

"I let you do that." He removed his hand from my face and stepped back. "So you see now, there's no price I won't pay to win."

He didn't smile now. His features were even, contained, his words almost businesslike. "There's nothing you can do to bribe me, nothing you can threaten me with."

Every movement of the yacht made my stomach turn, made the world spin.

"There's nothing you can do at all."

The swaying was too much, and my knees gave way. I slid to my backside, and the world grew quiet.

Haithem

PERHAPS ANGER FUELED my ruthlessness. I left her huddled on the ground and sought the solitude of my office. She'd fooled me for an instant. They'd chosen her so well. A sleeper no one would suspect, living in the bosom of her family, waiting for that one mission only an asset like her could fulfill.

She was smart, opportunistic, resourceful.

Not to be underestimated again, no matter how wide she could make her eyes. I placed the notepad she'd written on in the locked drawer of my desk. I'd promised to send an email to her family. Promised to alleviate their worry.

I lied.

Because the thing about my little stowaway was she had everything to lose. Assets like her always did. She might be groomed to place her mission above family—but that didn't mean weaknesses could no longer be exploited.

That was the difference between them and me.

None of my weaknesses survived. And if I didn't defeat her, neither might I.

I flipped open the folder Karim had left me and examined the contents. The headlines and articles tugged a knot beneath my sternum. I'd known after she'd passed out from fever that this was a possibility. Another day on top of the twelve hours she'd hidden away, they'd be looking for a missing person.

Now we could add the eyes of the world to those who hunted me. I slammed the folder shut, then jammed it back in the drawer. She'd almost won that round.

We were on.

There was a reason they gave prisoners with life sentences the prospect of parole—hope. Incentive drives a person.

I'd give her incentives. I'd give her promises.

Angelina would have hope—even though there was none.

I went to the window and peered through the blinds. She'd crawled onto a deck chair and curled onto her side. I rubbed the place between my ribs, because something deep inside ached just at the sight of her.

She's mine now.

I FELL.

Through darkness. Through gray-blue. Just like that necklace, I sank clean through the water without causing a single ripple.

Down, down, down.

I didn't scream. Didn't cry out. It was like flying. Freely flying toward my own death. I wasn't even afraid. In a way, it was a relief.

I breathed in deep. Water filled my lungs but didn't drown me.

"Angelina."

I kicked my legs, pushing up toward the sound of the voice. Light shone above me. I shot toward it then looked up to the surface and froze. A face looked down at me, obscured by rippling water.

I blinked, and the ripples cleared around the face.

My face. Except not. Me…but male. As if I was a boy. As though I'd been torn in half and made into two parts.

"Angelina."

Memory pushed at the edges of my mind, and I swam closer. I knew this face. I'd tried so hard to lock it away behind layer upon layer of repression.

He was there, above me, just on the other side of the water. He reached for me, his hand plunging through the water, stretching toward me. Urgency exploded through my system. Kicking my legs, I strained for him. My arms flung out—my legs flailed. I had to get to *him.* Before it was too late.

Before he was gone again.

The space between me and the surface grew. I screamed beneath the water, my voice a warbling roar. *"Josh."* The name left me, not from my mouth but from somewhere deep in my chest. The name almost forgotten by my tongue.

"Angelina."

The surface opened, and I sprang forward. Air rushed into my lungs, and I was once again on the yacht.

Haithem, in all his terrifying gorgeousness, leaned over me. "You shouldn't sleep in the sun—you'll dehydrate."

I rolled off the deck chair I'd curled up on and landed on my hands and knees. My joints shuddered with the impact.

"Fuck, you're dehydrated already, aren't you?"

Was that why I shook so hard I couldn't make it to my feet? My mouth pooled with water. I wasn't dehydrated.

"I'll get you some water."

Footsteps receded.

I couldn't move from my hands and knees. My limbs seemed locked in place. An image filled my thoughts, sent memories rushing through me.

A lifetime of memories.

I'd just invented time travel. Because my life from the first moment I could remember streaked though my vision.

Except all my memories centered around one person. *Josh*.

His name filled my brain, right there with his image. His name, which I'd banished from my vocabulary.

Footsteps approached, and a hand rested on my back.

I shook harder.

Because now the name reached my lips. The face swam in my mind. The soul loomed so close I could feel it next to me like a phantom limb.

So close, somewhere between here and memory.

Josh, my twin.

There was his name again. The name I'd not spoken, not once, not even in therapy, where I'd upheld my vow of silence. But somehow on the floor, shaking so hard I don't know how I kept my stomach from spilling, the name curled on my tongue, waiting for me to release it out loud.

"Here," Haithem said, and a glass of water appeared below my face.

A sob rattled my chest.

"Angelina?"

Another sob shook me, dragging painfully from my belly, up my ribs and into my shoulders. Strong hands pulled me up, helped me to sit, then hauled me against a chest as hard as steel, but warmer than the sun's rays beating on my back. His arms wrapped around me, and

I couldn't resist his embrace. I cried. I sobbed, heaving and ugly, jerking and shaking.

A year's worth of tears.

Haithem stroked my back, held on to me so tightly that he kept me tethered to sanity. I said nothing, just hiccupped and croaked, yet I could feel my secrets flow from me to him.

Evil bastard.

Holding me while I cried. Making me share things I didn't want to share. Apparently my heart wasn't as resistant to him as my mind was.

I cried harder.

He held me tighter.

Eventually, there wasn't anything left to cry. I didn't know there was a limit to how many tears one person can produce, but they did run out.

He held the glass of water to my lips, and I sipped. My head pounded with the onset of a migraine. No more tears flowed, but my breaths still shuddered.

"You've hardly eaten." He pulled me to my feet, let me lean against him. "Let's get you something."

He guided me into the cabin, sat me on the couch and draped a throw over me. I tipped to the side, lying against the soft pillows. Haithem walked to the intercom and barked something at the person at the other end of the line. I pulled the throw to my chin. My teeth chattered, but I wasn't cold.

Damp hair brushed from my face. His fingers smoothed over my temple and dipped behind my ear. Then his thumb swiped my cheek, pushing away the remaining wetness.

I hiccupped.

Asshole.

Wiping away my tears. Acting like my friend. Acting like someone I could trust. I couldn't trust him.

Yet he was the only one I'd entrusted with my tears…

Stupid.

Now he had a new power over me. The power of knowing I could cry. The power of having held my pain and seen just how heavy that bitch was.

"You know I'm not keeping you here simply for my own pleasure, don't you?"

I closed my eyes. I didn't want to see his bastard face. I had no freaking idea why he kept me. Only what he'd told me, which wasn't much, and I still didn't know what I could believe from him, anyway.

"I'm doing my best to get you home."

Home.

I shuddered again. My parents. Now that I'd started thinking, I couldn't stop. About Josh, about how we'd lost him. About how they wouldn't be able to take losing me, too.

I had to shut it down, turn off this thinking crap.

I'd done just fine the past twelve months—well, most of the past twelve months—blocking everything out. I still hurt. Still hurt every day. But I could make myself not acknowledge the source. I just needed to figure out how to do that again. Footsteps entered the room, and I opened my eyes.

Karim set a tray on the table, nodded to Haithem and walked back out.

Haithem collected the tray, returning a moment later with a bowl and spoon. "Eat some soup."

I shook my head.

Anything that went down now would definitely not stay down.

"You'll feel better after you eat." His voice went a little quieter. "I promise, just try some."

Damn him. Why'd he have to go and sound all caring?

Mind games.

He knelt beside me. I looked at him. His face reflected the warmth of his voice. The cool around me thawed. It was as easy as that—his eyes looking at me all softly, his lips pursed so tenderly.

As if he was someone else. As if he was someone who actually had a heart.

Where had that caring person been before?

How risky it was, how foolish I'd been, to give in to this softer side of him. I wanted to know what it'd be like to have him hold me now. Fondly, comfortingly. When I wasn't crying. But that would be taking foolishness too far.

I sat up and took the bowl from him. He rose then sat across from me. I lifted the spoon and brought it to my lips, sucking in a mouthful of hot, salty broth. The soup hit my empty stomach like a bucket of lead. I dropped the spoon back into the bowl. My stomach turned, hungry yet rebelling. I reached over and put the bowl on the side table next to the couch, then curled up against the pillows.

Haithem sighed but said nothing, only stretching his legs out in front of him. He watched me. Except his watching me didn't make me nervous. His watching me made me want him to come sit with me and let me rest my head in his lap instead of on fluffy pillows.

That settled it—I'd finally lost my marbles.

Hadn't that been what everyone had been saying behind my back for a year, anyway?

Angelina's cracked.

Well, consider me well and truly crack-a-lacked.

TWELVE

I MUST HAVE died in my sleep, because I awoke to the smell of heaven. My eyes flew open, and then I was looking at heaven, too. Haithem lying beside me in bed, relaxed in a shirt just like the one I wore, a wicked, sinful smile on his glistening lips. My heart beat way too fast for first thing after waking. Had he slept beside me? Had he been in bed with me without my knowing it? My skin prickled.

He raised a hand to his mouth, slid something brown and flaky between his lips and chewed. His jaw worked, the muscles on the edges popping out. I wet my lips. He still hadn't shaved. Tiny black hairs protruded from his skin, and I wanted nothing more than to feel them scrape against me. To touch them with my fingers. To drag his face to my throat. He swallowed. His hand moved again, and flakes fell from his fingers. I watched them fall onto the white sheet that covered us both to the waist.

A plate rested between us, piled high with three golden croissants.

Chocolate croissants.

Goddammit. My favorite. He was eating my absolute favorite thing in front of me. My stomach clenched, woke up and remembered the hunger it had forgotten in sleep.

"What are you doing?" My throat scraped, a husky morning croak filling my voice.

He picked up one of the pastries and tore it in half. Steam escaped, rising and dissipating from between his hands like a burst of delicious chocolate-filled magic. "I'm having breakfast in my bed."

His bed.

I shivered for real. Yes, I was in his bed. Half-naked in Haithem's bed.

He held half a croissant out to me so that the buttery, chocolaty scent washed over me.

"I thought you must be starving by now. So I had these baked fresh."

My gaze flicked between his fingers and his eyes. I couldn't miss the glint of satisfaction. He wasn't really hiding it. My heart sped up again. He'd had chocolate croissants baked for me. Some squealy, girlie part of me wanted to purr and rub up against him. Be all impressed.

The rest of me was just plain scared.

He'd known my weakness. This exact little weakness of mine. Of all the things he could have chosen, he'd picked so aptly. He'd known I'd just about sell my soul for a good croissant—make that croissant a chocolate one, and, well… He might be the actual devil. Knowing his position on contracts, I could picture him readying the paperwork now. My soul forfeit for the price of one chocolate croissant with the possibility of a proper fucking on the side.

"You're making a mess in the bed."

He grinned, flashed every tooth at me. "Angel, I've never minded making a mess in bed."

Heat exploded over my chest and face. I might not

have experienced it, but he made me want to find out—find out what a hot, messy fuck was like.

He held a pastry to my mouth. It warmed my lips. Tempted me to eat from his hand.

I wouldn't.

I wouldn't have been able to stop there. I'd be licking the butter from those fingers, sinking them into my mouth then dragging them down my body. Because, god help me, despite all wrongness, I was hungrier for Haithem than I'd ever been for food.

I reached forward, plucked the other half of the croissant off the plate and rolled out of bed.

He chuckled softly.

I sank into one of the wingback chairs in the corner of the room near the couch and pulled off a tiny piece of croissant and popped it in my mouth.

It melted on my tongue with all the rich loveliness of chocolate and good pastry. It took all my will not to moan. Haithem slid off the bed and walked toward me. I kept my eyes on the pastry. He set the plate on the small table next to me.

"You've forgotten something."

Jesus, did he expect a thank-you?

I glanced up, and he held out a cup. It looked and smelled suspiciously like a cappuccino. I'd have liked to resist. But we were talking about real coffee to wash down my croissant. There are some things you just don't say no to.

I took it from his hands.

"Thanks," I said, and had a sip. Then my gaze snapped to his. "Oh, come on, really?"

"What?"

I set the cup down. "Three sugars? How the hell did you just happen to guess how I take my coffee?"

"I didn't guess. I watched you put sugar in your coffee the first time I saw you."

He'd paid such close attention that day? What was it about *me* that made a man like him notice, made him pay attention? Whatever it was, maybe it had something to do with why he made such an impact on me. That *zing* between us. Zapping attraction. I'd experienced attraction before. I'd had butterflies a few times in high school. My heart had raced when I'd been kissed. I'd gotten wet when a guy had groped my tits.

I'd never believed in the kind of lust that made smart girls do stupid things. But here it was. I'd yet to understand chemistry. I'd only begun to appreciate just how deeply the desire to replicate was hardwired into my genetics. As though there was some genetic code that hit a magic sequence when it met its perfect counterpart and then—*zing*.

Cue the crazy.

I shook my head, picked up the cup and held it to my mouth. "I'm just going to have my coffee and croissant now, because I need it, and I'll try to pretend for five minutes that any part of this is normal," I said out loud but mostly to myself.

He sat in the chair opposite me and picked up a croissant.

I ate another piece of pastry. "Don't you have important secret business to attend to or something?"

"Ouch, Angel, you trying to get rid of me?"

I made a sound at the back of my throat.

"Business is mostly concluded, so for now, I'm all

yours." He dragged out the last part of the sentence, and I felt the words all the way down to my womb.

"Lucky me," I said, and scrunched up my nose at him.

"You wound me. And when I have such surprises in store for you today."

I laughed drily. "You know that sounds like a line right out of a horror movie, right?" I brushed crumbs off my legs, and my lips tightened. "I'm not sure I can handle any more surprises."

"You're determined to think the worst of me, aren't you?"

I looked up and met his fierce gaze. "You could always let me call my family and prove me wrong."

He sighed and put his pastry back onto the plate. "I've emailed your family, Angelina. They know you're fine. So you can stop worrying and relax until we can get you back to them."

I paused, fingers midway to my lips. "You have?"

"Yes, I sent it last night."

The croissant fell onto my lap. "Oh no, you've made it so much worse…"

"Worse?"

My mouth went dry. A fatty aftertaste coated my tongue. "My parents will never believe an email from some random guy saying I've run off with him." I shuddered. "They really will think something terrible has happened to me."

Haithem touched my knee and peered into my face. "Hey, do I look like an amateur to you?"

I blinked, his bold features swimming in front of me.

"I sent the email from your account, wrote it as you. Used all those things you said to me."

A pang filled my chest, and I gripped my forehead with my palm. "You said all that stuff about them smothering me?"

"Would you rather they think you're in a ditch somewhere?" He leaned back into his own chair.

"No," I whispered. My throat hurt.

They'd blame themselves now—my parents. And I'd disappointed them enough for one lifetime.

I picked up the coffee and took a small sip. It didn't taste quite as good anymore. "How could you even know my email address, let alone access my account?"

Haithem stroked his thumb under his chin. "Your résumé."

"You don't miss a thing, do you?" I let out a puff of air. "And my password?"

"I have a guy."

"You have a guy? Who the hell has a guy?" I held out my hands in an incredulous gesture.

He linked his fingers together and rested his elbows on his knees, hands dangling between his legs.

I wouldn't be getting any more answers on that topic.

I scooped pastry and crumbs off my lap and deposited them onto the plate, then picked up a small corner of croissant and looked at it.

Something occurred to me that had not before. "You had these baked for me, huh?"

"Yeah."

"You always so considerate, or am I just special?"

The way he focused on me—screw "special," he made me feel as if nothing existed outside the cabin.

"You're. Just. Special."

Me, special.

My stomach fluttered, and my reason for asking al-

most fled my mind. "Does that mean I can make re-
quests?" My gaze fell to his chest as though I'd suddenly
become fascinated by the way his first button hung
open. The way dark hair lightly smattered his olive
skin. "Is there a pastry chef on board?"

He remained silent.

I looked up and froze. I'd made another mistake.

"Angel, you don't want to play this game with me."
His top thumb tapped on his bottom one, and his lips
made a slashing line. "I'm so much better at it than you
could know."

"I—" What could I say? No, I wasn't fishing for information? No, I wasn't thinking what allies I might
find on this massive boat?

"I'm glad you're not stupid. But believe me, your
only friend here is me." He sat back, his hands moving
to his knees. "So you want to know how many people
are on board. Let's not pretend…go ahead and ask me."

I swallowed. "How many people are on board?"

"My captain and his two crew, the chef, two house-
keeping staff members, four of my security team,
Karim, and us." He smiled. "All members of my personal staff. All devoted to me."

Security team.

I studied him. He could have called them anything.
Squad, gang, associates, or even just *men*.

But he called them security.

Legitimate people had security teams. Other kinds
had henchmen.

People under threat had security teams.

There was more to his paranoia than keeping secrets—he was in danger.

Were we?

Maybe he'd given me that one clue, but I doubt he'd give me more."So, there're thirteen of us...isn't that unlucky?"

"Perhaps it is." He stood. "For the record, only Karim and I speak English. If you were wondering, that is."

He smiled wider, darker, then turned to the door.

"Wait—"

He looked back at me.

"Do I have to stay up here? Is it safe to go below?"

Haithem sighed and faced me. "It's better if you spend most of your time up here." He laid his palm over his chest. "But you are safe anywhere on this boat. You are safe wherever I am."

My shoulders rolled forward as though a rubber band had been holding them back and had suddenly snapped. "That's a relief, because I do remember having guns pulled on me."

"Won't happen again. You surprised my security, caused alarm."

I nodded. Somehow, the crazy freaking memory of armed security aiming shiny weapons at me lost its edge as Haithem explained it as if it were natural— reasonable.

What else would become reasonable, the longer I stayed here?

How many hours had I spent in the cabin?

Too many. All day. A full day on this boat without word from home.

Enough to educate me on exactly what is meant by the term *cabin fever.*

Idleness, for me, was like sitting on poison barbs. A thousand nasty images poked into me, their venom seeping into my blood. My mother's face all those weeks she'd sat by my brother's bedside—how she must be reacting now, thinking I'd run off because of her. Each thought carried its own unique brand of pain.

Wisps of images, snippets of sounds like my mother's sobs, clutched at me with spindly fingers, wrapped around me, dragged me into memories I couldn't revisit. Memories I knew would mirror almost exactly what my parents would be going through now.

I walked the length of the cabin. Fifteen strides with my legs. I knew how many steps, but I counted them again. One, two, three, four... Still, I heard it, the name, under all those other nasty little thoughts. A whisper.

Josh.

If I let it, that whisper would grow to a shout then a roar—a shaking, rattling, booming roar that would consume me.

I had to get out.

Had to. I didn't have a choice. I'd drown if I stayed in the cabin. I'd have a better chance of survival in the water. At least then I'd be busy trying to stay afloat.

I ran to the window. Nothing but blue stretching out to the horizon.

Pale blue sky. Dark blue ocean.

Haithem had said it'd be "better" for me to stay in here, but there was still a whole floor below me I hadn't explored. I left the cabin and went onto the deck.

A whirling sound buzzed through the air. I looked up. A helicopter cut through the sky, flying directly toward us. I froze, watching it grow from a small, toy-like thing to life size.

A helicopter...

My chest filled with breath, and I waved my hands

above my head in wide sweeps. The helicopter drew closer, the whirring louder. My hair blew around my face, tangling over my mouth. I added a jump to my movements, not even caring that Haithem's shirt flapped up to my waist.

"If I'd known you'd be this excited, I may have organized this sooner." Haithem's words boomed over the noise.

I jumped. The helicopter flew over our heads and somehow knocked the air from my lungs. The shirt whipped up to my armpits. I grabbed the fabric, hauling it down over my chest—over my fully exposed boobs. Haithem wrapped his arms around my waist, keeping me upright and my shirt in place.

Oh, dear lord.

The helicopter hovered over a space on the protruding lower deck, marked with a giant *H* in a circle. The wind eased, and I smoothed the shirt over my hips. Thank god my panties had dried, even if my bra hadn't.

Thank you, god—really. I couldn't have handled that indignity.

I turned and pulled out of Haithem's embrace. He laughed. Bloody bastard, and damn him, his laugh was just as captivating as the first time I'd heard it.

I pushed his chest then swiped hair out of my face. "Don't you dare enjoy this. I have no clean clothes, thanks to you."

He raised one brow. "No, if you truly fell into the lifeboat, then you have no clean clothes thanks to you being too stubborn to let me walk you to the dock."

I narrowed my gaze at him. "Oh, really, and if I'd signed on all your dotted lines and let you sweep me up in your romantic, ironclad contractual fantasy, would

I have clean clothes then?" I raised my own eyebrow, because, yeah, I could do that, too. "Or did you plan on keeping me naked the entire time?"

He lost his cocky expression, but the one that replaced it made my stomach do gymnastics. Reminded me exactly why I'd hopped on the damn boat in the first place. Reminded me exactly what I'd wanted from him.

What I still did want from him, if I were honest and let my mind drift there.

"If you'd taken me up on my offer, Angel, then no, you wouldn't have much need for clothes." He ran his gaze down to my thighs then back up. "But you would've had them. Karim could've taken you to collect some things, or I would've organized overnight shopping before we left."

Always with an answer for everything. But I didn't want to think about how different things might've been if I'd said yes—didn't want to imagine what I'd most likely be busy doing right now.

I glanced at the helicopter. The guards carried large packages out of the helicopter and jogged out of sight.

"You have a visitor?"

"A delivery," he said.

Geez, what could he be getting delivered by helicopter in the middle of the ocean?

Probably better I didn't find out. I tossed a lethal look at him and strode toward the cabin. Footsteps thundered up the stairs. My pulse jumped, and I ran the rest of the way to the cabin and slammed the door.

The door opened behind me, and I spun, linking my arms over my chest. One of the guards—one of the ones I'd "met" after I'd climbed out of the lifeboat— strode into the room. Haithem followed behind him. I backed against the wall, my gaze flicking between the dark-haired-cowboy, gun-wielding guard and Haithem.

Haithem gestured to the bed and said something in Spanish. I leaned against the wall and stared at the guard. *Spanish*. Haithem didn't usually speak Spanish. He spoke English or what I could only take a wild, un-educated guess and say was Arabic.

But I recognized Spanish. I knew Spanish.

Well… I knew *sangria*, and *paella de marisco*, and a few phrases learned from watching television, but that was beside the point. I knew something I didn't know before.

I'd learned something on my own.

Something Haithem didn't know I knew. That made me want to smile—but I didn't. Instead, I watched Spanish gun-slinging-cowboy-guard place several bags on the bed.

Another guard came into the room, this one with boxes, which he also placed on the bed.

They left, and I turned to Haithem.

"What—?" I paused as the two other guards came in, adding to the growing mountain of bags and packages slowly covering the surface of the giant bed.

The whirling intensified, and I looked out the window. The helicopter lifted off the helipad. The last two guards left, and the original two returned, bringing with them two final loads of what I'd only begun to verify as merchandise.

Department store merchandise.

Boutique merchandise.

Designer brand merchandise.

Shoe merchandise.

Because most of the bags had labels. Labels I rec-

ognized, although I'd never actually purchased anything from any of those fancy places. But given I was
the proud owner of a vagina, I knew a designer brand
when I saw one.

Perhaps Haithem was smuggling illegal contraband
stuffed in shoe boxes and perfume bottles?

The guards left the room, shutting the door behind
them. I turned to Haithem. He sat on the end of the
bed, the look on his face so supremely satisfied I got
the awful feeling this all had something to do with me.

He held a hand out, gesturing across the bed. "You
are welcome."

"What do you mean?" I stared at the Mount Everest-
sized pile of shopping bags.

Haithem's lips twitched. "Clean clothes... I believe
you were just complaining about not having any?"

"No way—you wouldn't get all this just for me." I
walked a step closer to the bed, but didn't touch any of
the bags—just let myself have a closer look.

"Can and *did*."

I glanced up. He'd pushed his shirtsleeves up to his
elbows, revealing his bronze forearms. I should've
known not to underestimate Haithem.

"You can start opening things. Nothing will bite."

I moved to the very edge of the bed and looked over
the bags and boxes, then dragged over one of the least
scary plastic department store bags and pulled out the
contents. I unfolded dark blue jeans and held them to
my waist.

Something in my chest uncurled, spreading warmth
into my body. I glanced at Haithem. He watched me
hold the jeans against my hips. I don't know what I'd
expected. A French maid outfit or a fishnet bodysuit?

Not this.

Not comfortable, practical and thoughtful.

Not something I couldn't resent him for.

"Thank you," I whispered, and folded the jeans. I hadn't tried them on, but he'd purchased the correct size. As if Haithem wouldn't. He had a way of knowing everything, even the things I didn't want him to know.

"You're welcome."

I hoped I hadn't shivered visibly. He didn't say things such as "you're welcome" the way normal people did. He didn't speak at you—he spoke to you. His voice so intimate you couldn't block it out if you tried.

I moved on, unpacking T-shirts, shirts, jumpers, jackets, pants, skirts, dresses, bathing suits, socks, essentially everything a girl might need on a yacht. Not to mention plenty of things she didn't—such as designer outfits I couldn't picture myself in, even if I had somewhere to wear them. He'd organized a year's worth of clothing.

He watched me the entire time I unpacked, not saying anything, his gaze traveling over every item I held up. I reached one of the lingerie boxes and pulled off the bow. I'd never owned lingerie that came in a box with a bow. I peeled back the tissue paper.

Bras.

Three beautiful bras, lined up one in front of the other. Black, white and pink. I checked the tags. Damn, he'd even gotten that right? I'd been putting my money on bras being the part where he slipped up. I wasn't a standard size. Buying bras was a bitch. Yet he'd worked it out.

I looked at him, pink bra dangling from my hand.

"You left a bra hanging in the bathroom," he said, once again using his powers of telepathy.

Of course, he'd leave nothing to chance.

"How could you even arrange all of this?" I looked around. "Who does helicopter deliveries to yachts?"

"Anything is possible, if you're prepared to pay for it." He got off the bed and faced me.

The bra fell back into the box. I could swear we were no longer talking about helicopter yacht delivery.

I turned away from him and reached for another package. Haithem fell silent again but stood next to me. I opened the lid to a bundle of pale pink fluff.

Oh, hell yes.

A giant plush robe. I tugged out the robe, hugged it, and then pulled it on, belting it at the waist. The robe swamped me in warmth and covered me down to my ankles.

This was my favorite.

This, I could wear night and day and never take off. More fluff rested at the bottom of the box. Matching slippers. I bent down and put them on.

Haithem looked down at me, a smile taking his face from attractive to completely goddamn lickable. "You like that, huh?"

"Yeah, I like it," I said then stood. "You thought of everything, didn't you?" I dragged across more bags and rummaged inside, finding toiletries. "Shampoo, cosmetics, everything."

Haithem just shrugged and crossed his arms.

One of the bags contained a hair straightener. I didn't even own one of those at home. I tipped another long white box out of a bag of toiletries. Make that two hair straighteners. I popped open the end and slid the plastic insert out of the cardboard, then gasped, my cheeks flushing hot.

Not a hair straightener.

My gaze snapped to Haithem's. I didn't even have words for this. Killed the *Pretty Woman* experience right there, though.

Haithem looked at the item in my hands, and his eyes flared. He removed the large flesh-colored vibrator from the box with a laugh. "Well, I did ask my shopper for everything a woman might want."

"So you didn't ask for this, then?"

He stopped laughing and took the box from me, as well. "No."

Of course not. Why would he give a girl one of these when he could give her...?

I grinned and snatched the vibrator from him. "Actually, I'll hang on to this." I let my eyelids bat softly and took the box back too, then held up the vibrator.

I shook it in front of him.

It wobbled.

Perfect.

"I've been getting really bored."

His face—*ohmygod*—was priceless.

My palm accidentally hit a button, and the vibrator sprang to life, buzzing, wiggling and twisting. "Would you look at that? Bonus features."

He frowned, and I'd never have believed Haithem capable of blushing, but his neck changed color. Yep, definitely went a shade or two darker than it had been. I choked back my laugh, shut the vibrator down, put it back in the box, and then stuffed it back inside the bag it came from. Then realized the bag also contained every kind of lube and love-oil solution ever made. Because nothing wins a girl's heart like gifts of lube.

I patted my chest, trying to keep the laughter in. After all this time, I'd be damned if I lost the upper hand I'd gained on Haithem. Even if it was a cheap, superficial upper hand.

I came to the last of the boxes. *Shoes.* The part of the experience that solidly confirmed to me that I was a fully functioning woman—because opening those boxes did physical things to me. I can't imagine the ways in which I may have disgraced myself with squeals and *oohs* and *ahhs* if Haithem hadn't been next to me.

I held it together.

Until the last box. Then I lost it in another kind of way.

My insides froze. I stared down at brown leather boots.

Boots I had at home.

Boots my parents had given me for my eighteenth birthday. Boots that took me out of the warped alternate reality I'd been existing in with Haithem and slammed me back where I'd been almost three years ago.

I'd gotten brown leather boots for my birthday. That morning, when Dad pulled back the tarp on Josh's Mustang, I'd been so thrilled for my twin. Josh needed special things. Josh had earned them. He'd suffered for them. But as I clutched my new birthday boots to my chest, maybe I was greedy, or selfish, or shallow, or all of those things, because I'd secretly hoped that maybe there'd be a surprise for me that day, too.

I looked around the room at the piles of things around me. Just things. Meaningless things. I, more than anyone, knew how unimportant things were.

I knew what really mattered.

But no one had ever gone to any effort for me. Not that I'd ever gone without. I got things when I needed them. A new outfit when I had a job interview, for instance. But I don't think anyone had ever thought about what I actually *wanted*—not even once.

I breathed deep, unable to catch my breath. Why did Haithem have to be the one, the first person to ever floor me by going to a little trouble?

"Something wrong with the boots?"

I looked at him. "Why did you do all this?"

"Told you—this doesn't have to be unpleasant. You could even try enjoying yourself."

I dropped the boots and scooped up an armful of clothing. "All of this?" I dumped them at his feet. "All this, just so I'd enjoy myself?"

I couldn't breathe deeply enough anymore, and I stalked the length of the room.

"You're angry?"

God, men, so clueless.

I stopped halfway across the room and walked back toward him. "Do you know, for my eighteenth birthday, all I wanted was to go and see *Les Misérables* while it was in Melbourne?"

Haithem didn't say anything, but his expression evened.

"I hinted to my mum about it for months." I stepped closer. "Instead, they gave me boots." I nudged the boots on the floor with my toe. "Not because we couldn't afford it or they had something against musicals, just because they couldn't be bothered—it was too much effort to take me, with everything else going on." I looked at

Haithem. His face blurred. "I'd have been happy with anything, really, if they'd just gone to a little effort."

I couldn't see Haithem anymore but knew I'd never seen someone stand so still. I tipped my head back and blinked until my vision cleared.

"So tell me, Haithem, why a stranger who cares little enough about me to keep me prisoner when he could've sent me home on a helicopter at any time, gives a crap about anything I might want?"

"What is it you'd like to hear?" He leaned closer, and my gaze flew back to him. "Do you want to hear that I feel sorry for you?" His voice became a whispering caress. "I'm sorry it worked out this way, but that's not going to stop me from doing anything I need to do." He straightened. "So enjoy yourself, Angelina, or don't." He turned and walked to the door, then paused. "It's up to you, but it sounds to me as if maybe this is exactly where you need to be."

THIRTEEN

AT A QUARTER past two, it hit me—no, Haithem had not been secretly hoping to sleep with me. I'd been alone, wearing holes through his bedsheets with my fidgeting fingers for a good three hours when I knew for sure. I could stop waiting.

He wasn't coming, wasn't going to sneak between the sheets for a midnight cuddle or a crack-of-dawn tumble. I glanced at the bedside clock. 2:16 a.m. Wow—that minute went hella fast.

Thank god he'd found somewhere else to crash, because if you're going to pretty much hold a girl prisoner, she definitely deserves the sanctity of her own sleep space. It turned out he had at least some sense of chivalry.

I looked at the clock again. 2:16. *Still?* I rubbed my face. This was the first night I'd actually gone to bed to sleep—as opposed to falling unconscious or being completely wiped out by some feverish or postcry coma—since meeting Haithem.

Actually, unconsciousness didn't sound so bad. I'd almost forgotten what this was like, this crazy, hyperactive, middle-of-the-night brain. It was the very reason I had a strict no-texting-after-midnight rule. The crap that goes through your mind when you're awake but tired in the middle of the night is best kept locked away in your own head.

I peered around the room in the dark.

Could someone please explain to me why, in the cabin of freaking luxury, there was no television? No television, no gaming console, no DVD player. Not even a radio. A girl could lose her ever-loving mind.

If she hadn't already.

I kicked my feet. The sheets were too heavy, yet not warm enough. For some reason, my calves twitched as though they wanted to run away. This was why, for the past year, I'd popped a sleeping pill at precisely nine o'clock every night, unless I was going out. Pill at nine, asleep by ten. No sleeplessness. No late-night musings.

No midnight psychotic rocking.

Pill and sleep.

Simple as that. The doctor agreed with this method from the beginning. It was the one thing I'd opened my mouth to complain about. Insomnia, they called it. I'm not sure I agreed. I knew what the problem was—too much alone time with my brain. I peeped at the clock.

2:16.

Are you freaking kidding me?

I leaned over and whacked my fist against the top of the clock. Pain shuddered through to my elbow. I looked and waited. The digital display flickered and then…2:17 a.m. Fantastic. Now only how many more minutes until dawn?

So why had Haithem managed to make a "right" choice on this one thing, and not slept in his own bed? Sure, given the circumstances, it'd be completely morally bankrupt or whatever, but like the guy had more than fifty cents in that vault, anyway. Wasn't I tempting enough to warrant giving it a go?

I sat up. In fact, besides a few saucy looks, he had

not put a single proper move on me since I'd awakened from that fever. What was up with that?

Maybe puking on him had put him off?

That's not real sexy...

Not that I'd sleep with him now, obviously. I fluffed the pillows and lay back down.

Except, maybe I should...

Maybe sleeping with Haithem would crack him. Just like a nut. Sex—and then *snap*, hard shell gone, tasty center up for grabs. I mean, Emma could get a guy to do just about anything with nothing more than the power of her vagina. I'd seen her do it a hundred times. She chewed them up, spat them out, and then moved on to the next one.

And *my* vagina and I had come here for the express purpose of getting laid. Maybe not *express*, but let's be honest, we'd wanted to be laid.

And Haithem was still superhot.

And no one was around to judge.

And after what he'd put me through, an orgasm or two—possibly three—wasn't too much to ask for, was it? If I were ever going to try meaningless, detached sex, what better time than right damn now with a man who infuriated me?

Except he still hadn't come on to me again—not even when I'd waved a vibrator at him. I flung my legs off the edge of the bed, jumped out and snatched my fluffy robe off the chair. At the very least, I'd get answers.

I marched to the door and tugged it open. A cool sea breeze filled my lungs, reminded me we were nowhere near home. The usual rules did not apply. In fact, there was no good reason why I couldn't take Haithem up on his offer and focus on enjoying myself for once.

I crossed the deck and reached the stairs. This time
I held on to the railing with a death grip as I made my
way down. Reaching the bottom, I scanned the lower
deck. A dark silhouette walked the perimeter. I couldn't
see which guard it was, but I didn't fancy another incident like the last time I'd surprised one of those dudes.

"Hi," I called, and waved, waiting for him to come
to me.

The silhouette approached at a steady pace. I
breathed out. He reached the bottom step, and I could
make out his features. Yep, Spanish-speaking cowboy-
guard.

"Hola." I understood that first word, thanks to *Dora
the Explorer* and my time babysitting, but not the rest
of the sentence he rattled off. I guessed by his tone
that it probably went a little something like "Go back
upstairs."

I pulled my dressing gown tighter, and because it
was most likely still 2:17 a.m. and the normal rules need
not apply, I cracked a smile. "Take me to your leader."

He looked at me blankly.

Either he was way too lame to appreciate my late-
night humor, or he really didn't speak English. I sighed.
"Haithem, take me to Haithem."

He frowned.

"Haithem said I could come down here."

He stared at me. I wasn't sure if it was my repeat-
ing Haithem's name or if the guard actually could understand, but he inclined his head and walked toward
a door. I followed, and he led me down a dim hallway,
then to a closed internal door. He nodded at the door
and waited.

I stared at the shiny wood-veneer surface. My stomach fluttered. The excess energy fueling my nerves dwindled a little. I glanced back at the guard. He nodded at the door again. Too late to back out. I held my breath, knocked, then turned the handle, stepped in and shut the door behind me.

A light flicked on, and Haithem sat up in bed, hair mussed, eyes narrowed and jaw set hard. A sheet pooled at his waist. My mouth pooled in response. He was shirtless. And what a chest, goddammit. Muscled enough to make me want to trace every ridge with my hands but not so muscular that it looked as if it took too much effort for him to be that way. My gaze flicked to where the sheet rested in his lap. Where dark hair gathered to a central tuft.

Possibly, he might've been fully naked under the sheet.

My skin caught fire. Went up in flames, as though someone had put a match to me. I swallowed twice.

"What's going on, Angelina?"

I stared at his lap.

"Why are you in my room?"

In his room? I glanced around. This room was more like a regular—but still nice—hotel room. *This* wasn't his room. I had his room.

"Why isn't there a TV in the cabin?" I blurted out the only question I could come up with.

"What?" Haithem scratched his cheek. He'd shaved. Damn him, he'd shaved—and showered, too, going by the smell of him. Because yes, I could smell him. He used some kind of scented man soap that made me want to crawl right onto his bed and rub my face all over him.

"Why is there no television in my cabin?"

He rested against the headboard. "I had the televisions taken out. I find them disruptive."

"Oh," I said.

"Is that all?"

I leaned my shoulder against the wall. "No."

"What then?"

"How come you've stopped hitting on me?" I glanced at my slippers.

Yeah, I played that cool.

"You're not here for the same reasons anymore."

I looked up, my fingers twitching. "I didn't agree to service your needs, you mean?"

His lips thinned. Odd, I used to think he was so hard to read, but now his anger blazed for me to see.

"That…and you're only twenty. I'm thirty, and I enjoy women who are at least old enough to drink."

Ouch.

That one hit me like a slap. Actually, maybe a slap would have stung less. Having Haithem look at me and imply a lack of attraction… I tried to shake it off, that old worry that I wasn't enough.

I smiled a bitter smile I'd seen on other women but never pictured on myself.

"Well, presuming we're still in Australian waters, not America, where clearly you're used to spending time—"

He twitched. Seemed as if I'd guessed what he hadn't chosen to tell me.

"Then I'm old enough to drink, to vote, to drive and to fuck." I smiled a little wider. "But if that's not enough to alleviate your conscience," I said, almost choking on the word, "then rest assured, I'll be twenty-one in a little over a week."

Haithem stared me down then met my smile with

an even more sarcastic one. He flipped back the sheet, exposing his hip and one long, long leg. I ate up the sight—Haithem naked, shoulders to toes. Oh, dear, merciful Lucifer. My insides did hot explosive things.

"By all means, come here then." He stroked the empty space next to him.

Challenge lit his eyes—*I double dare you.*

I almost dived onto that space, yet, for some reason, my heart revolted, made me shake with things other than lust. Maybe pride. Turned out that I needed to know he really wanted me.

"As stunningly seductive as that offer is, I'm afraid it fails to send my lady parts to their happy place."

I flashed a grin, watched his expression go blank, then I fled the room before I proved myself a total liar.

MAYBE MY JAB at Haithem's seduction skills prompted the pseudo dating, or perhaps he simply enjoyed eating sweets with women. He brought me cheesecake. Not a slice, not a mini cheesecake, but a whole damn family-sized baked strawberry cheesecake on a glass platter. At least I was more prepared than usual, lounging in a deck chair, looking extra sharp in designer sunglasses, high-heel shoes and a brand-new sundress when he set dessert on the table on the deck and called me to "breakfast."

I pulled myself up from the deck chair and walked over to the table, feeling a little taller next to him than I usually did. He set a bottle of champagne on the table, then went inside the cabin and came back out with two champagne flutes. He pried the lid off the bottle with a pop and eased the foam into a glass without so much as a drip, then handed me a full sparkling flute.

"Champagne breakfast?"

My fingers closed around the stem.

Haithem held on to the glass. "Well, since we are still in Australian waters, and you're old enough to drink…"

My heart did a backflip. He'd just given me something—knowledge. It wasn't lost on me. Nor was the fact that with him, such a gift would be deliberate. He let go of the glass, and I pulled it to my chest and sat in one of the chairs.

He filled the other glass, not looking up. "Why didn't you tell me about your impending birthday?"

"Like you didn't know. You saw my date of birth." I pushed the sunglasses back into my hair.

"No, I mean earlier." The bottle clinked on the tabletop, and he looked at me. The sun hit his eyes just right, showing me hidden highlights in what appeared to be total darkness. "When I asked you to come away with me, you said you had responsibilities." He sat cautiously. "You never said you had a special birthday. Is that it? Are there celebrations planned for you?"

My stomach dropped. A pile of bricks could've been placed on my chest, and there'd have been less pressure on my ribs. I pushed the glass to my lips and sipped. Bubbles tingled on my tongue. How do you describe something as being the exact opposite of a celebration? I took another bigger sip. Champagne burned up my nose and into my eyes. I hadn't done the sums when he'd invited me on his yacht, but if I'd realized I could be away from home for my birthday, maybe I'd have made a different choice.

I'd have made a different choice.

"Doesn't matter now. I won't be home for it, will I?"

"No." He said it simply. If he had any remorse, I couldn't tell.

I shut my eyes, tried to shut down the surge of relief. I shouldn't feel that way. I should want to be with my family on that day.

Josh's twenty-first birthday.

Because, let's face it, there wasn't room for it to be mine. Not in my heart, not in theirs.

I opened my eyes. Haithem cut a thick slice of cheesecake.

He handed me the plate, but I shook my head.

"Don't like cheesecake?"

"I like cheesecake just fine." I took another mouthful of bubbly. As though he hadn't already worked out that my love of sweet, cheesy baked goods came second only to my love of chocolate pastries. Not that I let myself overindulge.

Haithem sat and picked up a fork. "You shouldn't drink that on an empty stomach. It'll go to your head."

"Well, my mother taught me a lady never eats sweets for breakfast." I drained the glass then plonked it down. It hit the table harder than I meant it to, sending a jolt into my funny bone. I'm not sure what she'd say about champagne breakfasts. "And to save treats for once a week. So after yesterday's breakfast, I think I've met my quota and broken enough rules."

Haithem pressed his fork into the top of his cheesecake. It slid right through to the porcelain plate with a scrape. He glanced up at me. "And what happens if you're not a lady?"

I blinked, watching the fork rise, watching the strawberries on top seep down the fork before disappearing between his lips.

"You're not making sense."

"What rules do you need to follow in order to be a lady?" He licked the corner of his mouth.

I glanced at my empty glass, wishing it to refill itself. "No more than two drinks in a night," I whispered.

His fork sank back into the cheesecake.

"Never get in a car with a man I don't know."

No boys in the bedroom, but he didn't need to know about that one or how little I'd needed it.

"Home by midnight."

"Hmmm," he murmured.

"What?"

"The night you came here, you got into the car with Karim, and there's no way you could've gotten home by midnight." He swallowed and wiped his mouth on a napkin. "So, which is it, Angelina? Did you want to be a lady, or did you want to be bad?"

The sun heated my chest. My lips tingled. My pulse thundered in my ears again. I breathed through my nose. "I guess I wanted to be bad."

Haithem picked up his champagne and drank, never taking his gaze off me.

"And look how that turned out for me," I added.

He tilted his glass forward. "Then the real question is, if you could go back, would you run home like a good girl, or would you tempt fate again?" He leaned in, and rested an arm on the tabletop. "If there was no price to pay?"

"There's always a price to pay. You taught me that."

He smiled. Smiled and looked into me. Directly into me. Laid me bare.

I knew then why he was so irresistible. Not because he was so fine, so delicious no woman could walk away without soaked panties and a lost mind. I wanted him because Haithem was a glass of aged whiskey, a full-fat hot chocolate, a double-choc cheesecake, a triple-shot espresso, five-star fine-ass dining—he was gold in the kind of carats they have to blend to make jewelry out of. A blood diamond. He was all the fat, all the calories, all the sugar, all of the bad, wrong, decadent, sinful, greedy goodness I'd always been told I couldn't have—and believed I shouldn't want.

But I needed it.

I wanted it.

All of it.

Something purely for me. One thing, one moment that was selfishly, brazenly mine. There wasn't an instant in my life I could remember where I'd lived solely for myself. Not a second where I wasn't so bogged down in worry, or concern, or grief, or obligation, or numbness, that I could simply enjoy myself.

I'd hollowed into a defunct husk.

Now something blossomed in my shell. Maybe Haithem was tainted rain and maybe, eventually, I'd be poisoned—but right then, he watered me. Without him, i'd whither again.

I reached out and took the edge of his plate, and dragged the cheesecake toward me. He watched me, and the look that flashed across his face made my panties stick to my dampening skin.

He held out the fork, and I took it.

Consequences.

"I guess you can always fly in bigger clothes." I smiled and scooped up some cheesecake.

He laughed and watched me eat. I cleaned the plate, hardly tasting what passed between my lips. Someone had turned up the volume on my privates. I couldn't taste the strawberry, couldn't taste the vanilla. I knew it was there but all I tasted was sugar. I was too aware of what was going on inside my underwear to pay much notice to what was happening in my mouth. The scrap of fabric between my legs tugged like a humming live wire. Maybe I rocked myself a little.

I licked the fork.

The front.

The back.

Haithem's jaw ticked. I saw his control flickering on and off, and it filled me with a power I'd never known. I did that to him. If I could break him, I would. I'd take a hammer and shatter through his walls. If I was going to be stuck with him, if I was going to suffer the consequences of my lust, then I'd be damned if I'd let anything keep me from what I'd come for.

I needed him. Wanted him. I don't think anyone else could hope to understand. I was ready to break out.

"You said I could ask you for anything…" I rubbed my lips together.

"I did." His voice lowered, deeper than I'd ever heard it go.

I gave a half smile that tugged at the corner of my mouth. "Well, I know what I want."

"Then ask me."

You'd think I'd have whispered my request, but I didn't. I spoke clear and loud. "I want orgasms."

He laughed, soft and rumbling. "Orgasms? That specific?"

"Yes, orgasms."

Why lie? Why tone it down or dilute it with innuendo?

I wanted orgasms. I wanted to shake and come. To live and forget.

"I'm surprised you're still surprising me." His eyes narrowed slightly. "I'd have sworn if you were to ask me something like that, it'd be for lovemaking."

Lovemaking.

Images of Haithem as I'd seen him the night before, head to toe, huge and nude, but rolling in his white sheets with me in his arms, filled my imagination.

Tempting.

But something told me when Haithem and I came together it wouldn't be for lovemaking. Such a pretty word was too out of sync with what I felt for him.

They weren't sweet, warm feelings.

"I don't want lovemaking—I want orgasms."

Haithem pushed back his chair and walked around the table. My heart attempted to back out of the deal by making a quick exit up my throat.

"And what do I get in exchange for providing orgasms?"

"You?" I blinked. "You said you owe me, and I could ask for what I wanted."

"That was before you threw a million dollars overboard." He sank down on one knee in front of me, putting us at eye level. "And before you accepted all my gifts." He reached for my foot and pulled it into his lap.

Holy shit, was orgasm-giving starting right now?

Haithem tugged off my shoe and held it up. "Haven't I been very generous?"

I stared at the shoe. I'd worn good ones.

Why not? He'd given them to me.

"What do you want, Haithem?"

"Not much." He tossed my shoe then pulled up my other foot. "Just a little agreement."

"What is it with you and agreements?"

He grinned and threw away my other shoe. "I'm a born businessman."

"So, tell me what you want."

He pressed his thumb into the bottom of my foot. My back arched off the chair, and my breath caught. Fuck, if he could do that to me with one touch on my foot, what hope did I have?

"While I'm touching you, I get to ask questions, any questions I want, and I get the truth from you."

He rubbed his thumb up the arch of my foot. I squirmed, my muscles aching deliciously.

"One question," I whispered.

"Five." He pushed deep into the muscles of my foot.

Oh, lord help me, I might've called out ten if he'd just touch me more. "Two."

"Four," he said, and tugged my leg so my ass dragged down on the chair.

"Three…and a pass if I choose to use it."

He smiled and raised my foot, baring his teeth for a moment. "Deal," he said, and bit my big toe.

Bit it, the crazy fucker.

Yep, I'd just dealt the devil my soul.

Deal.

Sure, why not? It was only a soul.

He gripped my ankles and tugged again. I held on to the arms of the chair, my hips dragging forward.

"Shouldn't we go in the cabin?" I glanced at the open doorway.

"Why, who is going to see us up here?"

I looked at the man on his knees in front of me. Had

he ever been on his knees for a woman before? A little corner of my heart said no, he hadn't.

I was special.

"You nervous, Angel?"

I shook my head.

He dropped my feet to the floor and stood. "This isn't going to work if you lie to me. The truth, remember?"

"Then I'll take that as question one." I stared up at him. Thank fuck for champagne. "Yes, I'm nervous."

He smirked and pulled me to my feet before sinking into my chair and hauling me onto his lap.

My ass hit his legs with a jarring thud.

His arms surrounded me. I was enveloped. My head rested on his shoulder, my legs on either side of his. The fabric of my dress bunched at my middle. He touched my belly and the muscles there—who knew I had muscles under my belly?—clenched.

I might not have been able to see him, but I felt him behind me. Felt every movement of his humongous body. For some reason, I'd expected to be able to see him. To be a little more in control than I was in his lap.

"What's the matter, Haithem? Don't want to watch me come?" The champagne must have contained an evil spirit, because surely those words weren't mine?

"I get to ask the questions, remember?"

I shut my lips.

He ran his hands over my ribs then held them over my breasts. They seared through my dress, through my bra, pressed heat into my body.

"Was that another question? Damn, Haithem, you're running out fast."

He pinched my nipples. Squeezed them right between his fingertips.

I squealed, sensations rocketing into my core.

"Don't be cheeky. That wasn't one of the questions."

He rubbed over my nipples, soothing where he'd just tormented.

I kinda wished he'd pinch them again.

His hands moved, not messing around now, and he pushed between my legs. My hips arched off his lap. His fingers pressed over layers of fabric—skirt, panties, too damned much.

I'd asked for orgasms. You'd think he'd hop to it.

Then he did, he ran his hands to my knees and then ran them up under my skirt. His palms on my skin created a friction that made me twitch with desire. He reached my panties and brushed over my crotch.

My head went even lighter than it already was.

"Second question," he whispered, and rubbed two fingers over the top of my mound, lightly applying pressure over the place that demanded it.

"Why, if you don't want lovemaking, were you offended when I propositioned you?"

My head swam. My tongue was loose and pliant, and I spoke to him far more freely than I'd have liked to. "Because offering to pay me, no matter the reasoning, made me feel like a whore."

My cheeks heated, but I didn't have time to finish blushing before he pushed aside my panties. He touched me intimately. Went straight to the source of my heat.

"Good girl," he whispered. "I like it when you tell me the truth."

He touched my clitoris. Pushed right between my folds and stroked it with two fingers. I jerked, my knees snapping together. He caught one thigh in his hand, hauling my legs open.

"Last question, Angel, and then you get to come."

He rubbed over my entire pussy, from clitoris all the way down to my ass and back up again. Rubbed my own wetness all over me. I shuddered, a need so sharp it hurt crawling over me. My hips bucked fruitlessly.

His free hand moved to my chest. "I want to know, I want you to tell me exactly why you're nervous," he whispered. "Is it me? Or have you not fucked as much as you'd like me to believe?"

"Pass," I shouted.

He made a growling sound and pressed his teeth against my shoulder at the same time he moved his fingers up and pumped my clit.

I came. Came apart, really. I screamed, screamed from deep in my lungs. Must've been the shock. Nerves twisted, muscles stiffened and contracted. My insides turned outward, and pleasure bore down on me hard. I shook, clutching my thighs together, but his hand kept moving on me until I stopped shaking.

I flopped, panting, against his chest. His fingers still stroked me, but ever so softly now.

"You liked that, Angel?"

I gave him one for free. "Yeah."

Turned out I wasn't half the lady I'd thought I was.

FOURTEEN

I SHOWERED LIKE I'd never showered before. Lined up all the toiletries, cosmetics and beauty products Haithem had given me on the bathroom counter and made a plan to use them all.

It wasn't as if I had much else to do, but honestly, I was driven to do it.

I attacked my skin with body scrub and a loofah, put a conditioning mask in my hair, even took a razor to my privates. I'd never shaved my pussy completely, never needed to, and with my coordination there was always the chance I'd lose a flap. But I was careful, used one of the gentle razors for women and scraped myself clean.

Afterward, I blow-dried my hair and used a serum, gave myself a pedicure, then opened a perfume box set and used the scented body cream. I squeezed a dollop onto my palm then smeared it onto my arm. My skin soaked it up, the moisture, the fragrance. I put my cheek to my shoulder and inhaled. Maybe I was a little sleepy, because my eyes shut for a while.

I opened my eyes and caught a look at myself in the mirror. Squeezing more cream into my hands, I stepped closer to the mirror then spread the cream over my chest, wiping over my breasts. My nipples tingled under my palms, and a shiver ran into my stomach below my belly button. I used more cream. Ran my fingers over my middle. The first few days on the yacht had stripped a little flesh from my curves. Not much, but enough for me to notice a new tightness. I watched the mirror. Looked at every place my hands roamed. I'd never looked at myself like that before.

In the past, I'd allowed other people to make me feel that what I had wasn't right, wasn't enough, but gazing in that mirror, I saw what I had and I liked it—and I knew that anyone who didn't, didn't deserve to enjoy it. I rested my foot on the bath and moisturized my legs. Stroked over my thighs. My fingers brushed between my legs. The touch was electric, or maybe I was just that sensitive after what Haithem had done to me.

He'd given me exactly what I'd asked for. But, as with anything that good, one small taste only made me hungry for more. I touched myself again. My sex felt foreign under my fingers, hairless and so slippery. I looked at the mirror, watched my hand move between my legs, and hunger and need enveloped me again.

His hand had been here, his fingers here. Touching me where I touched. I rubbed my clitoris with my middle finger. Pleasure radiated into my core. Not like the pleasure he'd given me but pleasure, nonetheless. My pelvis tilted forward. Why had I only just discovered I could do this myself?

I made speedy circles over that nub until everything went tight then rippled in little waves of joy. My foot slid to the floor. It hadn't knocked me out, hadn't stolen my breath or made me scream, but I liked it. There were probably many things I hadn't discovered I could like—yet.

But now I could see them, find them, take them. I washed my hands and face again but didn't bother with makeup, only rubbed in a bit of tinted sunscreen.

Standing in front of the wardrobe, I pulled a sleek white dress off a hanger. One of the ones I'd worried I'd never get to wear because I didn't attend the kinds of events that called for dresses like that one. But why wait and hope I'd eventually go somewhere special? Normal rules needn't apply, right? I dressed and went out onto the deck.

Haithem sat at the table with a laptop. My heart skipped softly. After he'd done as he'd promised, I'd thanked him as though he'd just handed me a cup of coffee and then ran to the bathroom. I hadn't expected him to hang around. I approached the table and sat across from him, gaze fixed on the laptop.

Laptop.

Internet and emails.

The real world intruded on my bubble. And yes, the yacht was a bubble. A dangerous bubble, with new rules, and illusions that were so easy to sink into and forget everything on the outside.

Reflective ocean surrounded us—everything amplified, intensified—and I was trapped in the middle between reality and something that was part fantasy, part nightmare.

Haithem glanced up and his brow rose. He scanned me as though I'd changed skins. Maybe I had. His handiwork, really.

I cleared my throat. "Has anyone replied?"

"Replied?"

"To the email you sent?"

He shut the laptop and rested a fist on top. "Don't know, haven't been checking your emails."

"Hmm," I hummed, gaze trained on the computer under his fist.

My pulse grew louder.

He'd respected my privacy? I wouldn't buy that for one red minute.

"Let me have a quick look," I said, and reached across the table for the computer.

He unclenched his fist, and he held the laptop, dragging it closer to his body. "There's no connection." His eyes squinted just a fraction. Those sinful lashes concealing so much of his eyes. But it was his voice that got me—the quiver of tension.

The sliver of threat. I stared at him.

Water crashed against the boat, and voices drifted up from the lower deck. Between us, silence boomed.

"I'll try for you tonight." His accent got lost in the sharp finality of his words.

I held my breath inside. He lied. He was a lying liar. If he made nice with me he had his reasons.

I tugged at my dress. It was too tight. Why had I worn this stupid dress again? The sun bore down on us. My lips tasted of salt.

Tiny lines cut into the corners of Haithem's mouth. That's the thing with hard light. It shows up everything.

I'd missed so many things, but now they swarmed at me. All the things I should be thinking about. I'd succumbed to distraction—and I couldn't give up those moments of diversion, the tastes of pleasure. I'd only just started this game, each of us moving like pieces on a board, playing to our own agenda, and we all know—queen takes king.

"What day is it?"

"Tuesday."

I shut my eyes, guilt rising like a tide through my body. It was as easy as that—put a name to the day of the week and everything became real again. Tuesday, and on Tuesday there were things I had to do. Responsibilities and obligations.

People who would miss me.

"Does it bother you to know that tonight there will be an eight-year-old underprivileged girl who is going to be let down by the one person she thought she could count on?"

Haithem shrugged. "Perhaps, if I understood how that had anything to do with me?"

"I'm part of a Big Sister program, Haithem. On Tuesdays, I spend time with a girl named Sandy. Take her to the park or the beach. It's the one stable, regular thing she can count on." My throat ached as I explained to him. Dammit, it'd taken a good six months to get Sandy to open up. "Thanks to you, her trust is about to be shattered."

Haithem grew still. "Everyone has their trust broken, eventually."

"*Not by me*." I spoke through my teeth.

Haithem leaned back and pulled the laptop onto his knees. "And here I thought I'd caught myself an angel. Turns out, I've captured a saint."

I snorted. I'd busted my chances for sainthood the moment I stepped onto this yacht. Not that my motivations had *ever* been so pure or so selfless.

"You know things rarely end well for saints."

My nose screwed up, and I swiped the moisture on it with the back of my hand. "Go to hell."

"I'm sure I will."

I smiled. "Oh, I'd count on it."

"Careful, might stain that halo." He smiled back, a

narrow, closed-lips smile. "So then, my little saint, what other goodly deeds have you committed yourself to?"

I breathed in.

The asshole thought he'd figured me all out. But as I'd only just discovered in the past few days, not even I knew what I was really capable of. "Since I'm not busy coming, I don't think I owe you any answers, do I?"

His smile broadened, showed a little teeth.

I should've moved to the shade. The top of my head scalded.

"That's right. Angel has been flirting with the dark side." His gaze traveled me, examined me in a way that reminded me of every little touch he'd laid on me to make me come. "Let me guess then, volunteering with the elderly?"

Crap.

I tried not to blink. Not to confirm that I did just that. I scooped my hair over one shoulder, letting the breeze cool the back of my neck.

He leaned forward, his smile turning into a grin. "I know. Animals…an animal shelter."

Dammit.

I fanned my face and looked away.

"Yeah, I can picture that. Angelina cuddling all the poor homeless puppies." His voice lowered as though revealing secrets. "An adorable image, *such a lady.*"

Such an asshole.

I turned to him, my teeth snapping together. "Adorable? Shows what you actually know. There's nothing adorable about an animal shelter." I rested my palms on the tabletop. "Cuddling puppies? Try hosing out stalls and shoveling poop. It stinks, it's noisy and it's actually not a nice place at all." My lips tightened. "I hate it. How saintly is that?"

Haithem leaned forward, his expression smoothing as though things had not just been real weird or real heated, and covered the back of my hand with his. "So why do it?"

I swallowed. Tried to be distracted by his light touch. Tried to think about how naturally this man held my hand. Tried to let the stark contrast between home and here, buffer my proximity to the truth.

I knew why I did all those things, even if I pretended not to. But I'd never tell him, never tell Haithem I needed the karmic points just for living—for being the one to live. That if I got to be alive then I had to make sure I deserved it.

His thumb brushed the space between my thumb and index finger. I slid my hand from under his. He didn't hold me down, yet my palm felt glued to the table.

As though my body thought that he and I were friends. Like maybe after all this time surviving on my own, I needed his twisted version of help.

No.

He'd never know that in order to survive I'd had to drown myself in enough to bury my own memory. A memory that was beginning to crawl its way out.

My chin rose. "What would the world be if we only did the nice things?"

His mouth softened, and for the first time since I'd pushed the boundaries by reaching for that laptop, I knew we'd stopped playing.

"Now you're speaking a language I understand."

HE DIDN'T JOIN me for dinner.

I ate a chicken Caesar salad that Karim brought up on a tray, on my own. It should've been nice. Sunset on the yacht. Sky pink over amethyst sea, warm breeze, and solitude. No Haithem to annoy me. But too much alone time with my brain and all that... I chewed the lettuce. One of my favorite summer meals, made to order.

How's that for service? Lucky me. Spoiled rotten.

Rotten, all right, because my gaze kept flicking to the stairs, willing Haithem to walk up them. I set down the fork—my salad more tossed than consumed—and went back into the cabin. I fished a can of cola from the fridge and sat on the edge of the bed. A scrap of paper stuck out underneath the bedside table. I set the cola down and picked up the paper and flipped it over.

Blood rushed away from my head, making the cabin dip. The photo of me and Josh on our eighteenth birthday in his Mustang. A time branded in my mind.

A time when we'd actually believed things were looking up. He'd fought and won. We didn't know that it'd only been a warm-up for the real battle.

I placed the photo facedown on the side table and rubbed my forehead.

I'd sensed this birthday creeping up on me. Felt the days, the weeks, the months ticking by. Yet somehow I'd shut it out. I'd walked past Mum on the phone to the minister, organizing a memorial for our birthday—and it'd gone right over my head. I'd known but let it slide off as though I'd never heard anything at all.

Just as I blocked it out when I walked past his bedroom door. It was only a door. I paid no attention when a Maroon 5 song came on the radio. They were only songs, not songs that used to drift from his room to mine. When I looked in the mirror, I didn't see his eyes anymore—they were only my eyes now. I ignored my clenched guts, my hurting chest and my burning eyes. I ignored the desire to cry. I ignored the need I had to scream.

And I did something else.

But now there was nothing else to do. I picked up the cola and drained the can. There was no fresh air in the damn cabin, even with the door open. I walked to the intercom and picked up the receiver.

It rang half a dozen times before Karim answered. "Yes?"

"Put Haithem on the phone."

Silence met my ear. I hadn't asked nicely. Couldn't bring the "please" to my lips. Karim was less of a friend to me than Haithem was.

"Very well."

I let out a breath and waited.

"Angelina?" His voice was like a balm. It blunted the corners of my edginess.

"Don't I deserve dessert tonight?"

He laughed softly. "We had dessert for breakfast."

"Yet I still want dessert now."

"I'll see what's in the kitchen."

The line clicked, and I hung up the receiver then flopped into one of the chairs and stared at the ceiling. Footsteps padded across the deck, and Haithem walked into the cabin with a covered tray. I rested my elbow on the arm of the chair and my chin in my hand. He slowed, dragging the coffee table in front of me, and then he set the tray on top. He sat on the couch opposite and lifted the lid.

"Lemon meringue pie."

"Thanks," I said.

Pity there wasn't also a tub of ice cream on the tray. Haithem relaxed on the couch. I took the knife and cracked through the meringue top. The knife slid fluidly, catching on the biscuit base. I pushed down, dragged the knife along the bottom of the pie dish, then flipped the knife over and pried up a piece. I laid it on one of the two small plates on the tray.

With the back of the knife, I lifted the meringue top away from the curd and set it on the other plate, slid the meringue part across the table, took the curd plate, then picked up a fork. Haithem made no move to take the plate.

I glanced up.

He watched me from under his lashes. My gaze flicked to the plate I'd served him, and my blood just about solidified in my veins.

Shit.

I held my breath. My heart came back to life with a vengeance. The fork fell and clattered onto the plate. I knew what I'd done. What I always used to do. Pulled the meringue off for Josh.

Habit.

I'd done it instinctively. Except I hadn't done this kind of thing since the day he went. Hadn't left the bathroom light on for him to use after me. Hadn't said yes to the one-dollar Mars bar offers at the service station when buying milk. Hadn't set the TV to record *Top Gear*. Hadn't gone to his bedroom door at midnight with secrets and marshmallows.

None of it.

I'd stopped cold. As if I'd never done any of those things at all. Yet for some reason, I'd taken the meringue off the pie for him a little over a year later. I moved my plate aside.

"What's going on, Angelina?"

I looked at Haithem. As always, some deep, dark place inside me rose up to smother sensible thoughts.

I breathed evenly again.

"You haven't earned a question yet," the other Angelina, who only emerged around him, said.

He rested his arm on the back of the couch. "Is that what this is?"

I nodded. Who knew I could lie so easily. I guess what they say about the company you keep is true.

"Twice in one day. You're greedier than I thought." He made no move toward me.

If anything, he relaxed more. There'd be no kneeling in front of me this time. If I wanted this, I'd have to go to him. I'd have to get up on my feet and walk over to get what I wanted.

Somehow, I did.

Somehow, I got myself off that chair and went and sat next to him. Right under his outstretched arm.

He leaned toward me. "And you said something about me wanting you here to service *my* purposes..."

I smiled. "I guess this is karma then."

"There's no such thing as karma," he whispered, and grabbed my thigh.

His fingers squeezed. He didn't need to pull my legs wide; I let them fall open. His gaze tracked my body, landing on his hand on my skin.

He ran his fingers from the outside to the inside of my thigh. "Are you wet for me yet?"

Question one.

Heat lanced my cheeks, but I didn't look away.
"Yeah, I am. Have been since you walked in the room."

His nostrils flared, and he slid his hand higher. "I do
love this honesty." His hand moved up to my panties. He
brushed against my crotch. "But what I'd really like to
know is how you'd like me to make you come this time."

I felt like I was breathing some kind of smoke, because I almost choked. My hips rocked into his touch.

I'd happily come any way he let me. "Pass."

He grinned and pushed my panties to the side. "You
know what that means, don't you?"

"What?"

"That you have to answer my next question no matter what it is." He touched me. "And it means I'm going
to choose how this happens."

I sucked my lip between my teeth.

"Oh, Angel, you shaved for me." He swept over me
with his knuckles.

My pussy flooded at the ache in his voice.

"Get your ass on that bed. I'm ready for *my* dessert."

My skin tingled up and down my body, but I got my
ass up. Walked it across the room and sat on the bed.

He followed me.

He came after me and all I could do was wait.

"Take off your dress."

I shivered. My nice dress did a fine job at hiding
what I liked hidden, while showing off what I liked
to show. But I remembered how I'd looked in the mirror that morning and slid the straps off my shoulders,
pushed it down to my waist, then over my hips.

Haithem caught my foot as it came up to remove the
dress. He lifted my leg. My back hit the bed. He tugged
the dress over my feet and threw it over his shoulder.

The look on his face made my hips rise off the mattress. He grabbed them, sliding me higher on the bed and climbing on after me.

My panties didn't stand a chance. He jerked them down my thighs. I clamped my knees together. Not sure why, but I couldn't handle him looking at me there. I felt that if he saw, I'd never be able to hide from him again.

He didn't force my legs apart.

He could've. Hell, truth be told, it would have made me hotter.

"If you make me wait for dessert, I'm only going to take my time eating it."

Shit.

My pussy throbbed. I opened my legs, felt the lips of my sex open to him. Knowing this was it, I exposed all.

He made a sound like a groan. "Pull those knees up."

Moisture broke across my lip, and I gripped behind my knees, drawing them higher.

He cupped me with his entire hand and rubbed. "Just warning you, I'm saving my last question for later, because my mouth's about to be full." His thumb flicked across my clitoris.

My knees jerked, and pleasure shot through me.

"You good with that?"

I nodded. "Mmm-hmm."

He leaned between my legs, glancing up at me with a look so savage I forgot to breathe. His mouth closed over me. Sensations ripped into my core. He sucked with his entire mouth. A barrage of sensation, too much to process as good or bad—just a stunning feeling. My fingers clenched my knees, and my head dropped back. He worked my clit with his tongue—not with gentle licks or laps but with deep, aggressive strokes.

Muscles tightened up in my legs, across my stomach and through my shoulders. He released my clit and licked down my pussy. I gasped for air. His tongue pushed inside me.

My thighs jerked.

He withdrew and stroked his way back to my nub, then sucked. I moaned, dropped my knees, hands burying in his hair, hips lifting. A thick finger entered me. My flesh stretched, bursting with stinging pleasure. His tongue pumped my clit. Muscles clenched, everything bracing for an explosion.

The finger inside me thrust. It hurt with the same erotic satisfaction as stepping beneath a too-hot shower. Pleasure layered upon burn. He pressed his mouth harder and shook his head. My fingers stiffened, my body hardened tight enough to shatter—and then I did.

I shattered like a mirror falling against stone. Bursting and scattering into thousands of jagged parts. My hips jerked, but he continued eating me, drawing out every bead of pleasure until nothing remained.

I melted into the mattress. Sweat coated my skin like a blanket. I released his hair, my thighs flopping open. His movements softened. His finger left me, and he licked softly against a place so sensitive each tender touch zapped like the flick of an elastic band. I twitched, lacking the strength to stop him. Without the strength to fight the new wave of desire. He lapped me slowly. Made the tiniest little circles around my nub.

Deep, helpless sounds left my lips. He used his thumbs to spread my pussy wide, to access me completely. My head tossed, and I held on to the bedspread. I grew new bones, formed new muscles, and everything contracted again. My head twisted to the side, and my face pressed against the bed. Waves of ecstasy washed through me, over me, inside me and out. My back arched, and my body bowed. Ripple after ripple of pleasure. On and on and on as if it'd never stop.

I drifted away on the current.

FIFTEEN

HAITHEM KISSED UP over my stomach, his teeth nipping my breast through my bra before he lay beside me.

He tugged on my hip and rolled me toward him. I pressed my face into his shirt and inhaled. Man, spice and something just sharp enough in his cologne to make breathing him addictive. He touched my back, running his fingers from the bottom of my spine, up under my hair to the base of my neck.

I needed more. More than touching. More than playing.

More than dipping my toe in the ocean.

I tilted back my head and looked at him. His mouth. Hard and soft and irresistible. How long had it been since he'd kissed me?

Forever.

I pulled myself up. My naked stomach dragged over the fabric of his pants.

He watched me from under his sweeping lashes. Eyes so dark I could barely make out his irises. I brought my lips to his. He caught a fistful of my hair, tugging my head back. My hips pushed against him. He leaned in and rubbed his prickly chin against my jaw. My scent clung to him. The scent of my sex. A hum rose in my throat.

His mouth hovered over mine.

The beat of my pulse tapped against my neck.

"You owe me a question…"

The arm underneath my neck stretched then bent at the elbow, lightly squeezing my neck as he raised his hand.

I shivered.

The cabin had cooled while we were busy. He released my hair and passed something to his free hand.

My photo appeared between us.

"Who is this?"

I shut my eyes. My tongue went dry.

The paper ran over my cheek, a gentle scrape that made all my hair stand on end.

"A deal is a deal, Angelina."

My eyes opened. "My brother."

I gave him three long seconds of a look that could kill, then rolled away from him and scrambled for the dress he'd thrown on the floor.

"That's not a proper answer. I asked who this is, not what he is."

He spoke to my back.

I pulled the dress on, tugged it over my boobs and my hips with numb fingers.

"Josh, my twin brother, Josh."

The words escaped, and yet my tongue didn't fall out. I didn't catch fire. Didn't spontaneously combust.

My lips went numb as my fingers.

For a year, I'd kept that name in, sure that if I'd said it out loud I'd die, too.

I didn't die.

But I might throw up.

Cool air gusted into the cabin.

"Where is Josh?" Haithem spoke behind me. He'd followed me off the bed.

He knew, the bloody bastard. He knew for sure. That's why he asked me like this. If I could kill him, I would.

I straightened on jelly legs. "You only had one question left."

"Except you came twice. So I could demand another three."

I yanked the zip up and faced him. "I didn't ask to come twice."

He sighed. "Fair enough."

Fair? He said that without choking?

He glanced at the open doors then went and closed them. "Weather's turning."

The boat dipped.

My stomach roiled. I stumbled to a chair and sat, wrapping my arms around my middle.

Why didn't he push?

He was a pusher, but he'd dropped it. Cut me a break. I'd rather he didn't. Rather he gave me a little consistency, a little something more to hate him with.

"Did you check my emails?"

Haithem lowered himself onto the couch. "Not yet." He reached for the plate with the meringue then picked up a fork.

"Why?" I scooted to the edge of the seat, watching him eat the sugary pie top.

He took a bite, shrugged and swallowed. "I forgot."

"Bullshit."

He looked at me, finishing the meringue in a few large scoops.

"You don't forget."

He put the plate down and licked his lips. "You know me so well, do you?"

"I know you don't forget."

"That I don't." He smiled and sucked the side of his thumb. "Fine, I didn't forget."

I leaned in and rested my hands on the coffee table. My fingers bumped the knife. "Did my parents reply to the message you sent?"

"No."

"Liar." The word became a growl grazing my throat. "They'd have replied immediately. My dad has freaking email on his phone." My chest tightened; everything in my upper body did. "Tell me."

Haithem said nothing.

"Tell me." I slammed my fist on the table. The plates clattered. "Tell me." My voice echoed around the cabin.

Nice girls don't raise their voice, Angelina.

"Has it occurred to you that maybe everything I'm doing is to protect you?" His growl was deeper than mine—and so raw that it almost fooled me into believing him.

He took my hand. I tugged, but he gripped tighter. He turned my hand. A bright drop of blood trickled down my wrist.

I gasped. Never could stand the sight of blood. It was tied up with illness, hospitals and, inevitably, death. He picked up a napkin and placed it over the side of my palm.

I stared at my hand, the white napkin sucking up my blood. He removed the napkin and examined my cut.

"Breathe, Angelina. It's only a nick."

Don't be a wuss, Angelina.

I snatched my palm away. "Show me the email."

"I deleted it."

"What?" I clutched my injured fist to my chest. My

hand didn't hurt. I hadn't even felt the nick. But my chest did—my chest hurt as though he'd taken the knife to it.

"That's not right. You had no right to do that." I rubbed the place above my breasts with my fist but couldn't wipe out the ache. "No right at all."

My voice caught.

Oh shit, I was going to cry. I sucked it up—literally. Sucked in a breath and pulled back those tears. Pushed them down. I'd had a lot of practice. It was practically a part of my skill set.

"No right?"

The yacht rocked again. I clutched the arms of the chair, not taking my eyes off him as he rolled himself forward, unaffected by the movement.

"Look around. This is my yacht." He held out his hands, palms up. "And I'll let you in on a secret."

He didn't sound as if he was revealing a secret. His voice was clear and crisp.

"We just left Australian waters." He leaned back with a smile that cracked across his face like a clap of thunder. "Right now, this is my ocean, my world, my rules."

The world swayed under my chair.

"So stop worrying about what you think is right. Stop worrying about what rights you think you have. They mean nothing here."

Bile rose in my throat. Damn yacht.

Damn Haithem.

"The only thing you need to believe in now is me. Show me you can be trusted, and just maybe you'll earn some rights back."

I doubled over. The contents of my stomach rose into my esophagus.

I'd gotten lost in the game. Orgasms and questions. Pleasure and answers. Freedom and restraint. A game I'd fooled myself into believing I had a chance at winning.

How could I have been so stupid?

I might be queen in a game of chess, but Haithem wasn't the king. I couldn't sneak up and take him. He wasn't even on the board. He was standing somewhere above, moving the pieces.

He was the player.

I gagged. Nothing came up. The room tipped sideways. I fell off the chair onto the carpet.

My head rushed.

I needed to get out. Get off.

Escape.

Haithem took me by the arm and led me to the bed. I fell back against the cushions. He handed me the lid from the tray, turned upside down. I leaned over the tray cover, taking slow breaths. He knelt beside the bed and rummaged through the cupboard of the bedside table, pulling out half the crap I'd shoved in there.

He stood and tore something out of a piece of foil. "Here."

I eyed the small white circle in his palm.

"It's medication. It'll help with the seasickness."

If it weren't for the fact that I was about to go exorcist all over the cabin, I'd have told him where to insert his "medication." Instead, I snatched the pill from his palm.

"It's a wafer. Just dissolve it on your tongue."

I placed the wafer in my mouth. It melted in a little puddle of bitterness.

Haithem turned back to the mess on the floor, putting things back into the cupboard. He paused at the large bag, opening it and glancing inside.

I groaned. Fantastic. Why'd I shove *that* bag there?

He stared in the bag with the vibrator and accessories then finally glanced up at me. Just for a moment, his expression made me forget that I hated him all over again. Made me remember what we'd been doing moments earlier.

He closed the cupboard.

"I need to get off this yacht." I blinked, my eyes clouding with moisture. "Please put me ashore somewhere. Just leave me anywhere."

He sat next to my hip. "I can't do that."

"You mean you won't."

"Fine, I won't." He didn't say it in a mean voice as he had before; if anything, he spoke sweetly. "You think I'm a bastard—I am. I have to be."

The cabin tilted. Haithem rested a hand on my waist and one on the bedside table, holding us both in place.

I pulled the lid of the tray closer.

Goddammit.

"I didn't say those things for kicks. They're the truth. Don't expect me to do the right things, and don't expect me to play by rules I don't believe in." He released my waist.

I breathed deeply, trying to still the rise of my stomach.

"You'll only be disappointed, and we won't get along."

My stomach clenched. I retched. Nothing came up but spit. Tears spilled out my eyes. My stomach wrenched again.

Haithem climbed off the bed and went to the fridge, returning with a green apple.

"Try this."

"I don't want a fucking apple."

"They help." He took a bite then held it in front of me. The sweet scent hit my nose. "They really do. It's an old sea trick."

I took the apple and crunched through the skin on the opposite side to the one he'd bitten. It didn't make me hurl. I took another bite then rolled onto my back.

I finished the apple slowly and—curse him—my stomach settled back into its regular place.

He took the lid from the tray and the apple core from my hand, setting them aside. "Better?"

I turned my head toward him. "I need to get off this yacht." My chest hitched. "Please, it's making me sick. I'm going crazy. I need to put my feet on the ground."

He scanned my face then brushed my hair over my shoulder. "All right, tomorrow we'll get off the yacht. You can put your feet on solid ground."

"Really?"

I didn't believe him. How could I? Why would he turn around so quickly?

"Yes, tomorrow we'll go to land."

He stroked the hair out of my eyes. My stupid, leaking eyes. How could he do that? Good then bad, then back again. I was spinning. Didn't know which way was up or down anymore.

He must've had special mind-fuck training.

"Why did you delete the email?"

He traced my jaw with his fingertip. "Let it go. I don't want to do this, but I will."

"I can't."

His gaze dropped from mine to his hand on my skin. "It wasn't a nice email. Leave it at that."

My chest compressed. Not a nice email? It didn't surprise me. If Haithem had really written what he'd claimed he had, they'd be furious.

Absolutely, deathly mad.

"What did they say? I want to know."

"I'd rather not tell."

Oh god.

That bad. I dragged myself up to sitting position. If I didn't, I'd be crushed under the weight of my own anxiety. "I'd rather you didn't delete my emails."

His expression hardened.

"Please tell me." I dropped the attitude. Went for sad and pleading again. Not my favorite style. Yet Haithem didn't seem to realize he had a way of softening when I did it. I didn't want to think about why, but we'd done this enough now for me to figure out that sad eyes counted for something.

To an extent.

Enough for a little leverage. Not much, but a little.

"They're angry with you. Your mother replied." He looked across the cabin. "She said you'd worried them but she also criticized your behavior. She called you cheap, said she was disgusted you'd run off with a man."

I nodded. Tears trickled down my cheeks. Yep, sounded right. Worried but disapproving. Loving but concerned. Uninterested but controlling. I was only surprised she hadn't come right out and called me a slut. What with the way she'd taken to religion since Josh.

"What about Dad? Did Dad have anything to say?"

"He asked you to think about your mother and come home."

I wiped my face with my palm. "They'll expect another response."

"Already done."

My shoulders dropped. "Again?"

"Yes, I apologized. Said you were sorry to upset them but you needed to do your own thing for a while, and suggested they take the next few weeks to get used to it."

"You actually said that?"

I rubbed my arm. How strange he'd used those words. Words I'd thought but would never say. Words with enough truth no one would deny them.

Haithem handed me a handkerchief.

I wiped my face and let his words run through my mind. He could've said worse things. Now, at least, they'd spend the next couple of weeks thinking I'd lost my mind and grown some balls.

It'd be a bitch when I got home, but I could deal with that.

"You could, you know..." he said.

"Could what?"

"You could take this time to let them get used to it. Do your own thing."

I handed him back his handkerchief. "And you'd just slide right off the hook, right?"

"I'd call that win-win."

I relaxed back into the pillows. Somehow, I imagined Haithem and I had different ideas about what it meant to win.

SIXTEEN

I SAT IN the speedboat, gazing up at the yacht towering above us. Under normal circumstances, this would be considered a big speedboat. Much bigger than the one Dad used to take Josh and me out in. Mostly Josh—but sometimes me, too.

Next to the yacht, the speedboat could've been a toy.

The sea lay calm as a painting but so much more vivid than anyone could hope to capture on canvas. You'd never know it'd stormed last night. The sun blazed in the sky, and we in the speedboat were nothing more than a speck in the vastness of the ocean.

"You ready?"

To let Haithem whisk me off into nothingness?

Sparkling blue stretched around us. Not a scrap of the land he'd promised.

I nodded.

He reached underneath my seat, pulled out a life jacket it and handed it to me. I put it on and did up the straps as tightly as they would go.

He started the boat, steering us away from the sun. I held my hat on my head with one hand. The air cascaded over us. Haithem's T-shirt rippled over his back. I almost hadn't gotten into the boat with him looking that way. Pale blue T-shirt, white board shorts, bare feet. Casual, like some regular hunk. I preferred him in his immaculate, formal dress. At least that made him look like what he was—someone to be reckoned with.

Not sexy beach guy.

The boat hit a bump. My backside rose off the seat then slammed back down. A thrill ran from my knees to my head.

I laughed and gripped the edge of the seat.

Haithem glanced over his shoulder—striking me with an even deeper thrill. He pulled a lever, taking us faster. We rushed across the ocean, parting the air and water around us. My insides rose and fell, while my outsides flailed and bounced. He turned the boat in an arc.

My heart lifted.

I shook with laughter. Air swept the hat from my head. I lunged for it, but it blew into the water, disappearing from sight as we sped on. The boat slowed, and I glimpsed the so-called land.

Starting as a pin-sized island, it grew into something big and vegetated enough to outrank a sandbar, but it wasn't what I'd anticipated when I'd asked for solid ground.

We drew closer, approaching a small dock—the only evidence anything human had ever been to the island. Haithem stopped the boat and helped me out.

My feet hit wooden planks, yet the ground still didn't seem steady as it should be. I took a step, and the dock rolled. I stumbled off onto the sand and sat.

"Sea legs," Haithem said, carrying a basket and a bunch of towels out of the boat. "You'll adjust in a minute."

I kicked off my sandals and buried my feet in the hot beach. I'd been longing for the hard, unshakable security of land beneath me—concrete, bitumen, brick paving perhaps.

Trust Haithem to be sneaky.

"I'm not sure I'd call this land."

He dropped the towels and basket in a patch of shade. "If we go in a little farther, there's dirt. Dirt means land."

"You're way too tricky," I said, and lay down. The sand warmed my back like an electric blanket. "What do you plan on doing with me on a deserted island, anyway?"

He walked toward me, looking even bigger than usual from my vantage point with my back against the ground. "Whatever you want." He tugged off his T-shirt and dropped it beside me. "That's the point."

Holy bananas, Batman.

I made a sound, tried to pass it off as a cough. His big chest could've been airbrushed if it weren't for the hair spattered over his pecs and down his stomach. Perfectly sculpted yet not over-the-top. Muscles that screamed raw strength. Screamed for my fingernails to claw over them.

"But right now, let's take a swim."

I glanced at the water. It was probably warm on a day like this. "I'm not wearing bathers."

"Whatever will the fish think?" He took my hand and hauled me to my feet.

"I'll watch from here."

"Take off that dress, unless you want to wear it in the water." His eyes glistened. His chin lowered.

Excitement curled in my stomach. Today, Haithem was the one who wanted to play with me.

I stepped back and pulled my dress over my head.

He stepped forward. I shuffled back. He walked around me. I turned with him. He grinned then lunged for me.

I ran.

Made it to where the water licked my toes before they flew clear off the ground. My feet went over my head as my stomach hit his shoulder and my breath rushed out in a squeal. Haithem jogged into the water, turning me the right way up. I reached for his shoulders. He tossed me. My fingers slipped over his skin.

I crashed into the water, body sinking down, head submerged.

I kicked my legs and burst through the surface, gasping. Salty water streamed over my face. He hauled me to his chest. I panted.

He laughed, his chest vibrating against my skin. I pressed myself to him, absorbing the sound. He walked us farther into the water then grabbed my waist. This time, I held my breath. He lifted me high over his head and threw me. I dived down, turning underwater and swimming along the sand.

I reached his ankles and tugged his feet. He didn't wobble. He was unmovable, as though his legs had roots. I climbed up him from behind, wrapped my arms around his neck. He jostled me on his back, then pulled my legs around his hips and dipped us both underwater. I clung to him, letting him drag me along.

We came up in a burst of sputters and laughter. He dragged me from his back to face him.

I couldn't stand looking at him with the sun shining in his face—making him look like a golden hero. I closed my eyes and lay back, squeezing his hips with my legs. My back touched the water, and I floated. He stroked my belly. My muscles twitched. He traced my belly button then flattened his hand on my middle.

I had no delusions of tininess, but his hand on me was like the hand of a giant. I squinted at him. *He is a giant.* And I was a waif in his arms. I arched my chest, my forehead dipping below the water.

He didn't grope my breasts—even though my body bowed with invitation. My hands drifted from my sides. He held my waist and turned, spinning us around. I raised my arms over my head. The sea churned in my fingertips.

The world rotated, and I didn't close my eyes—I watched the earth move around us. Let the sun punch a brand in my vision.

He played with me.

Played with me for hours. Until then, I don't think I'd ever truly played before. Not like that. Not without caution or restraint.

Not with my arms stretched out to the sky.

WE COLLAPSED ON beach towels. My legs were like weights, but my stomach ached the most. Muscles deep in my core were activated from laughter.

Haithem pulled sandwiches and cans of soft drink from the basket. "Chicken and avocado, or turkey cranberry?"

I liked both. "Whichever."

Haithem narrowed his eyes and unwrapped both—swapping half of each sandwich for the other.

He handed me two halves. I ate the turkey, dulling the pang of my empty belly. Haithem ate leisurely, as though he hadn't just burned double the calories I had.

He still finished before me, only by virtue of his bite

size being four to my one. I gave him my chicken sandwich and watched him eat it.

I could've eaten the other sandwich easily, but I
must've been feeling generous. I sipped on a lemon-
flavored soda. My lips tasted like sunscreen.

Haithem finished and put the rubbish into the basket. I stretched on the towel and closed my eyes. Fingers brushed my left side.

I flinched.

The scars had faded better than I ever could have
hoped. Even with creams, lotions, massage, laser and
microdermabrasion. Must be that good teenage skin the
surgeon had assured me he'd do his best to preserve.

Still, direct natural light and all.

"What's this?"

I put an arm over my eyes. Maybe I could pretend to
be sleeping? His finger traced the curve of the biggest
scar, slightly silkier than the skin around it.

Was this the first time he'd noticed, or simply the
first time he'd thought to ask?

"Angelina?" He stretched beside me, rustling the
towel we lay on.

I took a breath and dropped my arm. "It's from a
kidney donation."

"You donated a kidney?"

"Yep." I cleared my throat and brushed sand off my
forearm.

Haithem rubbed his thumb over the thickest part of
the scar. "Ah, Josh?"

"Yes." My heart somersaulted as it did every time I
heard his name.

I examined my elbow. Not surprisingly, the joint
looked the same as always.

Haithem took a loud breath. "But he didn't make it?"

I dropped my arms flat. My ribs could have been soldered together the way they hardened around me.

"He made it..." Words jammed. I didn't do this— didn't talk about it.

Haithem touched my cheek.

I blinked at him. His face hovered over mine. Warmer than the sun behind him.

"The transplant went fine. He'd been in remission from leukemia for four years when we did it. But eighteen months after this—" I touched the scar with my index finger—"he wasn't anymore."

I sniffed. "He always did have the worst luck, especially when it came to being born at the same time as me." Wetness hit my lips, salt from my tears, salt from the ocean, chemical bitterness from sunscreen. "Everything that happened to him was my fault—"

Haithem grabbed my chin, made me look at him. "Who the fuck told you that?"

"Everyone. Not with words. But every time something happened to him, they froze me out." My nose trickled. "He was born little and weak because of me, because I was bigger and stronger. That's why he got sick, and I didn't." I swiped my face. "That's why he got kidney damage from the chemo, that's why no one ever asked me—" My breath hitched and choked my words. "That's why no one ever asked what I wanted. That's why no one who mattered ever asked how I felt about all the things I had to do, or all the things I had to give up. They all knew it was my responsibility because it was my fault."

I covered my eyes with the backs of my hands. My

head throbbed. Haithem dragged my hands from my face and held them both in one of his.

"Well, I'm asking. How the fuck did you feel?"

It was impossible to look away with his gaze boring into mine.

My temples pounded. Pressure built behind my nose and eyes.

I wouldn't have answered, couldn't have answered—if it weren't for the way he looked at me. Not with compassion, not with empathy. I'd had a shitload of that from everyone—friends, teachers, counselors—after Josh passed. Haithem locked gazes with me, watched me with every single part of his attention fixed on any word I might utter.

No obligatory patting on my back.

No temporary sympathy.

What I said *mattered*.

I swallowed the lump in my throat. "Pretty damn worthless. I'd have done anything for Josh—anything. Even when it terrified me. Because I *wanted* to, not because it was expected."

Haithem's fingers shifted on mine.

"We were the only ones who understood each other. We always knew with just a look what the other was thinking."

Haithem's features flickered softly, his eyes searching as though he had a direct view into my head. Not like having a twin, but I couldn't deny the connection—the way Haithem read me, knew me without me saying a word.

But I didn't know him.

I had no idea who this man was. Yet my heart screamed its secrets to him.

"Then he was gone, and no one had any clue the way it killed me." The words left a bitter sharpness on my tongue, but it didn't stop them pouring out. "How much I hated myself for being the one still standing."

My cheeks burned, and I lost control of my tears and they streamed. I pulled my hands free and wiped my face. "I probably sound so petty and self-obsessed. It's hard for people to understand what it's like to lose half of who you think you are in a day."

"No." He sounded as if he'd swallowed sand. His jaw muscles stuck out. "I know exactly what that's like. I lost my entire family in a day."

My tears froze half-formed.

Everything inside me stilled, turned around and centered on him.

His chest rose and fell evenly.

"What happened?"

His jaw ticked, but he didn't drop my gaze. "They were killed."

Killed.

Even covered in sweat beneath the sun's hot caress, my skin chilled.

Killed, not died.

"What killed them?" My heart galloped like horses in my ears.

He finally looked away. "Underestimating the power of greed."

His words rolled over me—low and chilling. I wouldn't ask more about it. He sat up and rested his elbows on his knees.

I dragged myself up beside him. "Where are you from, Haithem?"

He stared at the ocean. "Nowhere, not anymore."

"You live on the yacht?"

He gave a half laugh. "Fuck, no. I have a few places, an apartment in New York, another in Paris, a villa in Spain, but nowhere is home."

"Where was home?"

He glanced at me, studying me for a moment before answering. "Egypt, but my father's work took us around the globe."

"What was his work?"

Haithem's eyes narrowed. I didn't think he'd answer. "He was a scientist, among other things…"

He stared out at the water. Three times I tried to speak, but as soon as words got to my mouth, they seemed to get lost. I reached out and touched his cheek, absorbing the feel of him through my palm.

He went still.

Didn't move. Didn't react. Didn't recoil.

I'd always wanted to touch him this way. To trace the bones of his face. I ran my finger from his chin to his lips and back again.

Rough, soft, rough.

I rubbed my knuckles under his jaw then up to his ear and buried my fingers in his hair. Heat from his scalp radiated into me.

My heart fluttered like a jar of trapped moths. I trailed the touch to the back of his neck and tugged him in.

I didn't get to kiss him—he leaned down and kissed me. Kissed me as though I was something to eat. Tasted me. Tugged my bottom lip, then opened me and sucked my tongue. He took my head between his hands.

Heat flowed from his palms to my skin.

He poured into me—the clean taste of his tongue—

the musky scent of him—the spice of his breath filled my lungs.

All Haithem. Everything Haithem.

Deep, slow plunges of his tongue and soft, consuming drags of his lips. Every movement pulled at my chest. Every stroke seeped a sharp, bitter joy all the way to my bones.

He kissed me forever, overrode every system in my body so my senses only recognized him. Only the wet sounds of our kiss. Only the sight of him when I opened my eyes.

He released me.

I fell back. The sky spun. Haithem touched his mouth with his fingertips. A line creased between his eyebrows. I watched every movement of his features.

I could spend days staring at him.

He dropped his hand and met my gaze.

A weight settled in my throat.

I want you.

I tried to swallow that lump. Pretend I only wanted him between my legs.

"You shouldn't look at me that way."

"What way?" I whispered.

But I could feel it—the glossy veil covering my eyes, the droop of my lids.

"Like you're falling for me." He cupped my cheek and leaned in. "That would be very bad for you."

A chill brushed over me.

I wasn't falling for him. No way. He just gave me clit-tingles.

And maybe some other tingles.

A hopeless ball of insecurity ricocheted through me.

Why would it be bad? Wasn't I enough? Is that why he said that?

"Pfft, you're the one who needs to be careful," I said, and grabbed a handful of his T-shirt. "You're the one falling for me."

His eyes darkened. "You want that even less," he said, his voice thick and rough. "It'd be so much worse."

I let go. "Why?"

He stood, brushing off my question as easily as he brushed the sand of his shorts, then held out his hand to me. "Come on, there's one more thing I want to do."

We got back into the speedboat and took off. Haithem stopped not far out from the island.

"What are we doing?" I adjusted my life jacket.

"Catching our dinner." He looked at me.

I suddenly wanted to offer myself up as main course.

He produced a fishing rod, box and bucket from under a seat. "You fished before?"

"Yeah, sometimes Dad used to let me tag along when he took Josh."

He attached a lure to the line. "And now?"

"Now he goes with his mates." I sat down and gazed at the horizon. "It's boy time or something." I waved my hand.

"Do you enjoy fishing?"

I glanced back at Haithem. He stood with the fishing rod beside him, looking like a hunter.

"Actually, touching slimy things isn't my favorite. But I still put in the effort when I went out with them."

"Want a turn?" He held out the rod. "I won't make you touch anything slimy."

He winked. My heart jumped.

"I'm happy to watch."

Haithem cast the line. His biceps contracted.

Yep, the view was fine.

"What job were you applying for the day I met you?"

For an instant every part of my being went still. "You mean there's something you don't know?"

"Let's just keep that between us," he said, and the line went tight. Trust Haithem to catch something the moment his hook entered the water.

He reeled the line in. The fish never stood a chance.

He'd been so nice. This felt so nice. But then I bet the lure that fish took looked nice, too. My tongue tasted salty, like maybe I'd swallowed more seawater than I thought before. I'd learned one thing about him today but it was not enough. There was more to Haithem I'd yet to see.

I wouldn't push to see it now. "Copyediting."

He dragged a two-foot squid into the boat and dumped it in the bucket, and then he removed the lure.

"Hmm."

I sat forward. My ribs constricted over my organs. Did he know? "Hmm, what?"

"I would've taken you for something more creative." He cast the line back into the water. "Literature, art, theater studies, something like that."

My stomach dipped.

Theater studies.

Again, so spot-on. I'd dreamed of playwriting. "My parents encouraged me to do something that would result in gainful employment."

He wiggled the fishing rod but looked at me over his shoulder. "What did you want?"

I looked out at the water.

So many things.

Haithem

CONTROL. I NEEDED it back.

I sat at my desk and poured a whiskey. Drink muddles the mind, and I preferred mine clear. Yet, short of a sledgehammer, it was the closest I could come to numbing the pain.

I wasn't sure what she'd tell me. But that wasn't it. How could someone so selfless work for an organization as evil as the one after me?

I downed a gulp of whiskey, and let it singe the lining off my stomach.

But then they usually let recruits think they were something else—black ops intelligence, or some noble shit like that.

She'd have been so vulnerable. So ripe for picking. The vile assholes would have known exactly how to get to her.

I rotated the glass on the desk.

It didn't matter. I had to shut it down. Couldn't let her get to me. Had to stop thinking about her face. Her voice. Her body. The way my heart had squeezed when she'd told me her tale. The way my own story started to rush out. Whatever they'd used to get to her, I'd use better—more.

Worse.

I took a mouthful of whiskey and held it in on my tongue.

I could have everything. Take her heart and her loyalty. Give her what she longed for most. The whiskey numbed my mouth, and I swallowed, then walked to the window and looked out at the deck.

And I'd enjoy every moment of it.

She slept, curled like a kitten in the last of the sunlight.

My abdomen tightened.

The taste of her pussy hadn't left my mouth since the moment she'd let me between her thighs. Let my tongue in her cunt. I already knew the way she liked her clit stroked. I knew the way her breath sounded just before she was about to come and I knew the noises she made when she did. It wouldn't be difficult to slip under her defenses, get her where she was soft and weak—where she hurt the most. I wouldn't even have to lie—just steal from her. Steal that little heart she'd begun to open.

Then I'd be the one getting what *I* wanted.

That was only fair. She'd come to destroy me—but I was the one about to destroy her.

Her secrets were bubbling to the surface, waiting to be plucked. I'd pluck them. I'd give with one hand, even if I had to take with the other. Trust is overrated when you can have devotion.

The phone on the desk beeped. I snatched it up. "Yes?"

"It seems we have a tail," Karim said.

I dropped a palm flat on the wood desk. My head hammered. A swarm of blood and death clouded my vision. Memories so pure their copper tang blazed on my tongue.

Again.

It'd all happen again.

This time it'd be my corpse left to rot—and Angelina's. "You are certain?"

The secrets hidden on board this yacht trumped our lives. No one would take them from me. I'd protect them or die trying.

But I had no fucking intention of dying.

"We changed direction twice to be sure."

"How the fuck did this happen?" I hunched over the desk. "We were so careful."

"I have an idea, but you won't appreciate it."

My guts went hard. Like I'd swallowed a brick. Or a ton of bricks. Or eaten all the sand on the beach.

No, don't say it.

I forced myself to stand. To glance behind me at the girl on the deck. The sand concoction filled me like an hourglass, the feeling filtering all the way to my lungs.

"Send Emilio up here." I never wanted it to go like this. "Tell him to bring his equipment."

SEVENTEEN

"WAKE UP, ANGEL." The whispered command filtered into my dreams, and oh god—what a dream. I opened my eyes. The sun was orange behind him, and everything about him was warm and gold and beautiful.

I touched his cheek.

His bristles spiked my fingertips and all I wanted in the world was to have that face against my chest. Was to have that mouth on my mouth. I took him by the hair and tugged him closer.

"Wake up," he said.

Movement crossed the fading sun behind us, and drenched us in shadow. I sat up, the fuzz clearing from my imagination.

One of the guards—one I remembered in a nightmarish flash of needle-stabbing-terror—stood behind him. An itch pricked the hair at my temples and the base of my skull.

Why's he here?

I scooted back. "What's wrong?"

"Come with me." He took my forearm.

I jerked my arm free and glanced between them. "Why?"

"We need to talk inside." He took my arm again, and all the remnants of longing I'd had for his touch retracted back into my body like a snail's antennae.

He pulled me up and my body moved of its own accord. Our three sets of footsteps pounded over the deck and I heard each set distinctly.

My heart kept step, pounding in perfect military synchronization.

Why were we going inside? He'd touched me intimately out on deck. He'd said no one would see us on deck. Why'd we need to go inside now?

What's more private than my vagina?

The guard followed us through the doors and all the way to where Haithem released me. I stumbled against the bed, then caught myself and faced him.

"Who do you work for?"

The guard stood behind him. Not speaking. Not part of this conversation. A suitcase dangled from his left hand.

Why did Haithem need backup?

"Why is he here?"

"This is Emilio." Haithem didn't look back or gesture to the other man. He just stared at me. Stared at me in a way that had the back of my knees bumping into the mattress.

"I'd like Emilio to leave." He stepped in, and then the bed was a push against the back of my knees. There was nowhere to go. Not an inch of room with which to breathe or to flee.

"*You* want Emilio to leave."

I glanced over his shoulder at the guard. "Right then, sounds like you can go now."

"He doesn't speak English. I told you that."

Only Haithem could instruct Emilio to leave. He wanted me to know that. Why'd I need to know that? My hand flew out and gripped Haithem's arm. As if he were a safe thing to hold on to.

I squeezed the cotton under his elbow. "What are you doing?"

He glanced down at my grip. "I need to know who you work for."

I held on to his shirt so hard the fabric burned my fingers. Was this about the article? Had they found out I'd interviewed for *Poise*? Blood rushed through my body, even to the white of my fingertips squeezed tight. What would happen if I told?

My gaze darted to Emilio. He watched me but even though I stared him in the face our gazes never met.

No freaking way was I telling. They couldn't prove anything. Exactly zero good would come from this truth. I sensed that in the same way you sense lightning's arrival—that electric current in the air warning you to get your ass under cover.

I looked back at Haithem. His eyes were already trained on me. It took every bead of my concentration to meet them. "I don't work for anyone."

"You're hurting me. I'm letting you know that." His features tightened. He'd caught my lie before I'd told it. "But it's not going to make any difference that it hurts me to do this."

My heart shuddered against my ribs.

His head jerked toward the guard. Emilio set the suitcase on the bed. I didn't wait to find out what was inside it—I threw myself into Haithem's chest and shoved past him.

He seized me midlunge. One arm crossed my collarbone and hauled me against his chest.

"No," I shouted, straining the lower half of my body from side to side. "What's he doing?"

"Angelina, if there's anything on this boat that can be tracked, I need to know now."

It was weird he said my name like that, and often. Like he knew me. Like he knew me intimately. Like he knew me in the way of a man who'd licked me from clit to asshole and he still did this.

"No. I don't know." I struggled harder.

He held me tighter, his forearm my prison. "If you tell me now I'll forgive you."

I heard him as though through a wall of water, muddy and distorted. A sound like a piston—jerking breaths—shrieked through my eardrums.

"I swear to god, I don't know."

The suitcase popped open, and I felt the reverberation in the marrow of my bones.

"Is there anything on or in your person that can be tracked?"

"No, there's not. I swear there's not."

He held me tighter yet also softer, his other arm draping over my middle in a kind of absurd cuddle. "Sorry, Angel, I'm afraid I don't believe you."

Emilio pulled the device out of the suitcase. A plastic paddle with a light and a switch. My head swam. The entire room moved in a wave. They were going to electrocute me.

"Lift up your arms."

I couldn't do it. There wasn't the capacity in my limbs to keep me upright. Emilio approached and raised the paddle. Haithem caught my wrists and raised my arms up. My eyes clenched tight.

No!

The thing never touched me. A robot-alien noise

filled the room. I opened my eyes. Emilio ran the scanner over my body, down my arms, across my armpits.

The torture I'd imagined turned out to be in the form of humiliation.

I floated in a place of suspended reality where everything seemed distant. They scanned the backs of knees, my feet, ass and between my shoulders. Haithem turned me around and lifted my hair. They scanned the back of my neck and my scalp.

I buried my face in Haithem's shoulder and even though they inspected every inch of me as they would an animal, as though I were a stray cat, or a pig, or a sheep, this seemed like the safest place to rest my head.

I'd gone properly mental.

They finished, and I stayed right where I was in Haithem's arms. The intercom beeped. Emilio answered it, then spoke to Haithem in Spanish.

"The yacht has been swept. There's nothing here," Haithem whispered. He stroked my back as though we were friends again. As though we could go back to our question games. He took me by the chin and lifted my face. "It's time, Angel. You see there's nothing you can keep from me."

Fuck you.

"Say you understand."

I understood. He wasn't someone to be trusted. Not for all the orgasms and pastries in the world.

"I understand."

He leaned closer. "What do you understand?"

My lungs stung, bruised from holding my breath, but I'd play his stupid games. Maybe I'd win one.

"There's nothing I can keep from you." That move

required no lie—all I concealed, everything fortified in my heart and mind, eventually he'd have it all.

But not yet.

Not without a fight.

He kissed me—hard and consuming but without tongue or the majesty of his full passion. I held on to his biceps. He pulled back, leaving me midsway, then left the room with Emilio.

My ass fell back onto the bed.

I needed to find a way off this goddamn fucking yacht.

I WOKE BUT didn't rise. What I'd just gone through couldn't really be called sleep. More like an aggressive fluctuation in and out of consciousness. The idea that I would actually get to go home in two weeks seemed like a unicorn dream.

Unless I convinced Haithem we were friends.

That I was on his side.

That I would play by his rules. I'd do whatever it took to get home. To convince him I'd keep my mouth shut.

I'd bargain with whatever I could. Except there was literally only one thing I had that he wanted.

He wanted me.

I rolled out of bed, went to the bathroom and took the quickest shower of my life, then slipped on a dress. I glanced at the clock as I put on shoes.

Midday.

He hadn't brought me breakfast the way he always did. I went to the deck. The ocean lay flat and smooth, dark water wobbling like blueberry jelly. Pale clouds blotted out most of the sky, but the breeze warmed my skin.

I took the stairs to the lower deck, missing the last one. My foot slammed into the ground, jolting my knee. I winced and waved my hand to one of the guards, who turned toward me. He nodded, and I walked past him to Haithem's room.

The door was open, the bed made.

I glanced down the hallway. This deck was three times the size of the top deck, yet I'd seen none of it. I wandered down the hall.

More cabins.

Lots of closed doors.

The hallway ended at a room of mammoth proportions and exquisite style.

Parquetry. High-shine wood finishes. Emerald, gold and burgundy textiles. Rich leathery scents. Like a parlor from the *Titanic* or something.

A man cave.

And at the end of the cave, the man I sought lounged on a chesterfield sofa. I walked toward him. His fingers tapped the rounded arm of the sofa. Karim sat opposite him on another matching couch.

Haithem's voice wafted through the room.

Not the regular voice he used to speak to me. His foreign one. His native tongue, the one he would've used to speak to his mother and father.

The parents he'd lost—his parents who'd been killed.

I reached the sitting area, pausing at the edge. Karim glanced at me, but Haithem continued speaking.

The muscles in my forehead tightened. This could've been a movie set, it seemed so surreal. This was another world, with me standing on the outside.

Even on his yacht, Haithem was dressed in suit pants,

starched shirt, his feet pressed to the floor, his shoes polished to an inky gloss.

Karim flicked another look my way.

Haithem ran a hand over the side of his head. His hair didn't move; he'd groomed it so it lay perfectly, shining black.

I waited for the flash. The cameras, the film crew, the giant microphone.

The subtitles.

They didn't come.

Somehow, this was real life, and here I was, out of place and possibly out of time.

Haithem finally turned to me. I smiled, shaking off the strange vibe.

"Yes, Angelina?"

I halted my smile midway. *Yes, Angelina?* What kind of a greeting was that? Hardly "I had chocolate croissants baked for you this morning." Could he still seriously suspect me as some kind of spy? Hadn't last night's incident proved I'd done nothing wrong? He should be hard at work writing my freaking apology letter right now.

Not that I'd be forgiving, but groveling would be nice to watch.

"I missed breakfast."

Haithem turned back to Karim. "Perhaps you could show Angelina the way to the kitchen?"

Karim nodded and rocked himself out of his seat.

I stared at Haithem, and nothing on earth could've stopped my frown.

Not that he saw it.

"This way," Karim said.

I followed him into the hallway, looking back over

my shoulder. Haithem hadn't moved. Just continued to stare straight ahead at the empty sofa across from him.

"Is everything okay?" I asked.

Karim's gaze flicked to me. "Of course."

Of course.

Or, more accurately, *of course I can't expect answers from Karim.*

We turned a corner and went down a set of internal stairs to a floor where the air-conditioning was turned up way too high. I rubbed my arms and followed Karim down a white hallway at odds with the luxury of the rest of the yacht.

We came to large doors with portholes and entered an industrial-sized kitchen. A man in a pristine chef's jacket wiped down a stainless-steel bench.

"Bonjour..." Karim spoke to the chef in French.

French.

Freaking French. Just how many languages did these people speak? Ridiculous. I'd bet Karim was just as fluent in Spanish as Haithem was, and I'd bet even more that Haithem could out-French Karim. He wouldn't have the chef on his yacht, otherwise. Wouldn't have one soul he couldn't trust...

I shivered and glanced between Karim and the chef.

I might not be able to pull languages out my backside, but I had a master's degree in French as it applied to requesting pastries.

"Bonjour, puis-je avoir un croissant, s'il vous plaît?"

Karim's gaze flicked to me. He said nothing, but adjusted his tie.

I grinned.

He needn't know that therein lay the entirety of the grade-six French vocabulary I'd retained. The chef beamed, threw his hands up in the air and spoke one long string of meaningless words.

I caught cheese in there somewhere and went with it. *"Fromage, s'il vous plaît."*

The chef made me a plain croissant with cheese.

I raised my brow at Karim, who continued to watch me. I'm sure my smugness could only have been exceeded if I'd known how to say *tomato* in French. Then I'd have me a cheese and tomato croissant and the added joy of keeping Karim guessing.

I accepted the plate from the chef. *"Merci."*

Karim opened his mouth, but I brushed past him.

"I'll just take this upstairs." I winked at him and pushed open the doors with my back.

I PICKED FLAKES off my croissant. Haithem might just be busy. Something was probably going wrong with his business. He'd come up and talk to me, eventually. My heart seemed to sit high in my chest. He wasn't avoiding me.

Wasn't sitting down there plotting ways to break the stowaway spy...

I pushed the plate away and circled the room.

Made the bed.

Tidied up.

Wiped invisible dust.

I walked the perimeter of the room then stopped in front of the locked door. I reached out and twisted the handle. It turned halfway and jammed.

As if he'd actually forget to lock something.

I sighed and walked to his bedside table and opened it. I'd already inspected the contents well enough to know it didn't hold anything exciting. I opened the second drawer and paused.

A notepad.

I pulled it out then reached back inside the drawer for a blue ballpoint pen. I flipped through the empty ruled pages. How long had it been since I'd written something creative?

Years...

Not for university or work but just for the joy. I wandered out onto the deck and sat at the table. I used to write every day. Little plays and sketches. I'd written while I waited. There was always so much waiting—in hospitals, waiting rooms, at home on my own.

I ran my finger around the edge of a blank page.

Josh loved them, especially the funny ones.

We'd acted them out together.

I blinked, blinked back the name ringing through my head, and picked up the pen. My wrist moved, pressed the tip of the pen against the page and flowed a line of lettering from one end of the paper to the other.

MY STOMACH GAVE an empty gurgle. I glanced up. The sun hung low and orange on the horizon. The notepad was mostly filled, and blue smudged down the side of my left hand. I closed the notepad and put it away in the cabin then ventured downstairs.

I waved at the guard and walked directly to the room Haithem had been in earlier. The lights were off and the sofas empty. I walked around the room, ran my hand over the back of a leather chair, fiddled with the handle of an antique cabinet, then looked out the windows onto the lower deck. Only the dark forms of the guards paced outside. I went back down the hall and took the stairs belowdecks. I passed the kitchen and glanced inside. The chef hunched over the counter. I kept going, slinking down the stark hallway. Low, rhythmic thumping wafted toward me. I followed the sound to an unfurnished room.

Haithem stood at the far end, wearing only a pair of black shorts, the entire bronze length of his body glossed with sweat. His shoulders rippled with sharp movements that sent jolting thumps echoing off the empty walls. I stepped inside. Karim stood opposite Haithem, still in a suit—the guy probably slept in a suit—with his jacket off and sleeves rolled up, and holding a pair of boxing mitts. Haithem's fist connected smoothly with a mitt, and Karim let out a small grunt, pushing into the movement.

Karim barked a word, and Haithem leaped back. Karim tossed the pads to the side and Haithem spun on his heel, raising his leg in an arc. I leaned against the wall, pulse rising at the explosive movements. Karim blocked the move, rotated to the side and sent a kick flying toward Haithem.

He ducked, dropped down and swiped Karim's legs out from under him. Karim hit the carpet with a grunt. My heart did a backflip. A man that size shouldn't be so nimble—yet he was.

Big and fast, and so undeniably lethal.

I'd known that, yet somehow imagined him wielding a handgun as his guards did. He looked like the kind of man who'd know his way around a firearm. Now I knew that if he did carry one, he didn't need one.

Haithem helped Karim to his feet. Karim made a gesture with his chin in my direction. Haithem's movements slowed, and he glanced over his shoulder. Karim picked up the mitts and left the room, nodding to me on his way out. Haithem collected a towel and a water bottle from the floor near the wall and wiped his face, then laid the towel around his shoulders.

I approached him slowly. "Hey."

Haithem drank deeply from the water, the plastic walls of the bottle crinkling and concaving under the pressure of his gulps. A rivulet of sweat ran down his neck and over his shoulder. My mouth went wet yet somehow sticky. His scent reached me. *Damn you, you're supposed to stink when you're sweaty.* On him, of course, sweat only amplified the sexy, added a layer of something dirtier and muskier to his usual masculinity. Made me imagine this was how he'd smell after sex.

"What can I do for you?"

He didn't look at me when he asked the question. *What can I do for you?* As though we were strangers. But then, Haithem had a reserved way of speaking.

I frowned.

On second thought, he also had intimate ways of speaking—ways I'd become used to him using with me.

"I wanted to see if you were coming up for dinner?"

He put the top back on the bottle. "I'm busy today."

I resisted the frown tweaking my mouth. "I thought you said you were finished with your work?"

"You know nothing about my work."

Our gazes locked. A steely veil slammed over his expression. Still that wariness was there. One he had no right to be feeling.

I should be the one who was shitty. *Well.* He'd better get to girding his loins because right now I planned to stealth-seduce him so hard, he'd be choppering me home before he could finish his next stupidly suspicious thought.

"You're right, I don't." I stepped closer, rested the fingers of my right hand on the ridges of his shoulder. "But I haven't seen you today." I let my voice sink lower. "And I'm bored…"

His expression was all off. Vacant and detached.

"I spent yesterday entertaining you." He brushed my hand off his chest and leaned down. "I didn't realize you were going to be so needy."

I stumbled backward.

My cheeks went hot, then burning hot. A sinking sensation plunged from my throat to my belly. He could have said anything to me, hurled any insult, and I'd have taken it. But that one grated against open wounds. How many times had I heard those words in my life?

Don't be needy, Angelina.

When I'd tried to show my parents one of my plays, a report card, told them I'd had a nightmare.

Can't you see we're busy…tired…upset. Don't be so needy.

My eyes stung. And I'd learned not to be. Learned how useless it was to need things from other people. Until Haithem came along with his promises—until he invited me to ask him for things.

I pulled my jaw out of its sag. "Geez, Haithem, what happened to—" I held out my hand and put on my best Haithem voice "—'ask me for anything'…"

Okay, so the accent I affected was two parts Dracula, one part Gru from *Despicable Me*, but at least it added to the theatrical flair.

He scowled.

I tried not to flinch. He had a mean-ass scowl. I kept

going, anger the perfect antidote to the hurt. "I will listen to you talk for—" I paused, my eyes widening.

"Do you need someone to hear you? I will listen to you talk for days."

Fuck me. *The beach.* He'd played me just as I'd known he would.

"You goddamn bastard." I pressed my hands to my cheeks and shook my head. How could I be so stupid? So pathetic. I'd fallen right into his sadistic hands. "That's what it was yesterday?"

He could be a poker champion. While my lips shook like two windblown leaves, the only thing that moved on his face was another bead of sweat rolling from his temple.

"You playing me into this warped little fantasy you think will stop me from telling anyone about you?"

His cheek twitched.

My heartbeat rioted painfully.

"Well, you can stop." My throat scratched. "I don't work for anyone, and I'm not going to tell anyone about you." I looked away from him. If I had to see his satisfaction, this time I'd vomit on his bare feet. "Not for your sake, though. I'm not so stupid that I can't recognize you're poison. That breathing a word about you would only make my life that much more difficult." I tugged at my dress and stretched straighter. "So you can relax, stop feeling the need to fuck with me. My only agenda right now is to get the hell away from you."

I waited for him to say something. Prove me right, say *I'm so glad you understand* or some other patronizing bullshit. But he held his silence.

From now on, I'd go back to holding mine.

I'd like to say I could go back to holding everything the way I had before, but the emotions spilled from me, and I left before he could see me cry.

EIGHTEEN

I SNAPPED THE origami fortune teller game back and forth between my fingers, then shut my eyes. *Will this horror ever end?* I pried up a panel, then opened my eyes.

Highly doubtful.

The answer to the question blazed boldly in my own rounded lettering. I blew air between my lips and tossed the stupid game onto the top of the pile of chatterboxes I'd painstakingly folded, filled in, but not actually played until now.

I fell back onto the bed, legs still crossed. In two days I hadn't left this room. Not once. Hadn't so much as opened the door for a breeze. Cabin fever be damned. I'd rather go bat-shit-stir-crazy than suffer one more second of Haithem's hateful presence. I'd filled half of one of the notebooks I'd stolen from his drawer with journal-like rambles, and the other with something actually productive—less personal yet in some ways more so.

I kicked out my legs and the origami games, the same kind I'd learned to make to entertain Josh during the long hours he'd spent in waiting rooms, corridors and sickbeds, fell to the floor.

I wouldn't think about Haithem. *Nope.* Wouldn't cry again. Done with that.

Blinding rage was better company, and the only Haithem-induced emotion I'd tolerate at the moment. Except when I succumbed to sleep. Then everything was him—Haithem kissing. Haithem touching. Haithem holding. Haithem *listening.*

In my dreams he'd say again, "there's nothing you can keep from me," and in my dreams there wasn't. I'd tell him *everything.*

I'd say all the weak-willed sappy things my sleeping mind wouldn't deny. *Why didn't you want me?* Stupid things I should have evolved beyond. *Why aren't I enough?*

My subconscious and I weren't on the same page. We weren't in the same notebook, drawer, or even yacht when it came to Haithem.

The door handle creaked. I scrambled to sitting, but didn't look—didn't let my traitorous wanting gaze stray to him. I worried the red polish on my thumb with my index fingernail.

"What are you doing in here?" His voice rolled softly over me. A gentle enquiry.

Like he didn't know exactly what I was doing. I wouldn't dignify a response until he started asking better questions—such as, could I ever forgive him for being an unbearable douche-bucket? Except with more groveling. A chunk of red flicked off my thumbnail. The answer would be *never*, but I'd still enjoy the hell out of hearing it.

"The kitchen told me you haven't ordered any food since yesterday."

I ignored him. Pretended he was a big, annoying, asshole of a lump in the room. He touched my shoulder and sat on the edge of the bed. I clenched my teeth. Were my eyes still puffy? He shouldn't be allowed to see that.

"If you're doing this to punish me, you're only hurting yourself."

My gaze snapped to his. "Not everything is about you."

"Then stop being stubborn, and tell me what you'd like to eat." He leveled his do-as-I-command glare at me.

"Fine, I'd like some freshly caught squid." My voice could have cut glass.

He froze, and for a moment, I caught it—the briefest flash of emotion flickering across his face. I couldn't know if it was guilt or if he'd actually felt something when we'd been in that boat and he'd coaxed my life story out of me, but—stupid me—my heart lifted at the hint that maybe it'd been real.

My anger slipped, leaving me soft and hurting again.

He shifted and paper crunched, and he tugged a ruined chatterbox from under his thigh. "What's this?"

I stared at him for a long time. Stared at his duplicitous face. Warm and cold. Intimate and distant. My insides braced pain and a spark of anger still buried there. He sighed and lowered his hand.

I caught him by the sleeve. "It's a game."

His long eyelashes fanned tight around the dark of his eyes. "Is it now?"

My throat thickened. Haithem liked games. Games were his domain, but this time, all the games scattered around us were ones I'd made.

"Don't you want to play with me?"

Haithem

PLAY WITH HER—had we ever ceased? Challenge lit her eyes. A flash that crossed the hurt written over her.

Hurt I'd put there. If I could, I'd take it away. "I'll always play with you, Angel."

She released my cuff, slid to the ground, then rummaged through what I'd thought was litter, coming back up with one of her little paper contraptions. "This one I think."

"The rules?"

She smiled, kind of lopsided and not in her eyes. Did she find the idea I'd ask for rules ironic? I had rules. Many rules.

"The player picks a color." She indicated the colors on the four outer squares. "The dealer shuffles the chatterbox once for every letter." She opened the game back and forth. "Then the player chooses a number from inside."

I peered into the mouth of her chatterbox and at the numbers penned inside. "And then?"

"Then you open a flap and get your truth or dare."

I studied this pretty girl who'd somehow wormed her way under my skin and bored into my blood. This girl who'd caused every breath I'd avoided her with these two terrible days to die stale in my lungs. A girl whose motives were yet unproven.

Would this girl be the end of me?

With her tricks, her games and now this device to dare me with... My top teeth clashed on bottom teeth. Did she intend to steal my deadliest secrets with a child's toy?

I took the chatterbox from her hand as delicately as if it were an open rose. "And you wrote these truth or dares?"

Did she think she could dare me to let her go?

"I did." She blinked, one time only. Always so innocent with those eyes.

I looked into them, searched for a spark of deceit. "That all feels a little premeditated to me."

"Look around you." Her nose scrunched. "There's more than a dozen of these, and none of them were intended for you." She reached for the game. "But if you don't trust me pick another and I'll go first."

"Except you know what's under every number." I shifted the chatterbox out of her reach. "I'd call that an advantage, and I'm not inclined to give you one unless I know exactly what we're playing for."

Her lips tightened and she drew back. "Have you always been so suspicious?"

"Not always." I spat the words, English a clunky foreign mouthful for a strange instant.

She frowned, then her expression softened. "Look, it's just a kids' game. You don't have to play."

"I'll play, but I want to know, Angelina." I slid my fingers under the squares the way she had. "What do you think we're playing for?"

"The same thing kids do—amusement." She rested her palm on the bed between us and swayed toward me. "So we'll play by kids' rules, too. A dare must be fulfilled immediately. It can't be saved for later or prolonged. Truths are truths you would comfortably ask a child." She leaned in and the way her voice dripped could be sweet or it could be poison. "So there's no need to be afraid of me."

I laughed. But her poison struck. Perhaps I was afraid of her. She had weapons I could not armor against. "Pick a color."

"Red."

I knocked the chatterbox back and forth three times then opened it wide. "Choose."

Her eyelids fluttered. "You pick for me, just to be sure I'm not cheating."

"I'd have trusted you." A tick snapped in my neck. "But, I'll give you number three."

I pried open the flap and the title read *dare*. For a moment, a knot formed in my chest, and I wished for truth—if she were playing fair.

"Read it out."

"Angelina." My gaze locked on her. The rules, would she bend them? "I dare you to show me something you've never shown anyone."

She smiled, and brushed her hair over her shoulder. "Easy peasy, you saw my scars and I'd never shown them to anyone before. Other than doctors and that doesn't count."

I shook my head. "You didn't show me. I saw." Did she think the sympathy of that moment would earn her a free pass? "Show me something you've never shown anyone."

Her entire forehead wrinkled.

"The dare must be able to be fulfilled immediately." I dropped the chatterbox between us and hovered over it. "Again, Angelina, show me something you've never shown someone."

Her throat moved. "Seriously, what do I have to show you imprisoned in your cabin besides my physical body?"

Now I smiled, real, and wide. "Show me what's written in that notebook right there."

Her head turned in a jerk toward the side table.

"That's not what the dare says. You don't get to choose. I decide what to show you."

"Then choose something."

She glanced back to me and gripped the bedspread.

"I thought you said you weren't cheating." I had her. In whatever she'd tried to score from me in this silly game, I'd pushed, and I'd almost won. I should be content. As always what should satisfy me with her never seemed to be enough. There was always more. More I wanted. More I sensed. And the ruthless hunger to possess it. "Show me the notebook now."

She grabbed the notebook from the top of the bedside table and shoved it into the drawer, then took the other thicker one from underneath. "Fine, you can see one page from this one."

My gaze didn't stray to the thing she'd hidden. The thing I now wanted.

"Thank you." I took the notebook. "Preference for a page?"

"Whichever." Her arms linked under her breasts, and I didn't look there obviously, either.

"This was your game." I flipped open to a page of writing. "Remember, you wanted to play."

I scanned the words. Twice. Because this was structured. *Scene III.* A play. I glanced up. Her university transcripts. I'd thought she wanted to be an actress. But was this what it'd all been about. Did she want storytelling?

I read the lines, each one slowly. Until the words slunk into my mind, flowing like liquid. A laugh burst from my lips at a witty dialogue and I turned the page.

Her hand slammed down, open and splayed on top of the page. "You only got one."

"You wouldn't give me more?" I let her take her note-book. "Not for a dare but because I asked?"

Her gaze flirted on then away from me. She put the notebook in the drawer and picked up the chatterbox. "It's your turn."

"Green."

She made the five movements. "Choose."

"One."

She lifted the flap. "Truth. What's your favorite smell?"

"Pardon?"

"What's your favorite smell?" she read out again.

That's the question? She wanted to play for questions so trivial? But then maybe she hoped I'd get the dare. That I'd show her my unseen thing I would not be willing to reveal.

"I don't have one."

"Bullshit, everyone has one." She threw the chatter-box down. "I did mine, now you do yours."

My mouth curled down. "Pick another. I don't have one."

"You have to answer." She shuffled closer and put a hand on each of my shoulders. "When you close your eyes, what's the one thing you want to breathe in?" She squeezed. "Shut your eyes."

I did. And what filled me was her—her scent. Clean and uncontrived. Shampoo and soap and a faint under-lying sweetness of woman.

"Stop smelling me."

My eyes slit open.

She raised a brow. "You leaned closer."

"This is a ridiculous game." I shut my eyes.

She squeezed my shoulders. "Think about what you *want* to be there."

Memories plowed through me. A catalog of scents. Then one, just one, pushed through the rest. One I'd lay down my life to have again.

"What is it?"

My throat closed. "Rosewater."

"Like perfume?"

Pain drove into my ribs. "No, like Turkish Delight."

Rosewater in my mother's kitchen. The sweets she made for me. *Home.* Her voice when she sang at the sink. Not off-key—not through the ears of the man who'd last seen her. Not the man who never appreciated anything the way he should until it was gone. I heard her through the love-drenched ears of a child.

Something brushed my cheek.

I jerked back, eyes open and a burn behind them— one I also had not experienced in years. And there were her eyes, fixed on mine.

"Are you all right?"

She asked as though she hadn't seen. As though the truth were not on her face. As though she did not possess those same wants enough to have caught what I must've revealed. *Family—love—life.* So near, like the memory I still tasted.

The loss of those same things a reflection in her eyes.

She touched my cheek again, her hand warm and soft.

I'd give it all. Success, ambition, wealth. I'd lay it at the feet of anyone who could give my old world back. For a moment that world shifted, and I felt them alive in the way she touched my face and looked at me.

Her chin tilted forward and her breath flowed a new seduction into my lungs. *Purpose—vengeance—justice.* What did they matter with what we'd lost?

My will screamed—*Games*—I seized her wrist, and jerked her touch from me. Her breath caught, but her eyes went still. For all I've seen her earnest, this was the thing that had suspicion burning in my throat and dripping to my heart. *That look*. I held her wrist, caught like a speared fish between us. *That one*. The I-see-you-Haithem.

With her tricks and bartering. Her hand clutching diamonds over the ocean. Secrets for orgasms. Games and dares. None could claim to have known, or tested, or seen me the same. Not since I'd become this single-minded thing. Who could see past this shadow?

Angelina.

My muscles contracted and I tossed her wrist before I could squeeze it in a way I couldn't undo. "What are you playing at?"

THE PLETHORA OF things he'd failed to hide slammed closed as his jaw set in that familiar way. I rubbed my wrist, my heart a dull aching thump in my chest. Don't know what I thought I'd win from him, only that I'd pry whatever I could free.

"Truth or dare."

I hadn't expected to find so much. I hadn't expected to see grief as deep as my own. And I'd never have thought I'd find *hope*.

My fingers opened and closed, and even though he scowled I wanted to set my hand on him again. I wanted to see what else there was to him he wouldn't show.

"And what did you hope to dare? What truth did you want from me?" He stood. "Go on, ask me—maybe this time I'll answer."

The dull thump of my heart turned deeper, harder

and fuller. No he wouldn't. He wouldn't answer. He was hunting for ulterior motives.

"You accuse me of games, but you're the one who played me." I stood, too. My bare toes, inches from his black shoes on carpet. "You made me tell you personal things and pretended you cared."

His scowl turned further down.

"You made me think you really liked me." My bottom lip pulled in. I filled my lungs, because no, I wouldn't get emotional again.

His expression shivered, the anger and grit clearing. "I never agreed with what you suggested," he said. "If you're upset, it's because you've made assumptions."

His eyes were dark, and his gaze bored into me.

"What are you saying?"

"I'm saying I never said I was playing you—you assumed that." He touched his chin with his fingertip.

"Is this you trying to apologize? You're not saying you said that, but you're not denying it, either?" I leaned up a little higher. "That is not an apology."

"I'm sorry you're upset." He dropped his hand to my arm. A frown edged into his expression.

The warmth of his touch shot into my skin. I breathed hard, and the movement pushed my chest against my dress. The fabric suddenly didn't seem like much of a barrier between him and me. Neither did the tiny fraction of space between us.

My gaze flicked to his lips. I could still taste them. Still remember exactly how they felt against mine. Heat and need crawled through me, harder and sharper than I'd ever experienced.

"That is the worst apology I've ever heard, and it's

not even what you should be apologizing for." I hadn't meant to sound so breathless.

He'd played me in so many ways, but one was the most infuriating. He'd lured me here with something I'd desperately wanted. Something I hadn't been able to block from my mind or dreams even in my angriest moments. Something I still wanted and he should've damn well given to me already.

"Really? What should I be apologizing for?"

I brought my mouth so close to his he'd taste my answer. "You should apologize because I've been here for a week, and I still haven't gotten laid."

There could only be two reasons he hadn't been all over me. Either he didn't want me—or he was afraid of what would happen if he fucked me. A furious burn rose in my esophagus at the first possibility. And maybe my whole body did ache to have him, but what could *he* be afraid of? What would happen if we did? My heart raced at the idea. My core pooled with desire. Would it be like before, when I touched him and he couldn't keep himself inside?

Things couldn't get much worse between us, but maybe they could get *more*. Maybe I could have more. Be more to him.

If he gave in.

If I pushed him there.

"So, maybe you should shut your face and apologize to my vagina—with your prick."

I don't know how I came up with such vulgar words, but they worked. Air hissed between his lips. I wanted to feel okay again. Wanted to feel sexy and good and not shredded and anxious. I didn't need it to be sweet. I just needed it to happen.

The fingers wrapped around my arm squeezed.

"That's not a very nice way to talk." Each word he said tickled my mouth.

"Thought we established I didn't need to be nice with you?"

Haithem released my arm. "I'm going to get you something to eat." He strode to the door, then paused. "I hope you're done moping."

My pulse galloped and I watched him leave.

Big bad Haithem was afraid of me.

IT MUST'VE BEEN midnight when I heard the rustling next door. In the *locked* room. Strange, since I hadn't heard anyone outside on the deck.

And I'd been listening.

Ever since Karim delivered something that tasted very much like fresh-caught squid, I'd been listening. Wondering if Haithem would come back up.

Wondering if the chef had frozen squid somewhere, or if Haithem had sent someone out to catch some—or maybe he'd ventured out himself.

But the question running through my mind again was why Haithem, Mr. Balls of Steel, had chickened out of shagging me?

Either way, it wasn't fair—I couldn't stop thinking about him. Couldn't stop sitting there, staring at the wall, picturing what it'd actually be like to be taken by Haithem.

I'd lost a piece of my mind.

A beat thumped in my head.

Sex, sex, sex.

The same beat that had hummed away under the

surface of my skin since I'd stepped out of that damn elevator.

Sex, sex, sex.

Whispering in my blood dark with promises of what Haithem offered.

It was fucked-up, I'm sure.

I had hate and anger and pain all twisted up with a mighty lust. Yet that promise kept me going. The promise that had drawn me here, to his yacht, to him. *Sex.* I'd always been such a bloody good girl. Careful, dependable, *good*. Too bogged down in responsibility and grief to even know myself.

Another sound echoed from the other room, and I stared at the door.

I wanted to peel off my skin and see what lay underneath. That same skin shook with uncertainty—the fear of rejection. Even so, nothing he said or did could take away what I knew. He'd sought me out, brought me here—he desired me, too.

No amount of self-doubt could erase that.

That knowledge alone empowered me. That knowledge made me believe more about myself than I could have accepted on my own.

I am desirable.

I walked to the door and pressed my fist on the wood.

I'd use that desirability to my advantage. Because, fuck him—he'd messed with my life. He'd played god with my existence and had the audacity to deny me the one thing that had been an unspoken vow between us— that he would take me.

I raised my fist and knocked.

The room went quiet.

I knocked again.

The door opened. Once again, my heart faltered. Haithem, hair mussed, jaw rugged, shirtsleeves rolled up, freaking barefoot.

I pushed my way into the room and looked around. An office.

Big wood desk, wingback chair, a couple of arm-chairs. A bookshelf with glass doors.

Made sense, really—high-powered businessmen on yachts, maybe they'd need an adjoining office.

"I didn't hear you on the deck."

Haithem shut the door and pushed his hands into his pockets. "That's because I came up the internal stairs."

"There's internal stairs?" I glanced around the room. My gaze caught on a shut door across the room. "So, why have I been going down the outside ones?"

"Because you're not allowed in here."

"Not allowed?" I smiled. "I thought this time with you was all about being allowed to do anything." I walked to his desk. Picked up a narrow wooden box.

He stepped up behind me.

I opened the lid.

A letter opener.

I touched the edge. Rounded and smooth. Not sharp enough to be exciting.

"You're such a liar."

He took the box from me and set it back on the desk. "Never claimed otherwise."

"But you did say something about keeping prom-ises." I turned. "You were fairly adamant about your ability to keep a promise."

"And what promises have I broken?"

There was definitely something about being up late that gave me courage. "You said you'd give me whatever

I asked for." I stepped closer to him. "And I've asked you to fuck me, and yet I remain completely unfucked." I lowered my voice *"Liar."*

His teeth clamped shut with a snap.

Finally, a button.

Push.

I smiled, high on electric energy. "We both know I came here for one thing, but you lost your nerve."

His fingers twitched.

Push.

"You pretend to be so big and bad, with all your warnings—but I think all you are is one big bluff."

Shove.

He clenched his fists. "If I didn't know better, I'd think you were fishing for trouble."

"I don't need trouble. Believe me, I'm suffering enough." I looked up at him. "But if you think I'm scared of being hurt a little bit, don't worry—I'm used to being hurt a lot."

His eyelids drooped. "That's why I'm not doing this."

I laughed—tipped my head back and laughed bitterly at the ceiling.

"You care, do you?" I lowered my chin and stared at him. "You think I don't know what you wanted. Why you invited me here in the first place. To fuck me, use me, make me your little sex doll for two weeks?"

Silence pulsed between us.

His jaw ticked, once, twice, three times. "I didn't know you then. Now, I'm trying not to hurt you—a lot."

I wanted to hit him, to pound my fists against his chest like a lunatic. How dare he decide for me? I was done with that.

My choice.

I didn't need any more protecting.

I pushed his chest. He grabbed my wrist, stopped the futile action.

"No, you're being a pussy. Man up and fuck me."

His entire face twitched.

He jerked my hand up, turned me around and brought my hand up behind me.

He bent me over his desk.

My chest hit wood with a thud.

"Like this?"

His voice sent a chill into me—partly due to the underlying note of anger, partly because of the way it shook, as though I could snap his control with the slightest movement.

I wouldn't say no, wouldn't tell him this was not what I'd pictured when I'd thought of us together. Right then, though, any way we came together was better than being denied another moment.

My arm strained behind my back, stretching muscles in my shoulder. My nightgown was pushed up by the hand now manacled to the small of my back. Air flew back into my lungs. The silken fabric of his pants skimmed the back of my thighs. And his heat—his heat branded my skin. Made me hyperconscious of his body positioned behind me. Made my pussy wet and ready and willing. Made me all too aware of just what would happen now.

That he'd finally take me.

That he'd fuck me angry.

That he might fuck me roughly and callously, the way you take a woman who knows how to fuck. Because I'd shown him the most wanton side of myself. The side I hadn't really known was there until he drew it out of me. He didn't know that no other man had ever seen me naked.

And I'd rather he never found out.

The past week showed me I didn't believe in labels like *virgin*. I could demand cock and not blush. I wasn't innocent. I'd just never had the chance to take what I needed.

His knee drove between mine and opened my thighs.

Thought evaporated, leaving only lust in its wake.

"Is this what you want, Angel?" His hand moved between my legs, and his fingers curled around the crotch of my underwear.

I refused to let out the gasp that caught in my chest.

His body heat brushed the folds of my sex. His skin against my sensitive skin. His thumb moved, stroking my slickness.

My legs jerked.

"You want me to fuck you?" He tugged on my panties, slamming my backside into his hips and pulling fabric taut against my swelling clitoris. "Fuck you, use you, make you my doll?" His voice dripped with venomous sweetness.

He rotated his hips, and the full length of his cock rubbed against the curve of my ass through his pants. My stomach tightened, my core throbbed and my body reacted as if by instinct, rolling against that delicious hardness.

I moistened my lips, willing them to form the words to call his bluff. "So, stop talking about it, and do something."

I couldn't see his face, but his grip on my wrist tightened. I knew what I'd done—sliced a vein open in front of a shark and dared him to eat me.

You don't dare a shark—they have no soul.

He tugged my panties. The fabric dug into my hips, then gave way with a rip that echoed through the cabin. His hand covered me—his huge hand, fingertips hovering over my clit and thumb stretched all the way back to the top of my ass. My stomach squeezed. He rubbed a slow circle over my nerves. My eyes stretched open, pleasure lighting up my insides.

He moved his thumb, prodding against my pussy.

"So wet…" he said, and swirled his thumb in my heat. "You think you want this…" He delved back quickly, violently, jammed the pad of his thumb against my ass. "You don't know what you're asking for."

I jerked and gasped, breathing in air that tasted of varnish. My spine curled as if I was a cat. He pinned my wrist tighter to the small of my back, pushing me toward him. His thumb pressed deeper, the tip stretching my entrance. My hips twisted.

"All you have to say is no. All you have to say is stop."

I sucked in more air, torn between the need to yelp and the need to beg for more.

"Say it." He leaned over me, his fingers slipping and brushing my clitoris. Sensations streaked through me.

I squirmed, involuntarily releasing a sound.

"Say you've had enough." Haithem released my wrist. Blood rushed back into my shoulder muscles. He brushed hair from my face with his free hand and leaned over me, then sank a fraction farther into my ass.

I squeezed my eyes shut, bracing against the fullness.

"Just push me away," he whispered, his breath rushing against my temple.

My pulse raced hard and fast.

He was right. I had no clue what I'd asked for. Even the thrill couldn't combat the system overload.

I couldn't have imaged he'd do this—want this.

He rocked his fingers simultaneously against my ass and my pussy. The tension in my pelvis coiled tightly and urgently, caused my vision to blur. Even half out of my mind, I knew he held back. He toyed with me, still tried to scare me away, convince me of his badness—prove I couldn't handle it.

But I wanted his wickedness. Needed it to balance the bleakness inside me.

I breathed out slowly, expelling all the air from my lungs. Forced my muscles to relax, to comply with his invasion—then I pushed back.

I stretched. His thumb sank in to the first knuckle. He stilled behind me and whispered a foreign word against my hair.

Playtime ended.

He impaled me with his thumb, rubbing my clit with two fingers. This time, I couldn't control the squeal that burst out of my chest. He stroked hard and methodically, no playing, no teasing. My slippery flesh quivered under the pump of his fingers. My insides strained, my pelvis jerked, every cell contracted, stiffened—then let go.

I screamed, the hoarse sound grating against my throat. Raw ecstasy smashed into me. I pulsed, vibrated, unraveled. I thrashed as though stung with electricity.

My breaths slowed, and the hand between my legs slid free. His weight left me, and cold touched my rear. I rested on the desk, arms over my head, muscles limp and useless.

I turned my head to the side.

Haithem stood beside me, staring at me as if he either wanted to devour me or tear me apart. Passion streaked his features. Something opened inside me, and energy flowed in. I climbed off the desk and onto the floor in front of Haithem.

He towered over me, all hard man. I placed my hands on his thighs and leaned into him. At any other time, I might have been nervous, but now I realized this was where I'd always wanted to be.

I became catlike around him. No bones, just stretching, arching muscle, desperate to rub against him. I wanted to lie at his feet, had felt it the moment I saw him. Like some primitive response to his masculine energy—everything female in me desperate to crawl to him. I rested my cheek against his pants, his erection reaching me through the fabric. My hands stroked toward his belt, but I couldn't resist—couldn't resist the desire to bite that bulge. I scraped my teeth over a hardness that could have been made of metal.

He grabbed my chin, turning me to look at him.

I saw it in his eyes—no going back.

He jerked off his belt and yanked it free of the loops, tossing it to the floor, and then he undid the top button of his pants. I watched, fascinated, as he slid the zipper, exposing the taut, smooth skin on his abdomen.

Commando.

I should have known.

Jet-black hair coated his pelvis in a downward trail. He shoved open his pants and his cock sprang free. Every part of my attention focused on that magnificent organ nestled in a crown of midnight curls. His cock rose, a sweeping arc, daring me to touch it.

I lunged, mouth open—possessed.

Haithem grabbed the back of my hair, holding me still. He took his huge cock in his hand, only a breath from my face. The scent of him teased my nostrils, musky and male and enthralling.

My mouth watered.

I wanted him in me, in my mouth, in my pussy, anywhere he deigned to put it.

He tugged my hair, forcing my neck to crane, and brought his cock to my lips. I opened my mouth wide, struggling toward it.

"Fuck," he whispered.

Haithem tapped his cock on my lips. "Show me that sexy pink tongue."

I stuck out my tongue as far as it could go. He stroked the head of his penis over my tongue and into my mouth before snatching it away. I thrust my chin forward, trying to get him back.

"You want it, don't you?" He tightened his grip on my hair. "You want my cock in your sweet little mouth."

He let me have it, pushing himself past my lips. I extended my jaw, straining to accept his girth, and took all he gave me.

He wasn't kind—he thrust deep, hard, until he hit my throat.

Coughs racked my chest, the muscles of my throat spasming around him. But I didn't spit him out—didn't push him away. I succumbed to him, drowning in the taste, the smell, the power of him.

He pulled out, and the fist in my hair loosened, held me gently. He surged back into my mouth. I sucked with my tongue, my cheeks, my throat, drinking in his salty flavor. He pushed past my gag reflex, pulled out and made me gasp for air.

If I didn't know him, I'd think he was callous. But I did know him, knew why he did this to me. He wanted to take me, overwhelm me, take me to within an inch of what I could stand—because now he knew the real me, too.

His other hand came to cradle my skull, to hold me in place as he fucked my mouth. I did my best to suck, to use my tongue and lips, but mostly I just held on, just let myself get lost in the feel of him, the need overwhelming us.

He stiffened under my hands, between my lips.

I curled my hands into the fabric on his thighs and squeezed everything I could around him. He surged deep, made me splutter, made my eyes water and my lungs burn.

His fingers curled against my scalp. He shook and spurted salty heat into the back of my mouth. I had no choice but to swallow—not that I'd have done differently. I'd take any part of him he'd give. I drank him, closed my lips over his length then sucked gently on his tip. I ran my tongue over his seam, licked over his ridges, curled my fingers over his base. I could do this forever. I would do this forever.

I'd been pumped full of energy. Had inches added to my height, decades to my life. I was Superwoman. I was his angel—and I was a fucking queen.

I made him shake.

I made him come.

I made him lose control.

He softened in my hands, but I stroked my cheek against him. He massaged my scalp, then ran his touch down my jaw and tipped back my head. I gazed at him, knew my eyelids were heavy, my lips swollen. I gazed up at a man I'd never seen before.

A man whose heart beat only for me.

He swallowed, and his Adam's apple moved under all that dark stubble.

"What is happening to me?" he said, and stroked the sides of my face.

I'd begged to be taken, but it looked as though I was the one who had just taken him.

NINETEEN

He carried me into the bedroom and set me down on the floor beside the bed. Then he moved to the wardrobe. I couldn't think straight. I'd expected to be placed on the bed and ravaged instantly. He emerged with a thick blanket and spread it over the bed.

"What's that for?"

He turned to me, linked his thumbs under the straps of my nightgown and pushed them over my shoulders. The fabric caught on my breasts.

"It's for the mess I'm going to make out of you."

My body heated as though I'd been tossed next to a bonfire.

Oh, merciful fuck.

He pushed the satin over my breasts, then took them in his hands.

"What mess?"

He squeezed my nipples. I shivered, chills flowing from my chest into my nether regions.

"Knowing how tight your little pussy is, I'm going to have to take extra special care of you." He shoved the scrap of my panties over my hips, scooped me up and laid me on the blanket. "And that, Angel, is going to get messy."

He ran his gaze over me, then walked to the bedside table.

I leaned up on my elbows and tracked his movements. Oh lord, this should not be happening straight after his incredible blow job. He was way too together, his actions too methodical, too thought out.

He pulled out the "special bag."

My heart kicked up three notches.

I swallowed and fell back against the blanket. If he tried to use the giant vibrator on me, I'd die. I mean, I'd let him do it—at that point, I was up for anything—but I might die.

I stared at the ceiling; it really was well crafted.

The bedside table door shut, and my gaze snapped to him. He set a purple bottle and a condom on the bed.

Haithem looked at me, his eyes narrowed, and then he glanced back at the side table. A grin stretched his face, and he climbed over me. "And you accuse me of bluffing."

Bloody mind reader.

I grabbed his shirt collar and tugged him down, bringing my face to his. He brushed his lips over mine, then pulled back and removed his shirt, then his pants. I ran my hands over his bare chest. I wanted that chest against me. Wanted to slide against him like a snake— drag my skin against his skin, feel our bodies touch from head to toe.

He finally kissed me properly.

I wrapped my arms around his neck and kissed him back. He swept his tongue into my mouth, and opened his lips over mine. My back arched, and the hair on his chest brushed my nipples. His heat seeped into me, but I was already hot—so hot. Our mouths moved together, but I couldn't keep up. He drank me, sucked out the sane, freethinking part of me.

He made a fist in my hair, tugged back my head, and

moved his mouth to my jaw—kissed the line from my
chin to my ear. His lips closed over the lobe. My hips
jerked. A thread of pleasure streaked from my earlobe
to my nipples. He sucked, and my consciousness folded,
focused on nothing more than how searing, wet and incredible his mouth was.

He moved down, scraped his stubble over the side of
my neck and nipped me. His teeth pinched, sent a static
bolt ringing through me. I buried my hands in his hair.
It slid between my fingers.

My hands in his hair, his in mine.

He sucked hard over my pulse. My heart must've
pounded against his tongue. His other hand moved
down my side and gripped my thigh, hoisted my leg.
He moved to my breast and tongued my nipple.

My breath hitched.

Pleasure rang between my legs. He released my hair
and teased the hard, beaded peak of my breast. My pelvis arched off the mattress. I dragged my nails down the
back of his scalp. He sat up, and my hands fell from him.

My wet nipple drew tighter, stiffer, in the cool air. He
flicked it with his thumb, then reached for the purple
bottle. He popped off the lid and turned the container
over my stomach. Liquid hit me, made me gasp, like
ice on sunbaked skin. It pooled in my belly button, cascaded down my sides.

He held the bottle higher, squeezed it in his fist and
squirted more across my breasts. The sticky wetness
smothered my chest and dribbled down to my armpits.

I twitched, my system flashing from burning to chill
and back again. He held my thighs open, and a jet of
fluid lashed between my legs. I gave a shuddering gasp.
He saturated my mound, covered me so completely it

trickled down my ass. I clenched my hands in the blanket under me.

He tossed the bottle aside and grabbed my hips, dragged me closer, brought my ass up hard against his thighs. His cock hovered above my open knees. So close, all he'd have to do is lean down, and he could put himself inside me.

I opened my legs wider, exposing myself to him. He touched me. Not where I wanted, but placed his hands flat on my abdomen and stroked his palms across my skin, over my belly, between my breasts, over my chest, up my neck. He stroked his thumbs down the center of my throat. I dropped my head back and absorbed the soft, commanding pressure. He smoothed over my shoulders, then rolled his palms around the outsides of my breasts, pushed his hands over the dip of my hips, stroked down to my sex.

He brushed my folds, his fingers scraping over my clit.

My thighs jerked.

His touch glided—there then gone, up then down.

Whatever he'd put on me made me tingle—made my skin prickle and shiver—sent me from sensitive to raw. He stroked over my ass, tilted up my hips and rubbed back up over my pussy. Tension coiled in my core, and my toes stretched. He ran his hands over my stomach, then caressed my breasts. My head fell back, and I let him touch me. Let myself feel every exquisite movement.

I shut my eyes.

Over and over, around and around, my entire body unraveled under his caress. I arched and bowed, and breathed into his touch. My muscles loosened, and my heart beat hard but steady. He ran a finger down my seam. Somehow, I managed to get wetter. He pushed the slippery finger inside me. It glided in, filling and stretching.

Wicked heat rolled in my pussy.

He pressed up, and pleasure flared in my womb. I moaned, my eyes closing again. He stroked inside me, slowly then faster. Tension coiled, unlike anything before, bone deep. His pace increased, his palm slammed against my clitoris. My hips rocked. He splayed his free hand on my mound and pushed down. I couldn't breathe out, only in, one small breath packed on top of another.

His finger pulsed against some hypersensitive place inside me, and all I could do was let my muscles clench tighter and tighter from my core to my limbs.

Slap, slap, slap.

His palm connected with my flesh. Heat rolled through me in ripples, and all my breath came rushing out in one long moan. Ecstasy burned over me, and I contracted, every cell bursting. Haithem grabbed my hips, holding me down as my body tried to roll. My knees flew up to my chest, he still pressed between my legs.

I rocked, and twitched, and gasped.

The bliss carried on, one bone-shattering wave crashing and another rising to take its place. Sounds released themselves from my tongue. My thighs slid together, slick and so slippery I couldn't know if it was the stuff he'd used or something from me.

I collapsed, still shuddering but without the energy to squirm.

He *had* made a mess of me.

I was a mess.

He hovered over me, brushed damp hair out of my eyes. Salty moisture trickled from my upper lip and into my mouth. I looked up at him. His face defined what satisfaction looks like. I tried to master that breathing in and out thing, but he still touched my sex.

He pushed another finger inside me. Pain cut through the haze, and I made a noise then grasped his wrist.

Haithem stilled. "Ouch?"

Had I said that out loud?

"It shouldn't…" He looked down my body, and his expression shifted, satisfaction morphing into something much more horrified.

He pulled my thighs apart, peered between my legs. I squeezed my knees together, but nothing could be more fruitless than trying to stop Haithem. He spread my folds and touched me gently.

His forehead wrinkled.

I hadn't thought there was a pulse rate faster than the one that had been rushing under my skin, yet apparently there was.

He glanced up, then rose over me. "Is there something you'd like to tell me?"

His lips shook.

My heart shook.

"No."

"I think there is."

"It doesn't mean anything." My tongue darted out, tasted my own sweat.

His chin dropped. "It. Means. Something. To. Me."

Each word hit me like a little punch in the ribs.

It did?

I don't think I'd ever considered that. At first, I hadn't told him because I didn't want my inexperience to put him off, and then I'd *stayed* quiet because I didn't want him going easy on me. I wanted to know what it was really like to be with him.

His emotions, that he'd *care*, that it'd *mean* something to him—that never crossed my mind.

"How is this possible?" He leaned back, rubbed the top of his hand under his chin. "The things you've said…"

I lunged forward, cracked my palm against his cheek. The sound rang louder than it should've, considering how little muscle I'd put into it.

But it worked, and my Haithem rose back to the surface, furious gaze locked on mine.

"Don't you dare go all honorable on me now. I didn't choose you because I thought you'd make a good boyfriend." I touched the red marks already fading from his face. "I chose you because I knew you'd make it incredible…"

His features evened, and he rested over me on his forearm.

"I want to feel all the things, Haithem." I ran my fingers into the luxury of his hair. "Please let's not think." I leaned up, touched my nose to his. "Let's just feel."

His face softened. It showed me beyond a doubt, for the first time, that the person behind all his many shields was real and raw and tangible.

He kissed me. Rested the full weight of his body on me, held one side of my face with fingers behind my ear.

A kiss like falling and drowning and flying, all at once.

He didn't crush me, although his size should have been too heavy. It felt right, his weight compressing my ribs against my heart. His other hand moved between

my legs, an area still so slick and wet and tender. I
opened to him, let my knees fall wider. He pressed two
fingers into me. I cried out into his mouth.

It stung—in the same satisfying way as overscratch-
ing a bite stung. A bit good, a bit bad, a bit perfect. His
hand moved faster, and suddenly my system glided right
back to where it'd been before. Curling and needing,
hot and out of control.

My pelvis rocked, gearing toward another explosion.

"Not yet," he whispered against my lips.

He sat up between my legs. I clutched at him, trying
to keep my hands on him. My fingers trailed down his
hard belly, and I grasped his cock. Let its rigid weight
fill my hand. His fingers moved again, once, twice, then
withdrew. I squeezed his hips with my knees and tried
to guide his hand back to my pussy.

He reached over and picked up the condom.

I couldn't stay still. Could only writhe and wiggle
as he unwound my fingers from his cock and covered
it with the rubber.

He took himself in hand and pressed his cock against
me, rubbed up and down over my folds. Maybe you're
not supposed to look, but I couldn't help myself, I had
to see, had to lean up on my elbows and watch that magnificent thing stroke me.

He flicked the ridge of his crown over my clit.

Flick, flick, flick.

My stomach muscles squeezed, and I pulled my
knees higher. He dipped down and pressed the head
against my entrance. My eyes strained wider; I couldn't
look away, had to watch this happen. He pulsed against
me, pressed in slightly, a hint of fullness, and then he
pulled away. I clutched his waist, tried to draw him in.

His thumb moved to my nub and stroked. Pleasure bubbled over. I dropped back onto my elbows, body twitching toward implosion. He surged inside, sent something sharp and brutal cutting through the joy.

I fell flat against the blanket.

My chin lifted to the ceiling, and my limbs braced. His hand came down next to my ear, and his warmth hovered over me, but all I could focus on was the shifting, searing pressure inside me.

Fingers wrapped around my throat, broke through my prism of tension.

"Here, Angelina, come back here."

I lowered my jaw and looked at him.

He stared down at me and moved, pushed in deeper, stretched me fuller, strained the fibers of my walls.

My lungs filled with air, and my head spun.

His hold on my throat shifted.

"Here," he whispered.

My eyes refocused, and I breathed out and met his gaze. He leaned back just enough to touch me again, to stroke that magic little place of mine. Sensations packed one upon another, filling me with red-hot need. A need for more. A need for friction. A need that would fling me out of my body if it weren't for his hand on my neck. I placed both my hands over his and held him there, held the anchor of his fingers to my throat. His expression shifted, his nostrils flared, and he pulled out and then drove back in.

Pleasure flared in my pelvis. My body adjusted, complied, accepted. He fucked me, drove in and in and into me. Kept me captive and present in my body with his touch and his gaze. My muscles tightened, and I held on to his wrist with both hands as I convulsed, and shook, and screamed.

My eyes stayed open, watched him watch me with wide-open eyes, even when every other part of me contracted. Just as I'd thought I'd experienced the full spectrum of pleasure, the way he looked at me filled me with some deeper ecstasy than any bodily touch could deliver.

His hand left my throat, and he guided my left leg up and over my right. He slammed into me, his pelvis driving up against my rotated backside, cock sliding into me at an angle that sent sharp, sweets bolts of delight through my core.

His jaw twitched, the muscles on his shoulders bulged and strained. I reached for the hand holding my hip to the side, held it as his thrusts shook my body. He fucked me for himself, took what he needed—what I gave.

The veins on his neck stood up, and he rolled my leg back over and settled above me. His hard abdomen slid over the slick, lubed-up skin of my stomach. I rubbed myself against him, wound my arms around his neck and absorbed the glide of his chest against my breasts as he moved in me. He thrust hard, his neck and back stiff under my hands. I drew my knees higher, and he sank deep—pushed in and ground his hips against me.

A low growling sound rumbled from his chest. He grabbed my ass, squeezing me to him. I scraped my teeth over his shoulder, tasted his skin and his sweat, inhaled his scent, taking in everything of his that I could.

He rolled us to the side. I closed my eyes. His hands moved to my hair, smoothed it all back from my face. He pressed his lips to mine, just a soft little kiss.

I opened my eyes.

He kissed me again and again.

Light little pecks while he held my face. My chest filled with warmth, and I no longer knew what I felt with my heart, my head, or my body, only that I was, indeed, feeling *everything*.

TWENTY

EVEN WITH HIS heat radiating against me, my skin eventually cooled. I'm not sure how long we'd lain there—could've been ten minutes, could've been an hour. I'd always expected he'd be the kind of man who'd shag and leave. I didn't need that much experience to know that there are very different ways things like this can go.

That some men are cold, and others are not.

I didn't think he'd keep touching me after we were done. His fingers trailed down the curve of my spine. I almost wished he'd stop. Almost wished he'd stop holding me as though I were precious. I pushed my cheek deeper into his chest. If he didn't stop, there was a good chance I wouldn't be able to stand it when he eventually did. His heart throbbed against my ear. I hurt in places I didn't know I had.

From the inside out.

He stroked down the back of my arm.

I shivered.

He drew back and looked down at me. "Well, look at this."

Cool air brushed my chest, and the surface of my skin prickled. He touched the bumps on my breast, then ran the pad of his index finger over my nipple.

I shivered again, in a different way.

"I might have to keep you cold if you keep this up."

I swallowed. I couldn't speak, didn't know what I'd

say. Didn't know what I could say. My head was a jumble, my brains scrambled.

Crazy things lurked in there.

He rested his hand on my shoulder. "You feeling okay?"

No.

"Just sticky."

He laughed a soft, intimate laugh that pierced my heart.

"Come on then, dirty girl."

He slapped my backside lightly and helped me off the bed, led me into the bathroom and turned on the shower. I stepped inside, and he stepped in after me. There was room for us both, yet he took all my breathing space. Haithem and me, the hot water raining down on us, the steam, the glass walls wrapping me in.

I moved back and leaned against the tiled wall.

"Where are you sticky?"

He rubbed soap between his hands.

"Everywhere," I said.

He washed me. Washed me with soapy hands—*everywhere*. Lifted my leg and washed my foot, pinched my toes. He touched every corner of my body, as though he couldn't touch me enough. Nothing had ever felt as good as this part, this sweet, tender part I hadn't prepared for.

I'm not sure why his touch made my organs squeeze as though massive organ failure were imminent.

I fell against him and wrapped my arms around his waist, buried my face in his shoulder. Water poured over my head and face. He paused in his ministrations and moved us out of the stream. He tilted up my chin to him. He looked as if he was going to say something but stopped and rested his forehead on mine.

His chest expanded against my chest. I breathed with him, as though his breaths were my breaths. I imagined the surface between our skins shivered. His heart beating against me became my heartbeat.

Something of my old life flowed down the drain.

Haithem

SHE'D DRAGGED ONE of the sun loungers halfway inside the cabin doors, catching the breeze but not the sun. I'd been stuck there, at the top of the stairs, immobilized. Watching the hair pulled over one of her shoulders flutter.

Watching her expression change as she scrawled in that notebook she'd refused to open.

What was she writing about? *Me?* She sat with one leg bent, notebook against her knee. My lungs stung as though I'd breathed too much when I certainly had not. What would she say about me if brutal honesty was required?

She ran the tip of her middle finger down the center of her tongue, then flicked the page. A hungry shudder ran through me.

That tongue of hers flashed a hundred times in my head. Running the length of my cock with her eyes unflinchingly on mine. Moistening her lips as her breaths grew frantic—desperate. Her mouth opening wide as her throat arched, straining, exposing the blue veins on her neck.

My fist closed against the railing.

It was almost too easy to forget what we were doing

with each other. Almost too easy to forget that a smaller yacht had been following us for the past three days, not getting closer, not getting farther away.

That in two weeks she'd expect to go home.

She glanced up, then slid her sunglasses into her hair and gazed back at me. I moved across the deck, fluidly as though a moment before I hadn't been soldered in place. She snapped the notepad closed and placed it on the floor. My gaze flicked to it and then to her. What, she didn't want me to see?

Does she still think she can hide from me?

When I'd looked into her eyes while buried inside her and seen her soul? There were secrets there. More that she hadn't told.

Her dress rippled on her thighs, even the breeze luring me to her pale skin. There was so much more to her story.

I sat on the end of the sun lounger.

"Hi." She shuffled back. Her cheeks went rosier. Funny that. When she could look me in the eye and suck my cock, yet now she blushed when I approached her. Awkward now we had this intimacy.

"What were you writing?" I placed my hand on her knee, voice soft but grip firm, and pressed her thigh to the side.

Her muscles contracted for a moment, an instant of resistance before giving in. "Nothing important."

Nothing for me you mean.

It didn't matter, whatever was in there wouldn't be what I needed. I'd only wanted to see if she'd tell me. If she'd trust me. My gaze flowed between her legs, and I smiled, then touched a red prickly rash on her upper thigh still raised from where my face had been. Her thigh twitched under my fingers.

I ran my touch to her cunt. To the pretty white lace between her legs, then ran my knuckles over her sweet spot. "I'd prefer you didn't wear panties while on my yacht."

Her eyes widened but a scrap of lace wasn't enough to stop her heat seeping against me.

"I'll take that under advisement." She crossed her bent leg over the straight one, trapping my hand between her thighs. Trapping, so far as I allowed her to.

She lowered her chin and leaned half a foot closer to me. "Haithem, when you come up here to me, I require you to be without a shirt." Her voice lowered and her gaze flicked to my collar. "It interferes with my ability to see muscles. I prefer to see muscles."

A laugh ripped through my chest and came out as a chuckle. *Look at her.* Like she made the rules. How would we be if she did? *Wonderful.* I clutched her knee with my free hand and yanked open her thighs again.

Life does not get to be wonderful. And the rules were mine to make or break.

I shoved her panties aside and pushed two fingers up inside her. Her reaction was instant. My hand went slick. She clenched her jaw and leaned back. Allowed her legs to be opened.

She turned into sex the way dry ice turns to smoke in hot water—instantly and with majestic beauty.

I twisted my fingers sideways to get her clit with my thumb. She made a choking sound and gripped the sides of the sun lounger. This wasn't going to be sweet today. I went for her G-spot ruthlessly. Until she screamed loud enough everyone on board would know what I did to her.

Until she chanted my name in broken shouts.

Until she came in a way that drenched my hand.

Let them all know she's mine.

She fell back panting and shaking. Fuck, I'd never seen a person come the way she did. The way her whole body spasmed as though there was no thread of control she clung to.

She was abandon.

"Oh, wow." She smoothed hair back from her face, her chest still moving fast. Her gaze fell down on me, then went to the cock pushing hard on the zipper of my pants. I knew what she wanted.

I let her put her little hand on my cock.

"Why hadn't you fucked before me?"

Her fingers froze midcaress. "I told you."

"No you didn't."

She rubbed her chest against my shoulder, then slid her hand farther, tormenting my balls. Lust pounded through my veins but so did the thirst for something more.

"I said I knew you'd be good." She cupped me hard through fabric. "Plus, you're very sexy."

"I didn't ask why you fucked me." I clamped my hand over hers. "I knew you were hot for me the moment you set eyes on me."

She went still.

"I asked why you hadn't before me." I tucked in my chin, trying to see the face she'd turned away, looking down at our hands on my crotch.

"You know my parents have expectations." She

tugged her hand free. "And with my brother and everything. Now was just the right time."

Why?

I watched her. Still lying. Still making excuses around the truth.

"I know you're a good girl, Angel." I slid my hand against the back of her scalp and tugged her hair, tilted her face to me. Gripped her with just an edge of roughness the way she liked. "But you're a very dirty good girl."

She couldn't hide under my direct scrutiny. Her tongue darted between her lips. "The time was right."

"Why was the time right?" I angled her harder, looked closer until our noses almost brushed. *Tell me it wasn't your job.* "Why wasn't it right until you met a man you believed would leave the country the next day?"

Her eyes darted in their sockets, away from mine, looking somewhere vaguely down. "Maybe it's better to break the rules when there's no risk of someone getting hurt."

"You ever thought I couldn't hurt you?" I didn't mean to laugh but I did, and her eyes sparked with inner fire when they landed back on me.

She brushed aside my hand and sat back. "Maybe *I* didn't want to hurt *you*."

My blood froze. *No.* "What do you mean?"

She scooted off the sun lounger. "Nothing."

"I think you're not being honest with me." I drew myself up to standing.

She picked up her notebook and started inside. "Frankly, you're free to think what you like."

I went after her. *Tell me.* My heart boomed. *Tell me.*

My head throbbed. *Tell me.* I followed her around while she put things away, slamming drawers. She managed not to tread on me but I did not make that easy to avoid.

She spun to me. "Why can't you just fucking let a thing go?"

"I don't let go." I growled, and then I had her again, by the waist.

Tell me.

Her chest rose high, then flopped down.

My fingers gripped her waist. My guts clenched.

Don't tell me.

"Honestly, Haithem. My actual twin, womb sibling, was terminally ill most of my freaking life." Her teeth pressed together. "Do you really think there's not a really good chance that I have fucked-up genes. That one day I won't be the sick one?"

What?

My grip dropped from her waist. What about the espionage agency who recruited her? What about them? "That's ridiculous. You're healthy."

How could she not know her genes were perfect?

"Really?" Her eyelids flared. "Because the way I see it we have the same exact parents, and if you haven't heard of it there's this thing called DNA."

A rock-firm absolute certainty settled in my bones. "That will not happen."

I would not allow it.

"What if it did?" Her eyes glistened but a snarl moved into her lip. "Do you have any fucking clue how awful that is? Watching, no, *experiencing* someone you love—it's not even dying, it's decaying."

The living breath ceased in my body. "Angelina…"

I reached for her.

"You think I'd do that to someone?" She knocked my touch away. "If I was bald, and bloated, and sick, and dying, what would you do?" She shoved me between the ribs with her palm. Her dimples pinched along with her lips. "Would you want to fuck me then?"

Our gazes collided in a tangle of agony.

In that quaking instant I knew her. Knew her the way I never knew my dead father—dead mother—relative or friend. Never had I known myself so well.

"I'd still fuck you." I grabbed her by the back of the neck. "But it's never going to fucking happen."

I kissed her.

Drove every inch of my will into her with my lips and tongue and spirit.

I reached between us and broke open my fly. Then I was on her, tearing her panties to shove into her before her ass hit the bed. Let her try to argue there'd ever be a time I wouldn't take this. Her rejoinder—scraping nails, biting teeth and arching hips—was stark desperation and utter longing. And yet still secrets persisted. In that soul-tight bond, I felt it there. The more she didn't tell.

TWENTY-ONE

THE INTERCOM BEEPED. I was coming to hate that stupid beep. I might just take the screws out with a knife and disconnect the wires next time he went downstairs. Haithem pried himself from my arms and crossed the room to answer the handset.

I rolled onto my back.

"Cut the engine," Haithem spat.

I sat up.

His gaze fixed on me, naked on the bed with the sheet up to my hip. "Invite our guests on board."

He hung up the phone, lingered with his hand on the receiver for a moment, and then went to the wardrobe. I leaped up and followed him. Someone was here? No one was ever here.

"Who's visiting?"

With Haithem's trust issues, this could only mean friends—family. Other people who knew him.

"Put on clothes." He pulled on a clean shirt and pants. "And wait for me in this room."

Huh?

So he still wasn't trusting me? I still hadn't earned the right to know about his life or his business?

After everything we'd just talked about and how I'd shared. Things I hadn't even acknowledged until he made me say them.

I'd given him more than I'd ever given another person. Not just the sex—but yes that, too. I hadn't saved myself up like a present or wrapped a bow on my hymen. But, with or without my problems it'd taken this long to let myself get here. And now I'd done this thing, there was a gnawing ache in my stomach. A kind of hopeful grief—could he be the wrong person? Because I'd wanted fun. *Liar.* I'd wanted pleasure.

Haithem gave me that and then some. He hadn't taken anything from me, but he gave me intimacy. I hadn't expected this connection but now we had it I needed more.

"I'll get dressed and come down with you."

He looked up from zipping his pants. "You'll stay here."

He tried to use that this-shit-is-final tone on me, but he didn't quite have it anymore. Too much had changed. Just look, I'd followed him around shamelessly, butt-assed naked. Wasn't even flinching over my own nudity. *This isn't enough.* I wanted the entire caboodle. His heart, trust and devotion.

"And what if I don't?" I tore a dress off the hanger.

I wanted to know what happened in two weeks when he let me go. Would this be over?

How could something like *this* be over?

"You stay." He pistoled his finger at me.

I put on the dress and stomped after him to the doors out to the deck. "Or what?"

He spun around, then backed me up a step. "Don't push me, Angel."

My chest tightened. *Or what?* My heart said he bluffed but my mind screamed you-don't-know-him-enough. There was a gaping void in the middle of us.

A chasm of knowledge of things neither of us would part with.

I wanted his honesty. Yet I hadn't given my own. He didn't know me the way he thought he did. There was that other thing. The bigger deception. Worse than anything I'd been forced to say. The one thing I could never ever tell him.

Not the article. Not the magazine.

I'd have to tell him about *Poise* eventually. This I never could.

A burning shame filled me from core to surface.

I hadn't let my mind dwell or stray to that place since I came here. He saw me so well. What if he saw *that*?

What if he sensed *that*?

Nothing would ever be the same. He'd never look at me the same way.

Never look at me like I was beautiful.

Never call me perfect.

I wanted to be perfect if only to him. If only for him. *We can't keep doing this.*

"I'll wait." I sat myself down in a deck chair and crossed my legs. "But don't bother coming back up here if you don't bring cake."

He smiled, but for once I saw everything underneath it, and today it was all sadness. "I wouldn't dare."

Haithem

I TOOK THE stairs two at a time. Karim, in typical form, knew what was to be done without instruction.

Spirits. Ice. Cigars. Caviar. Subtle instrumental music.

Everything prepared and ready for the arrival.

I yanked up the knot on my tie, flipped down the shirt collar, then folded myself into the center armchair.

"They're boarding." Karim stood behind my chair, a white towel draped over his arm, though a butler he was not.

"How many?" I braced my fingers on the rolled chesterfield arms—opening my chest.

"Seven."

"Fine." It wouldn't matter. They could outnumber security, but they'd find some things and some people aren't so easily overpowered.

They walked in armed, except for one, a white-haired man I knew at once. Rude, when I'd been so polite already.

I didn't stand, instead held out a hand to the couch opposite. "Sergei Ivankov, welcome."

His step faltered, just a small shortening of his stride. Of course he'd be surprised I'd recognize him on sight. The leader of the world's most cunning criminal espionage agency ought to walk around secure in his anonymity. Or he wouldn't be leader for long.

But I didn't keep friends like Avner Malfancini for nothing.

"Mr. Soltan." He took the seat.

His men lined the couch behind him, weapons held across their chests. My gaze didn't shift from Sergei, but I had them locked in my peripheral. Along with Emilio in the corner and my other two men. The third stood at the door.

"Mr. Soltan was my father." I let that statement linger.

Sergei didn't blink. For too long.

Of course he wasn't the one who'd killed my father—

that man was dead. In the end all these people were implicit because their goal was the same.

"Call me Haithem." I gestured to the drinks tray, and Karim stepped forward. "Ice?"

Sergei nodded and accepted the whiskey.

"Caviar?"

"I didn't come for caviar," he said, and swirled the glass, letting ice clink against the sides before downing the whiskey in one swallow, then slamming the cup on the coffee table. "And I much prefer vodka."

I laughed, clipped, but guttural. If he wanted to break etiquette, so be it. This was still more civilized than painting the walls with blood. They wouldn't do that today. Not in the beginning anyway. Not if they could secure my cooperation. The only reason why they'd wanted us to see them coming, and why we'd let them on board. Why this all didn't simply end with a missile in my hull. "Of course."

Karim took the white spirit from the bar freezer and refilled Sergei's glass.

"My clients are willing to come to the party." He sat back with the vodka.

I smiled. "I'm not taking partners."

"They're not seeking partnership as you well know." He sipped from the glass, then glanced at the contents. "This is good shit."

"Of course."

His gaze flicked to me. "They want to buy you out."

"I'm not for sale."

"You haven't heard the offer."

I set elbows on my knees. "There is nothing that can be offered."

His jaw moved left then right. Then he set the glass

down and joined me in leaning forward. "Then things will become more unpleasant."

"I think I've proved I'm up to the challenge."

"This is a nice yacht you have." He looked up. Around the room and at all the furniture. Then opened his jacket and set a handgun on his lap, his fingers resting casually on top. "That's a pretty girl you have hidden up there." He pointed up to the roof with a smirk, then bit his lip.

Adrenaline spurted through my veins.

"I keep good pussy, too." I forced the smile to remain carved into my cheeks. "Would that be more to your taste than caviar, I could summon her?"

I tugged the sleeve of my shirt. Looked like there would be blood today after all.

He snorted. "It's not pussy I came here for, either."

Relief should have knocked my heart back into correct rhythm. It didn't. Considering perhaps he knew she was here because he'd put her here, if not because he'd spied her on deck. Perhaps he was here because she'd led him to me.

No.

Not her.

Not like friends who'd sold me out. Allies who'd been planted in my life. She wouldn't betray me. She wasn't a spy.

Suspicions would eat me alive and destroy us both. "How did you find me?"

"It doesn't matter how, only that we did." That smirk was back. "We will always find you. Just like I will find your cargo no matter how well you think you've concealed it." He caressed the gun like a pet in his lap.

"Then I will fuck your pretty piece of pussy before I put it down."

I hadn't twitched, or moved, or blinked, or stayed too still. *He knew.* Must have been my eyes. I'd warned her my affection was a terrible thing. And here it was— that danger realized.

I scooted forward, feet flat and ready to push off the ground. "Do you think I'd make myself dispensable?"

Sergei's smile spread to one side, and he gripped the handgun, measuring it in his palm with gaze cocked at me.

"You'll find it won't be easy to stop me." My voice dropped low. Only Sergei would hear me. "But if you do, I can promise it won't be by bullet."

The safety clicked.

Energy exploded though my thighs. Muscles snapped along my arms, his head in my hands before his finger could twitch on the trigger. His body bounced off the coffee table, then thumped to the floor. I hadn't known how natural it had become to end a man until Sergei's neck snapped in my hands.

I rose on braced knees to barren silence. My pulse boomed.

Emilio stood behind the sofa, lowering the last corpse to the ground. He caught my gaze. I held it and nodded. There was a reason Emilio had been the Spanish Central Intelligence's best. They'd called him silent death. Now he worked for me. Taught me the precise art of breaking a neck.

I scanned the room. These dead men were killers, mercenaries, assassins. They had no duty, their highest purpose was the bidder. I swiped my mouth on the back of my wrist. They'd have taken the very thing my family died for. What I'd worked and bled for. They'd have killed us. They'd have killed her.

Yet no matter how many times death visited me it never grew less shocking.

Today was worse.

It'd come quietly. Not a drop of blood to wipe away. A woman waited upstairs for me. I'd killed for her and she'd never know it.

SWEAT COATED MY ARMS. My thighs were damp. It wasn't just the pacing back and forth, it was me. He couldn't keep everything from me like this. Couldn't keep me locked away like this forever. I was done waiting. Done expecting he'd grow reasonable. There'd be a way to contact home. They needed to hear things from me. I snatched the library card from the drawer and walked to the door of Haithem's office. He was downstairs with guests. This might be the only chance I'd ever get.

This had to be done.

I shoved the card between the door and the door frame, level with the handle. It took some jostling but then the card slid right behind the latch.

I pushed on the door. It swung—creaking.

His office was just as I remembered. Neat, organized, luxurious and all him. I ran to his desk and started on the drawers. Rummaged through stationery and other useless things. No phone. Nothing useful. I tugged on the large bottom drawer. It stuck. *Locked.* I fell to my knees and tried my library card trick. The card banged against the bolt. This was an entire other kind of mechanism.

I set the card on the desk, eyes coming level with

his closed laptop, so fancy and thin I almost missed it. I sat in the chair and opened the lid slowly.

My fingers shook on the keys.

Have to do this. Have to.

The laptop started up and to no surprise of mine required a password. I started with the obvious, although Haithem wasn't stupid, and in a moment of pure narcissism even tried my own name.

I exceeded attempts. *Wait thirty seconds.* Tried again. *Wait two minutes.* I leaned back in the chair and ran my hands into my hair. My knee knocked against the locked drawer then I stood, ran to the bathroom and came back with hairpins.

I took a pin between my teeth and bent it open, then slipped the open end into the lock and wiggled.

"You know I almost fell for everything." The voice was so sharp it severed my nerves in two.

My blood thickened, becoming oil like in my veins. How the hell could he be so silent?

"I knew better, but you were so believable." He strode into the room. Tie he'd left with gone, shirt collar open.

"I can explain." My stomached churned.

Could I?

His fingers opened and closed. Rage rolled off him. He rotated his shoulders. Something else flowered over him, a drop-dead-lethal current. "Who do you work for?"

There'd be no lying to him now. No diffusing this suspicion with something trivial.

"I'm sorry." I swallowed and stood, leaning on the edge of the desk. "I planned to tell you on the first night." I dropped the pin and splayed my hands. "I was planning an article on you for *Poise* magazine."

"The media hasn't begun to know about me." He inched closer. "If they did, I can guarantee we wouldn't be having this conversation.

I backed up, the desk still between us. "I pitched you as an idea after meeting you in the coffee shop." We moved sideways. "But when you asked for a confidentiality agreement I dropped the idea."

"Yet here you are." He took a step. "Stuck on my yacht. Rifling through the office you broke into."

I stopped still, then stomped the ground. "I need to speak to my family."

"Who do you work for?" In a breath he was around the desk.

I leaped back. "No one."

"I *know*..." The words slipped between his teeth. "I know all about the six weeks you were *gone*."

The muscles in my calves contracted as though I'd been touched by a cattle prod. He did not know.

Impossible.

"Where were you?"

My heart let loose an out-of-beat thunk.

No. I'd never say. *Couldn't*.

We'd been so discreet. How could he find out?

My mind jolted as though he'd grabbed my head in his big fists and given me a shake.

He walked around me. I danced with him again. That dark dance of hands-thrown-out-for-balance revolution. My knees softened, but I turned. His thumb flicked under his chin. A swinging scythe blade, slicing arcs of tension through the air between us.

No.

"Nowhere. I was at home."

His nose scrunched and he walked faster. *Liar.* He saw it. I couldn't conceal it.

My heart choked my throat. How did this peril between us survive when I knew I was already there— already his—already transformed.

Past mistakes were irrelevant, that was *before*.

He moved. A blur. He'd always been so fast.

I squealed. He didn't touch me, but I was knocked sideways by the force of my own shock. I fell against his desk. The desk I'd tried to break into.

"Where the hell were you for six weeks, Angelina?"

Pictures flipped through my head. Flick, flick, flick. He couldn't know.

Oh, the shame.

Bile in my throat. I couldn't say. Fumes in my throat. I remembered them. Now they were back, a dirty seduction to sleep. That Mustang, the one I loved and hated. The top up, hose in the window. I couldn't breathe.

"I had to—" I shook my head as though there were a bug on my hair. "I had to go somewhere."

He seized the top of my arms. "Where? Tell me, where did you have to go? Where did they take you?"

I sagged in his arms. He kept me standing. Didn't give me the mercy of hiding away. Yet his urgent tone burst with longing—longing for my truth.

"I hurt myself."

His grip slacked.

Everything went quiet. I stared at his collarbone. Numbness spread through my chest. Wetness soaked my throat.

Then there was sound again. And all I could hear was the wet, wet sound of my own breath.

"You had to go away because you hurt yourself?"

I'd never heard him speak like that before. As though whispering to someone in the night *are you awake*?

"Mum came home early and heard the motor in the garage."

I couldn't meet his gaze. Would he look at me the way they did? My shoulders drew up as though I could push them over my head. Would he talk to me like I was damaged? Treat me like I couldn't be trusted with myself?

Like they do.

"But, Angelina." He squeezed my arms, and then I had to look at him. Had to face a kind of suffering I'd felt but never seen. "I looked everywhere and there's no record of you being in any hospital."

My own parents so ashamed. How could he not be?

"They didn't want people knowing." I rubbed my arm right below where he gripped me. "Not after Josh. They let it be private and admitted me in my cousin Cara's name."

Everyone knew about the town mayor's poor dead son—but not about the broken daughter.

Better for all of us it stayed that way.

"Because of Josh? Is that why you hurt yourself?"

"No." I swallowed. I'd been well for so long. Time didn't seem to matter. "Josh was the rock I hit at the bottom. I was generally and overwhelmingly unhappy in a way where it seemed like nothing could ever be good again."

His hands changed on me, suddenly holding not gripping.

"And now?" His voice crackled.

I breathed. I *could* cope. Could cope with this and everything. "Now I know it can be better—it does get better. I'll never, ever be that way again. I can survive anything." I tried for a smile. "I'm basically indestructible."

I watched every word be absorbed by him through his eyes.

"I would have that be true."

He pressed his lips to my mouth. A hovering kiss that took nothing and tasted of salt.

So would I.

TWENTY-TWO

"I SAID DON'T MOVE."

Haithem had me by the little toe, but I had him by something more significant. He paused, nail-polish brush poised above my foot. "I only do this for special birthday girls, you know."

My birthday.

The words rang through me with equal measures of grief and excitement. A strange feeling, that. I was just glad it was happening here. Happening my way. Happy to be twenty-one and a woman enjoying her lover.

I couldn't bring myself to think about what would be happening right now at home. It probably made me a terrible person, that I didn't want to spend my twenty-first birthday pandering to everyone *else's* feelings about what the day meant to *them*.

"Promise." I made a cross over my heart. "No more moving."

He'd turned me into a little liar. Something I'd never pulled off before.

He lowered the brush.

I wiggled my toes. Pink polish streaked across my skin. I laughed, and he grabbed me, dragged me into his lap. I straddled him. My hair fell into his face. He didn't brush it away.

"You are very lucky it's your birthday, or you'd be in big trouble."

I laughed again, wrapped my arms around his neck and dragged my pelvis over his. Through his pants I could feel that big wonderful organ I couldn't get enough of.

Mr. In-control.

Mr. Powerful.

He was soft with me. And I knew why.

He grabbed my hips and pushed his hardening cock firmly against me.

Call me a squirrel, because I'd cracked myself a hard nut and made me some butter. He didn't realize it yet. Yep, Haithem was butter in my hands. I'd let him think he was still in charge, because the man had his ego and his stubbornness—but he was soft for me.

Haithem groaned and patted my thigh. "There's something I have to do."

I rolled off him and lay back on the deck of this new smaller yacht.

"I'll be back soon."

I frowned—pouted, actually. Never, ever thought of myself as a pouter, but there you go, the strange things getting some good cock will do to you.

He kissed me. Quickly. Then he gave me another, slightly more lingering one.

We'd left the old yacht and all the staff but Karim and Emilio by helicopter in the night, a week ago. Taken a speedboat from one island to another before slipping onto the new yacht in the dark.

Unspoken tension throbbed between the men, yet the kind between Haithem and I had altered.

I'd be leaving soon.

Like the yacht before it, the main cabin of this yacht

occupied an upper deck. But this boat was lithe. Ripples jetting out around us as we cut through the water.

Clouds folded over the sun. The water turned gray. I sighed.

Footsteps pounded up the stairs, then Haithem was back beside me. "Okay."

"Okay, what?" I bolted upright.

He grinned, truly grinned, made me tingle.

"Come on."

I rolled off the sun bed.

His excitement infected me, sent urgency racing under my skin. He spun me around, and red fabric fell across my vision. He knotted the blindfold behind my head.

I touched my face and the soft covering. "Kinky."

"Later it will be." His voice growled against my ear. I'd hold him to that.

He led me across the deck. My feet flew off the ground as he hoisted me against his chest, one arm around my waist and another under my knees.

I wrapped my arm around his neck and held on. We descended the stairs. He didn't set me down at the bottom but instead managed to open doors without dropping me. Eventually he lowered me onto something soft and supple.

"You ready?"

I exhaled. "Always."

He undid the blindfold, and I blinked, staring at a blank wall.

I glanced around.

We were in the big downstairs sitting room. I sat on one of the sofas, but all the furniture had been cleared from in front of us.

"Happy birthday, Angelina."

I scrunched up my nose, not sure what I was supposed to be seeing. He sat next to me and handed me a plastic case.

"You got me a present?" I opened the lid and pulled out a small pair of gold-and-black binoculars with a handle on the side.

Theater binoculars.

My heart lifted. He'd remembered what I wanted. How'd he even manage that with the moving? I flicked the binoculars from side to side. When I went home, I'd use these. Wouldn't wait for someone to take me. Wouldn't wait for a reason to justify the expense; I'd just go to the damn theater.

"Thank you. These are lovely." I leaned forward and kissed his rough cheek. He'd shaved, but his skin always had a little bite to it.

He pulled something from his pocket and pressed a button.

Sound boomed around us, vibrated up my bare feet.

The wall in front of us lit up with images. I glanced up. A projector had been screwed into the roof. Along with speakers in the corners.

"What...?" The image on the wall projected a stage. As clearly as if we were sitting front row at Melbourne's Regent Theatre. On-screen curtains parted, and I slipped back against the sofa, glancing from the screen to Haithem and back again.

No way.

He couldn't have. This wasn't the movie version. This was the real thing—the theater production.

Les Misérables.

I'd never seen it. Never let myself watch the movies,

because I wanted to save seeing it for the stage version. But I knew without a doubt what we were watching.

Karim entered and shut all the blinds, then wheeled a trolley next to us. The scent of fresh popcorn filled my nose. He pulled the cork off a bottle and filled two glasses, then left the room, shutting the door behind him.

I couldn't draw a full breath. Haithem wound an arm around me, and I leaned into his side to watch something I'd always wanted to see. Experienced something I'd always longed to experience. Haithem's yacht might not be the same as sitting in the live theater, but somehow this was so much more special.

I glanced up at him.

My chest hurt, a pain gnawing in my breastbone.

I'd never been so afraid that I'd wake up, and this would all be a fantasy. That I'd crash back to reality, where no one could know me so well, care for me so much, give to me so freely. The show finished, and I wiped my face. I wasn't sure if the tears were from watching the saddest freaking thing ever conceived— or not.

"Was it what you thought it would be?" He brushed my cheek with his thumb.

I sniffed.

He never seemed able to let a tear sit on my face.

I rested my palm on his chest. "More." My breath shuddered. "Thank you—" I couldn't get more words out, just climbed into his lap and pressed my face into his neck.

He wrapped his arms around me, rocked us a little from side to side.

Everything rushed through me. Feelings that began

in that shower, when I'd fallen in love with him without knowing, became tangible. Now I loved him out loud—even if only to myself. Loved him with the places I couldn't control and the places I could. I loved him with fear and without it.

I loved him completely.

He stroked my hair.

I leaned back, my lips hovering over his for the space of a sigh before I kissed him.

He opened his mouth to me. I tasted him, tasted my tears, tasted us together. Wanted to cry more. Instead, I paused to unbutton his shirt.

He said nothing, just shrugged out of his shirt without taking his gaze from me. I undid his belt, watching his chest move up and down, faster and faster.

He knew.

He knew everything, because these feelings, they cascaded from my heart and through my body, and then out my skin. I slid down his zipper and pulled out his cock. It was iron in my palm. I squeezed, lifting my hips. I needed him. Needed him moving in me with the same urgency as my emotions. He made a sound and grabbed my waist, flipping my back against the sofa.

My dress pooled at my hips. He crawled over me, kissed me hungrily. My lips smashed against my teeth. I jerked his pants over his backside and pulled my panties to the side. He entered me swiftly, cock brushing against my knuckles as the head pushed inside me. Even with an edge of pain, pleasure stole my breath.

We moved fast and hard and as violently as our grazing lips and clashing teeth. He filled me, filled my pussy and my heart. My feet slid against the leather sofa. I dug my fingers into his backside, orgasm breaking over me in a wave of crushing ecstasy.

His mouth never left mine, but his thrusts went from urgent to wild. My head knocked against the arm of the sofa, bending my neck. My muscles tightened around him, my thighs twitched. He stiffened and pulled out, shoved my dress over my chest, and spilled onto my belly. My abdomen contracted.

The sight burned into the back of my eyes—Haithem suspended above me, cock in hand, coming all over me.

Warmth trickled over my skin.

I gasped, one loud breath after another.

He rolled off the sofa onto the ground and dragged me on top of him. I went limp as a flower that had just gotten more than her share of sun.

Whatever he may not say, whatever he may not have asked me, whatever we may not have discussed, one certainty rose inside me—Haithem was mine, too.

TWENTY-THREE

Haithem's laugh rang through the cabin.

As always, it filled me with glee, even if the cause had me nervous.

I licked an edge of paper, then folded it, trying not to look at what he did. He turned the page on the notepad. It would probably be rude to jump up, rip it off him and set it on fire.

Yeah, there were social rules about setting things people were reading on fire.

He read my play.

Read it not two feet away from me.

No one but Josh had ever wanted to read anything I'd written before. His reading my work made me itchy, as if I could scratch the entire surface of my skin off.

Also other things.

Hot and shaky, and as though my muscles couldn't settle into a stationary position. He'd been reading for over an hour. If he'd wanted to demonstrate an effort, I'd have been impressed at the fifteen-minute mark. I folded in the corners and sides of the paper, then leaned closer to him, tried to see where he was up to. He glanced at me and held his arm out. I rested my head on his shoulder and pulled out the corners of the paper. His arm ran around my hip. I pulled more corners out of the back. He held the notepad with both hands on his lap.

I read a few lines.

The part at the very end, where my protagonist, an aspiring news anchor, makes a stellar Freudian slip, then goes wackily off script in an attempt to cover it up—and actually pulls it off.

Haithem's chest rumbled against my ear. The notepad jiggled.

He leaned down and kissed the top of my head. "You're very cheeky, you know that?"

I set the paper water lily on his chest.

He closed the notepad and put it down on the side table. "How long have you been writing?"

"Since I was about seven or eight. Around the time Josh got diagnosed."

"Why not do something with them?" His fingers ran from my elbow to my shoulder and back again.

I shook my head. Pipe dreams, that's what my parents called them. "It's pretty competitive. Nothing would come of it."

"I'd pay to see them."

I looked up at him. "That's because you enjoy fucking me."

He smiled one of his panty-exploding smiles. "That I do." He leaned in, his lips brushing mine. "I'd still want to see them."

"You don't think it's a silly hobby?" I leaned on his chest and picked up the flower. "Like this?"

He took the flower and studied it. "Why would you call it that?"

Then he looked at me, and for once I could read *his* mind.

"They're not all bad, you know. They just had a lot

to deal with. They didn't have the energy for anything they thought of as nonsense."

He put the flower on top of the notepad then touched the tip of my nose with his index finger. "They can't be *all* bad—they made you."

I laughed. "Oh god. You didn't just say something so cheesy. Who are you?" I laughed again and slid my thigh over his legs.

His smile shifted. "I'm not sure I know anymore."

The room grew warmer.

I MEASURED HAITHEM'S breaths with the palm of my hand. His secrets bubbled away under his skin. I could almost touch them. Now we were so close he couldn't hide the things he used to. I knew they were all there— his many dark secrets. I'd seen the looks flash across his face when he'd stare out at the sea, as though at any moment some great threat would appear on the horizon, cannons blazing. Whatever he'd done, however hard he'd tried to keep me away, no matter how underhanded it may have seemed, now I understood.

He protects me.

I ran my fingers over his stomach.

His secrets, whatever they were, were far more dangerous than he'd ever been. I didn't need to know them.

He took my hand from his shirt and kissed my fingers.

Pressure built in my lungs, thoughts and words catching in my airways.

I'd thought loss had shown me my capacity to feel. I'd had no idea—my heart was so much bigger, so infinitely more receptive, than I'd ever imagined.

Haithem showed me that.

I was better, deeper, stronger than I could have known.

Those words again.

I love you.

Words tattooed in my breath, so I'd wake from sleep and worry that I'd said them out loud.

Words he'd warned me not to say.

Words he'd warned me not to feel.

He turned onto his side, facing me, and kneaded my hip gently with his fingers. His hands had a way of gravitating to me. There couldn't be less than three feet of space between us without him laying them on me.

"I love you."

The words left my lips. Slowly and carefully. Filled the cabin with their truth.

I didn't whisper, and I wouldn't repent. Even if he cast my feelings away. Even if he threw them back at me. Denied me words of his own.

I wouldn't be sorry to have been open and to have loved. Even if it hurt, I couldn't be sorry for that.

His features shifted.

He gripped my face, thumbs lining my jaw. I braced myself as best I could. Held my breath and waited for the assault of words I never wanted to hear.

He didn't love me.

Because he'd warned me about this—not to fall for him.

"I love you, too."

He released my face, his features drawing into tight, angry lines.

The declaration hit like the drop of a guillotine—sharp, brutal and final.

My pulse stuttered.

Had I misheard? Had desperation caused me to imagine words? Because he didn't look like someone who'd just professed his love—he looked like someone who'd just been spat on.

He rolled off the bed and put on his clothes.

"Haithem?"

He turned his back on me, then walked to the cabin door.

I sat up.

The door shut behind him, and thumped closed.

Haithem

MUSCLES BUNCHED IN my shoulders. Karim knocked the mitts together then spread his arms. I sprang forward, fists driving into one mitt then the other.

He braced, his rear foot sliding. Impact shuddered down my elbows. It wasn't enough.

Karim shoved back at me with the mitts. "Enough."

I brought my fists to my chin, pulse slamming through my system like a stream of cannons. "Too much for you?"

Moisture gathered on my eyebrow then dripped into my right eye.

"You should have left her behind. It's no longer safe to travel with her."

My biceps seized. *No.* I tore off the gloves.

"She is not safe for us." Karim dropped the mitts. "Something must be done."

Pain shot into my chest. *Something.* Anything. Nothing. She loved me, and damn her, she'd made me love her, too. There were no easy answers and no simple solutions for us. We might both be ruined.

I jerked forward and threw the gloves across the deck. "I'll decide what has to be done."

Karim, my old friend, didn't flinch. "What does she know?"

"She." I glanced up at the upper deck. "Angelina doesn't know anything."

"Keep it that way. For the love of god, for everything we've done, for the peace of your parents—keep it that way." He shook his head, then bent and picked up the equipment.

I swiped at my dripping face. *No.* He was right. I'd never tell her. I glanced up again. Imagined her in my room, in my bed. What was one lie in the face of the rest I'd told?

Angelina had no idea what I'd done to her life.

"How long until she's supposed to be home?" He knew but he asked.

Days.

I pinched my nose. The stink of my own anxiety clung to me thicker than the sweat.

"Right now you're infatuated with a girl you think likes you." Karim tucked the gloves and mitts under one arm and set a hand on my shoulder. "But before this week is done, you'll be dealing with something else entirely."

Karim went upstairs.

I drove my bare knuckles into the side of the yacht. The panel gave a warbling boom. Cracks split the fiberglass. The sting burst through the bones of my hand. I opened my fingers and stared at the broken flesh there.

Once again in my life, I was about to lose everything.

I DREW CIRCLES on a brand-new notepad. That was about the extent of my creativity. My mind seemed much more interested in watching the clock.

Tick, tick, tick—six days left.

Yet another ending I couldn't avoid.

Maybe that's why I was so reckless. Maybe that's way I tried to bury my roots in so deep with Haithem that it'd take more than an ocean to wash me away.

I threw down the pen, itching to wander belowdecks. But I didn't. Clearly, he needed to process.

Typical bloke.

I could only hope he figured it out.

We'd already lost half a day, and I couldn't stand to lose another hour.

The thud of a door burst open. I uncrossed my legs and stood. Haithem stepped in, looking even bigger, even more male in only his black shorts and bare feet.

He walked directly to me, his chin down, gaze fixed on mine.

"Say it again."

I backed up a step, grabbing onto the armchair behind me. "Say what?"

He reached me, grabbed the back of my head, and tugged me into him. My breasts crushed against the wall of his chest. His scent surrounded me. Sharper and more pungent than usual. As if he'd hit high on the pheromones just to ruin my willpower.

"Say it again."

I blinked, and my lungs burned with joy and pain. "I love you."

"Again," he growled.

"I love you."

He dropped his head, gaze tearing across my eyes. "Again."

"I love you."

His features scrunched before his jaw clamped. He

spun me around. Cut off my view of his face. "Are you sure?"

"Yes."

His breath rushed against my hair. "How do you know it's love?" He jerked my hips back against his and slid his hand between my legs. "How do you know it's not just this?"

Moisture streamed into my pussy. My senses homed in on his touch.

He pushed my panties down and ran his palm over me. "You love what I do to this, don't you?"

"Yes, but I *love* you." Puffs of air flew between my lips, drying my tongue.

He sank two fingers into me. "How do you know?"

I moaned, muscles clamping around his fingers. He rocked them inside me, played me like his very own violin.

I grabbed his wrist, willed my tongue to speak through the sensations. "I just feel it."

He withdrew from me and pushed my dress down my body. "I love you, Angelina."

I fell forward and gripped the armchair in front of me. His words struck a need deep in my soul.

"I love you." He said the words again, and my core tightened.

There was no doubt in my mind this man could talk me into orgasm.

A zipper creaked behind me. The zipper of his pants. I leaned my arms on the armchair and dropped my head, pushing my ass out.

"Tell you how I know?" His cock grazed my ass.

I thrust backward.

He seized my hips, held me still, and ran a hand up

and down, from my lips to my ass and back again. "I know because everything I have is now yours."

He hunched over me. Ran his palm up my arching spine. His cock nudged my clit.

I moaned.

"My body, my heart—" He scraped his teeth over the back of my shoulder, then he held my throat. His fingers circled my neck, almost meeting at my nape. "My life."

I reached my hands behind me, trying to touch him even as I dissolved.

"I'd pay any price to protect you—any."

He loves me.

I drowned in oxygen, my lungs taking in too much. More than I could process or filter.

He loves me.

His hips rotated, bringing his cock to my entrance. "Can you say the same?"

"Yes," I shouted, rising up on my toes to take him.

He slid up, head nudging my back passage. "Swear it."

"I swear." The backs of my thighs quivered.

He plunged down, driving himself into my vagina. I stretched, taking the pleasure and the burn. He pulled me up off the armchair, so I stood balanced on my toes, pinioned on his cock. If I could've breathed, I would've cried. Because he'd promised me everything.

Now I wanted everything.

"Will you always remember that?" he whispered against my ear.

I drew air again. "Yes."

He moved in me. Wrapped his arms around my middle and bucked. Pleasure radiated from my core, but the sensations flowing from my chest were the ones that made my head spin. His hand moved to my pussy, and he rubbed with flat fingers on my clit. Fast movements. Deep friction. My limbs stiffened, and my chin curled to my chest. I came on his cock, muscles pulsing. He slowed, rocking himself into my orgasm.

I fell forward, suspended in his arms. He stepped toward the bed, laid me down and rolled me onto my back, then moved over me.

He scooped me up, my head resting in the crook of his arm, his other arm under my back. I lifted my knees, and he sank into me, watched my widening eyes.

He settled to the hilt and squeezed me tight. "I love you."

I stared up at him, seeing that love in the softness of his eyes more than I heard it in the roughness of his voice.

"I love you," I said.

He pulled out and pushed back in, knocked against my womb, then pulsed there as if he could squeeze into my soul.

"I love you," he said again.

My arms tightened around his neck. My chest heaved. Sweat rolled across my temple. He gave it to me. Gave me everything and more. Pushed and pushed until I thought I'd break. Until I came so hard I cried. He shouted, crushed me in his arms and ground his cock deep, coming inside me and flooding me with his heat.

I wrapped my legs around him and held him there. Absorbed his shudders and groans. I was born for this. To lie here with him in my arms. Maybe it was a gift from fate, giving me back a little of what it'd stolen. Without him, I'd never be complete.

We rolled to the side, but he didn't leave me. Didn't pull out or withdraw.

"I'll come for you," he said against my cheek.

I breathed in, tasting us. The scent of our sex. Maybe even the glow of our love tingled on my tongue. "What?"

"In five months." He moved his face, dragging the blunt tip of his nose over my cheekbone to rest against the button of my nose. "I'll come for you in five months."

I clamped my teeth together. Shut down the tears that threatened to choke words.

He's going to come back for me.

He wasn't going to leave me. Wasn't going to send me away.

He was mine—my man—my lover—my soul mate.

I nodded but couldn't hold the tears back.

"Can you do that—wait, have faith for five months?"

I laid my palm on his jaw. "I'd wait five years."

He kissed me, and I tasted my tears on his tongue.

TWENTY-FOUR

It must be a sin, surely, for anything to taste so good.

Haithem pushed the spoon between my lips. A spoon dripping with molten chocolate and cream. I chewed, gooey cake sticking to the top of my mouth.

Cream—lord, how I'd missed cream.

There was just never a good enough reason to eat cream. Bad enough that I ate the pastries, pies and cakes. I didn't need the cream, as well. So I'd scrape off the delicious dairy.

You can't have your cake and eat it, too.

He took another scoop from the bowl. Chocolate dribbled from the spoon and spattered on my neck. My mouth closed over the spoon. Haithem ducked and sucked the sauce off my skin.

I laughed and gripped his hair as his hot, wet tongue stroked me.

Almost as good as chocolate lava cake in bed.

If I didn't know better, I'd think he loved my ass so much he'd decided to try to expand it. Not that such tactics were working. God love him, no matter how much sugar he lay on my tongue, he sweated it off me in bed.

But even with the most decadent things available, sometimes I still craved something clean and simple.

He held out another scoop.

I shook my head. The cake sat heavy in my belly.

"My teeth are going to fall out if we keep this up. To-morrow I want fruit for breakfast."

He ate the scoop of lava cake, then dipped the spoon back into the bowl. "Fruit?"

"Yeah, those things that grow on trees and bushes," I said, watching him finish the cake. "Berries and mangos go good with yogurt."

"Yogurt." He glanced at me with a look as though he'd sniffed something bad. His gaze trailed down to where my robe opened on my thigh, and he smiled. "I'll concede berries and whipped cream."

"Deal." I laughed, then reached for the coffee on the bedside table. The rich foam stuck to my top lip.

I licked it off.

This cappuccino wasn't skim.

I still drank the coffee. I'd spent too much of my life worrying about getting fat, knowing I was a little predisposed to roundness. Yet with Haithem—who, when I'd first met him, had seemed all things shallow and vain—I'd found something that extended beyond the physical.

As much as I adored his face, there was so much more to enthrall me now. I set down the cappuccino. I didn't need him to be beautiful. I didn't need yachts, helicopter home delivery or dessert disguised as break-fasts.

I'd take him and me alone in a room, any room, any hovel, if it meant us being together.

Haithem sucked chocolate off the side of his thumb. My gaze followed his lips.

The blast of a horn sounded outside the cabin. I slid my legs off the bed, went to the window and drew back the curtain.

My hand paused midway.

Buildings and skyscrapers filled the horizon. The sea swarmed with boats, ships and yachts like bees returning to the hive.

I dropped the curtain and turned to Haithem.

He lay on his back. The sheet pooled around his waist.

"I thought we still had five days?"

"We do." He put an arm behind his head. "We're stopping for supplies."

The knots twisting up my insides loosened. I walked to the bed and sat next to him. "Are we getting off for a while?"

"No." He said it fast, then took my hand. "In fact, until we're done, it's best we both remain indoors."

I frowned. "Seriously?"

"Seriously." He had his old Haithem face on. The one that reminded me there were parts of him I didn't understand but still trusted.

I exhaled. "Where are we, anyway?"

"Malaysia." He let go of my hand.

I stared at him. Perhaps I'd misheard? *Malaysia?* He reclined so casually, biceps bulging next to his head. *Nothing strange going on here.* Except now I knew him. Knew the way his mouth flatlined when he held things in. I drifted off the bed and returned to the window, this time sweeping the curtain wide.

The landscape hit me like a strange spice.

The sheer scale of the buildings in the distance. How foreign. The subtle differences in the lines and curves of the cityscape, like an architectural accent.

"How do we get home from Malaysia?" My heart

padded in my chest like two sets of little feet. "I don't even have a passport."

Haithem sat up and patted the mattress next to him. The sheet dipped, revealing dark pubic hair. Tension flowed into my pelvis. As always, I couldn't resist his summons. Questions screaming in my head lost their volume.

I went to the bed and sat next to him.

He took my face in both hands. "Angelina, I said I'd get you home. I'll get you home."

His hands radiated heat into my skull and closed my peripheral vision.

"How?"

"Private plane. Then a domestic flight." His thumbs brushed my cheeks. "It'll be fine. It's done, organized."

He kissed me.

I leaned into the touch of his lips. He pushed his tongue into my mouth, covered my ears, and his face filled my vision until nothing remained outside of this.

He let me go, and I rested beside him.

"I've never been outside of Melbourne before…"

Now I lay in a yacht in the Malaysian sea, not even knowing where we'd headed—ready to sneak back into my own homeland.

There had to be a crime in there somewhere.

I'd gone from breaking curfew to breaking federal law.

"One day, Angel, you're going to see the world the way you deserve to." He pushed hair behind my ear. "And I'm going to be the one to show you."

I tipped back my head and looked at him. Searched his serious gaze.

Cake filled my stomach like stones, the cream now surely curdled.

He'd show me when he came for me. After leaving for five months to do whatever he was doing. The thought somehow disturbed me so much more than the idea of breaking the law.

I missed him already.

Felt that gnawing emptiness of impending loss all the way down to my toenails. I balled my hand against his chest. Wished I had invisible claws to sink into him, to keep us together.

Five months without him—how would I survive that?

Haithem

ANGELINA SLEPT AGAINST my side. Her breath caught on a snort. A smile made its way up one side of my face.

Perhaps I should tell her she snores?

Then I could watch the fire light behind her eyes, woo her all over again. So fun to tease her—maybe because she bit back.

She rubbed her cheek against my chest. I ran my hands down her back, then over the full, round peach of her ass. Her skin was soft as a fruit.

I could eat her.

Perhaps, in the end, I would.

A knock tapped outside. I extracted myself from the bed, shoving feet into pants from the floor and scooping up a shirt. I opened the door then slipped outside. Emilio's face greeted me, mouth a pinch. He didn't need to speak. I followed him downstairs, halting halfway, looking out at the bobbing sea.

We've stopped.

I did the final button on my shirt and took the remaining stairs in a few strides. Karim waited in the bridge, papers spread across a table.

He glanced up. "I warned you she'd be no good for us."

My limbs went stiff. I approached the table. The sight sent a heart-slam of vision-blurring blood to my head. Everything went bright. I stared at the pictures.

It couldn't be.

"You swore when you made this decision against my advice that you'd do what had to be done."

No.

When shit hit the fan in my life, it tended to go atomically explosive. I'd always been able to pick myself up, even from the worst.

There'd be no way back from this.

A burn gnawed in my guts. "I can't."

Our gazes locked like horns. The deference that had always been there from him to me wavered.

"How many people had to die for our purpose?" Karim drove his palms onto the table. "Would you risk it all for a girl?"

Adrenaline burst into my hands. With a shout, I grabbed the edge of the table and flung. Karim leaped back. The table flipped, hitting the ground with a floor-rattling bang. Pictures scattered the floor.

I stepped through the debris. "I can't."

"You won't," he spat, then left the bridge.

Emilio stepped aside to let him pass.

My fingers pumped. My mind fought with my body. Fought the urge to tear the yacht apart.

"Sir," Emilio said. "Which way do we go?"

Broken promises.

Lies.

I'd pay for them all and more. Because with one piece of news, my well-laid plans amounted to nothing. Good intentions dissolved into sea foam.

"I don't know."

Falling in love came with a dreadful price.

I RUBBED SUNSCREEN up my leg, swiped it across my thigh and glanced over my shoulder. Haithem sat on a large cushioned deck chair, staring out into the water as though he were reading code from the waves. I swapped legs, pumped cream into my palm, put my other foot up on the railing and leaned down to my foot.

The narrow briefs of my bikini shifted on my bent backside, narrowing dangerously toward a wedgie.

I looked back.

Haithem tapped his fingers on the wicker arm of the deck chair, gaze still drifting outside the yacht. I dropped my foot. He'd been quiet since yesterday. *Distracted.* Even from me. And if my wedgie bikini ass didn't get a reaction, then frankly, that scared me.

I wiped my hands on the towel I'd hung over the railing and went over to him. He glanced up, rested his chin between his thumb and forefinger. I stood in front of him, then reached behind me, undid the clasp on my bikini and slid it off my shoulders. I tossed it on the ground beside him.

His smile crept up one cheek. I rested a knee in the gap between his waist and the chair, then pulled myself up and squeezed my other knee into the other side. I ran my palm around the back of his neck and pulled his face to my chest.

He pressed his face between my breasts. Took long,

deep breaths from my skin. He cupped my breasts, one in each hand, and nuzzled. I stroked his hair and pushed my chest out, let him have them.

If you could bottle this, it'd outperform any prescription pharmaceutical, I'm sure. He pinched my nipple, rolled his tongue over the other. My head fell back. He sucked me, licked me, teased me, enjoyed me.

My need for oxygen increased, but each breath pushed my breasts deeper into his mouth. I'd done this for him, yet now the place between *my* thighs ached. Now I was the one who needed help.

I didn't seek it, though, just gripped his hair and let him feast on my chest. Kept my hips still when they wanted to rock. Squeezed the muscles of my empty, aching pussy. He reached his hand between my legs, pushed aside my briefs and sank his first two fingers inside me and his thumb against my clit.

My back arched.

I looked down. Got an eyeful of Haithem suckling from my tit while gazing up at me. My abdomen contracted, muscles winding tighter and tenser.

I'd tamed a lion.

Trusted it enough to let it eat from my hand.

He pumped me. I clamped my teeth on my lower lip to keep sounds in. He pulled his fingers out and gripped the crotch of my bikini bottoms with both hands. Tore them at the seams. He really did enjoy breaking things—especially my underwear.

I reached down and opened his pants. His cock sprang out. I grasped his thick length, rubbed him against me. He slipped in my juices so perfectly.

I sank onto him.

One inch—another.

My walls strained.

I gripped his shoulder, then stopped. Breathed hard, unable to move.

"I'm stuck."

Haithem laughed. His body vibrated, and his cock jerked in me, slid in another fraction.

I gasped, my spine stiffening.

"You are not stuck."

I held his other shoulder and shook my head. "I am a human shish kebab."

"You've just never been in control before," he said, and leaned back against the chair, sliding his hips forward. He held my waist. "You're not stuck. You can take more than you think."

He rocked gently, changed the pressure inside me until I adjusted—until I felt myself give—and I slid down completely.

I breathed deep, my stomach filling as well as my chest. Tried to breathe around the invasion, then moved.

Just a little. A sway forward then back.

Then more.

Circular rotations.

Continuous sensation.

Pelvis forward, he pressed against that spot, rolling up—sweet, maddening friction, hips back and down, then breathtaking fullness. And again. And again.

Momentum.

My skin warmed around me. Forward, up, back, down. Pressure, friction, fullness.

His open zipper scraped my ass, grazed my skin, and still I ground against him hard as I could. Took him all in. Tried to keep myself together when a frenzy bubbled through my system.

His head fell back, his chest rose and his abs tightened.

I watched him and moved. Pressed my hands against his stomach and rode him.

He groaned, breathing faster.

I'd never doubted how much he enjoyed fucking me, but I'd never seen him take pleasure like this. Never seen him give in—surrender himself to me.

An orgasm built, but I held it back, pushed it down. I wouldn't let anything distract me from this moment.

The thighs under mine stiffened, and I slammed myself onto his cock. He lunged forward, wrapped his arms around me, buried his face in my neck and a fist in my hair. I held him, rocked my hips, pleasure rippling through my core.

He made gruff noises against my throat.

Vibrations shivered into my blood.

His grip on me relaxed, but he still held me, still rested his face in my neck.

I laughed, softly then louder, joy cascading over me.

He groaned and grasped my hips. "Are you trying to kill me?"

I laughed again. Knew my muscles contracted around him when I did. He looked at me with the face of a man who had just awoken from a deep sleep. I kissed him.

A whirling sound whistled above us.

I broke the kiss and glanced up. A small airplane soared through the clouds.

Haithem exploded into movement.

Standing with me still in his arms, he ran to the cabin. He set me down and turned to the doors, his pants still open, and peered outside.

He panted, stared up at the sky then moved to the intercom, doing up his zipper.

I scrambled for my robe and pulled it on, belting it at the waist.

"Close the curtains," he said, glancing at me before switching languages as he spoke into the intercom.

I ran to the windows and drew the curtains, then sat on the edge of the bed.

Haithem put the intercom receiver down and crossed the bedroom toward his office.

"What's going on?" My pulse rushed, but not from the sexathon.

He paused and came to me, leaned over and held my face. "I'm not sure yet. Just sit tight. Don't go outside."

He didn't give me a chance to answer, just kissed my forehead and left.

I threw my hands up, then flopped on the bed. I stared at the roof and my head swirled with possibilities of all the things he'd never tell me.

TWENTY-FIVE

Haithem

I STORMED THE BRIDGE.

Emilio stood at the helm. I set the instructions beside him. "There's been a change of plans."

He glanced at the instructions and nodded.

I folded my arms and stared out at the view. Watched the sea part for us as we cut a new course.

Footsteps raced to the bridge. "What is this?"

My jaw set. I offered no response. None was owed. This was my war, my mission and my heart.

Karim approached the helm and skimmed the instructions. "What have you done?"

"What I had to." My chin curled. This was the only way. "I'll do what it takes to protect her."

He strode up behind me.

"Your destiny is greater than this, my friend." A firm hand took my shoulder. "There's no hiding from it."

I took in a breath that filled me to the bottom of my aching heart. No, there was no hiding. There was no escape. Not for me.

Angelina's destiny had now been sealed as firmly as mine.

But there was one last choice.

A choice only she could make.

A terrible choice.

"I'd never try." Even if it broke my heart. There was no hiding. I'd protect her.

Even if it killed me.

TWENTY-SIX

HAITHEM SPOKE TO EMILIO. I watched them from a distance. We had three days remaining together, but I may as well have lost him already.

He'd slipped away from me.

Days ago we'd been so close that my lungs filled when he breathed in, and he tasted whatever passed between my lips, but now the space between us seemed indomitable.

Ever since the airplane, it was as though we'd already said our goodbyes.

Haithem's gaze flickered from Emilio to where I stood, but he continued speaking, didn't acknowledge me standing there.

My ribs ached.

Maybe this was for the best. Maybe he was trying to ease out of us gently.

Because in three days, I'd be going home.

As much as I dreaded leaving, I also craved it, needed to extract myself from this closed-in world and go home, put myself and my family right.

Then I could look forward to the day when we'd be together in the *real* world.

Start a real life.

On land.

With friends and family.

Because I missed them.

I missed my mum and dad. Missed my home. Missed Emma. I owed them all a proper explanation, one that was actually from me.

For the first time, I had the nerve to do it, too. Put everything in my own words, be honest. I didn't blame them for not being perfect.

Not anymore.

Haithem and Emilio finished speaking, and Haithem moved out of sight. I waited for him to come upstairs.

He didn't.

My body didn't want to move. Everything felt weighed down, heavy, painful. Kinda like I'd been run over—run over and now had a gut full of hurt and road rage.

I'd be leaving tomorrow.

I dug in the wardrobe for the boxes and bags I'd stored in there. Pulled out all the boxes, unfolded all the good-quality cardboard and linen bags and sorted the plastic ones. Shoes first, back in original boxes. I stacked them in the corner of the room, then moved on to dresses.

I tried my best not to crease them.

Because yes, I'd be wearing them again.

Yes, I'd be taking them with me.

Even if Haithem was too chicken to spend this precious time with me, I wasn't leaving anything behind.

This was all mine, from him, just as he was mine.

Even if he acted like an ass.

I packed underwear, maybe even sneaked one of his worn shirts in with my bras. Packed the special bag with the toy inside, too.

I'd be needing it.

Celibacy no longer suited me.

I stacked the bags with the shoes. The cabin door opened behind me. I kept moving, although my spine seemed to stick for a moment.

"What are you doing?" His voice filled the room.

If I'd ever doubted his feelings, they all rang out in that one question.

I cleared my throat. "Packing, since I'm leaving tomorrow."

"Stop."

I turned, dropping a bag. "Why? Aren't I allowed to take anything with me now you're done?"

He came toward me, picked up a bag and dumped the contents onto the bed.

My stomach twisted.

He opened a drawer and shoved things randomly inside.

"Don't you want me to leave?" I said, following him to the drawer and scooping out what he'd put in. "Could have fooled me, the way you've been avoiding me."

Maybe I was cruel, but I needed him to say it—that he'd miss me.

That he didn't want me to go.

That this killed *him* inside, too.

"No, I don't want you to leave," he said, then he turned to me. Hit me with a gaze both breathtaking and immobilizing. Half old Haithem, half my Haithem. "There is so much you don't understand."

I found my voice and threw the clothes on the floor. "Then explain it to me, or must everything be a complete goddamn secret?"

His jaw set. Now he was completely old Haithem. "You won't like my secrets, not most of them."

There was no way to miss the warning, not with the

hairs prickling up the back of my neck or the way his words slithered through the room.

"I never thought I would." I stepped toward him. Went against the current pushing me away. "I always knew there were things about you that would hurt me."

I reached him. My bare toes knocked against his polished shoes. "I love you anyway."

His chin curled, but he only stared at me.

"You don't need to be perfect, because you're perfect for me." I took a handful of his shirt. "So, I'll take the good with the bad."

He made a sound in the back of his throat, then leaned down and kissed me. Grabbed me by my nape and kissed me as though he could wipe the slate clean with sweeps of his tongue. My lips bruised against his mouth.

I kissed him back.

Kissed him as if it was the last time.

He walked me backward until my knees hit the bed.

I pushed against his chest. "No."

"No?" His hands came off me as though I'd caught fire, the look on his face as though I'd just kneed him.

"No," I said again and found balance on my feet. "You asked me once how I knew I loved you." I ran my hand down my stomach. "How I knew that it wasn't just this."

I cupped myself.

His fists closed at his sides.

"I know because as tempting as it is to lose myself in what you make me feel, as lost as I already am, I want to know all of you." I took his fist and held it between my hands. "I want to love you with my eyes open."

His hand opened between mine, and he pushed his

fingers between the fingers on my right hand. "Do you really want to know?" He stared at our joined hands. "I'll give you that choice. Let you choose." His fingers flexed, squashed mine a little. "I'll tell you everything—put all my secrets in your hands."

I nodded and flicked my drying tongue between my battered lips. "Yes."

"It'll hurt more than you think it will." He pressed his lips to my knuckles, then rubbed them. "I could lie. Protect you. Make you happy. It'd be nicer."

"I've had enough nice. I want real."

He caught my gaze, held me there with it. "Very well." He let go of my hand, held my waist and just stared at me. "Tell me you love me."

"*I love you.*" The words ground, raspy and raw, from my throat.

His chest rose, then fell. "One more time."

"I love you."

"Come then," he said, and touched my bottom lip with his thumb. "Come and see all the things I have done."

TWENTY-SEVEN

HE LED ME to the bowels of the yacht. Down to a place that could only be for maintenance, into an area we had to crawl inside. I breathed in the stagnant, metallic air.

Haithem opened a cupboard and pulled out a beaten tin toolbox.

I wasn't sure what I'd expected him to show me. A dungeon full of slaves or some other heinous discovery.

Not an old toolbox that wasn't even big enough for the most modest pirate's booty.

We went upstairs to our cabin. He set the toolbox on the table.

Queasiness rose in my belly.

Because now my mind raced with possibilities. Tried to explore all the monstrous things one might hide in a toolbox.

He flicked the latch.

The box creaked open with a groan.

I stepped closer, peered inside.

The contents shocked me—truly they did.

Tools.

All kinds.

How unexpected.

A hammer, screwdrivers, pliers, a wrench. Others I didn't know the names of, because let's face it—I wasn't exactly a carpenter's apprentice.

He moved the larger tools aside and fished a large box of nails from the bottom. My heart beat faster.

Perhaps the tools were to pry up the tiles, floor-boards, wall panels or whatever, and get to wherever he'd stashed his secrets.

He opened the box of nails—and slid out a black device the size of a pack of cards.

I stepped into his side, staring at the object.

He held the device out to me, and I took it.

This was *it*.

The big secret.

I turned the box over in my hand. "What is it?"

"What do think it is?"

I glanced at him then back at my hands. The smooth surface cooled my palm. A bit like aluminum but perhaps sturdier. I turned the box and looked at the end. There was a finger groove. I pressed my index finger-nail to the groove and slid it open.

A counter flashed a series of numbers.

"Holy fuck." My hand shook in an effort not to drop it. "Is this an explosive?"

"No," he said, a frown sweeping across his face. He turned the device over and opened the other end. "Try again."

A plug, similar to the one in the center of my lap-top charger.

"An adapter?" I looked back at the counter. "It measures something?"

"Closer," he said.

"Contains something?" I looked back at the plug. "A portable charger?"

Haithem smiled, although it didn't reach his dark eyes. "Almost. It's a self-replenishing energy cell."

I glanced at Haithem, and suddenly everything clicked into place. "Self-replenishing, as in it doesn't run out?"

"No, Angel, it doesn't run out." He took the device. "It's a whole new energy technology."

"Oh my god," I said, watching him slide one end closed. "So, it's like a battery that lasts forever."

The end closed with a soft click. "Not forever—like all technology, it has a life expectancy." He closed the other end. "Ten years, fifteen at most for this."

He laid it on the table, and my mind whirled. The little black box looked way too innocent for something so revolutionary.

"What can it actually power?" I gasped. "Could it power a car?"

"This particular cell," he said, touching the top, "could power a hospital or a large shopping mall."

Excitement sizzled in my blood.

I'd expected ugly secrets, not an epic treasure.

How could something so small be so powerful?

"Should we be handling it?" I asked.

Haithem's lips curved. "It's perfectly safe."

I glanced back at the innocent-looking device. So much energy in one place had to be volatile. "What if I smashed it with that?" I pointed to the hammer on the table. "What would happen then?"

"If you smashed it with a hammer, it would break." He moved the hammer, placing the tools back in the toolbox. "Break...and no longer work. Not break and explode."

I pushed my hair behind my ear. "This is insane."

"The insane part is that I'm five months away from being able to mass-produce these." His voice grew lighter. "In a year, I can have one of these in every home in Australia and the United States for the price of a new smartphone."

I glanced from the energy cell to Haithem, the full impact sinking in.

My heart lifted.

Five months.

Now I understood.

Why had I been so worried some terrible thing was happening?

"Three years and I can supply the world. Five, and I'll have a modified version for all automobiles on the open market."

Automobiles.

Replacing fuel.

"I can't imagine how valuable this must be…" My heart skipped. "There must be people who'd kill to get their hands on it." *Click, click, click.* "That's why you were so secretive. Everyone must want it?"

"No." Haithem turned to me fully. Looked right down at me. "This isn't valuable—it's invaluable." His voice grew so cold it could have frosted the windows. "I'm not worried about the people who'd kill to have it." He took me by both arms. "What worries me are all the people who are desperate to ensure no one ever has access to it."

The chill seeped into my heart, freezing it for a moment.

"The ones who'd do anything to destroy it." His eyelids hooded. "Kill me, you, anyone who'd ever heard of it and anyone who they ever even thought had."

My pulse came rushing back with a vengeance.

He hadn't simply handed me his secret.

He'd handed me power.

Knowledge that could kill him.

He trusted me that much—with his life.

I pressed myself forward and hugged him. "Do you know what this means, Haithem?" Tears welled. "You're saving the world."

I loosened my grip on his middle to look up at him and grin. "You're a real-life Captain Planet."

Haithem's features clamped tight, and he pried my arms from around him. "No." He backed away from me and dragged the empty nail box closer and fished inside. "This, Angelina, was the hero."

He handed me a small photo.

Haithem, younger, softer, with a man who was a shorter, grayer, broader version of himself.

"My father spent his life working for this."

I held the image closer.

The Haithem in the photo smiled freely.

"His greatest dream was that his legacy would become my legacy."

I glanced up from the photo.

"But do you know what I was doing instead of working with him on what I thought of as a fruitless pipe dream?"

I frowned, seeing something on his face I'd not seen before. Something I recognized from my own life—guilt.

"I was off making my fortune halfway across the world." A snarl moved to his lips. "And make it, I did. With gadgets and apps and useless things that make our privileged lives more entertaining."

He took the edge of the photo and tugged it from my fingers.

"The day I returned home for my mother's fiftieth birthday, my father and I worked together for the last time. I saw the problems he'd been too close to see, and we finished it together." He rubbed the photo with his thumb, then pushed it into his shirt pocket. "He'd asked me so many times to come home and work with him, but even though I had his scientific brain—my heart was all business, all greed."

My breaths sped up.

His pain was palpable. I wanted to reach out to him, touch him, but I wouldn't stop him speaking. Not this man who so rarely spoke. Not like this.

He stepped back, picked up the empty nail box. "That night, I flew back to resume my business in the States, excited at the new possibilities for us." He put the energy cell back inside the box. "But I understood greed well enough to appreciate the need to proceed delicately."

He looked down, his fist closing around the box. "Father didn't understand. Greed wasn't his thing. Sharing knowledge was." He moved again and slid the nail box into the back of the toolbox. "They were dead within the week."

The toolbox closed with a slam.

"This only exists because my father entrusted his research to me. Knew I was the one who'd bring it to life. Because I was the one with the resources to be careful and the cunning to prevail." He finished his tale, his voice brittle and cracked.

"It's not your fault, Haithem." I stepped forward and touched his arm. "It is not your fault that bad people did bad things."

The full, devastating power of his gaze landed on me. "But what about the terrible things I have done?"

My chest felt as though I'd breathed smog, something poisonous creeping into my lungs.

His voice grew soft again yet still as insidious. "My love, you said you wanted to love me with your eyes wide-open." He moved to the wardrobe and collected his briefcase. The locks popped open with a snap. He removed a file thick as a magazine and laid it on the table. "So open it. I'm no spandex-covered hero."

He slid the file toward me.

"What is this?"

I stared at the folder.

"It's the full, ugly truth of who I am and what I will do, Angelina."

Now this file, this was the thing I knew would explode if I touched it.

I didn't want to touch it.

What could it give me?

I tore my gaze from the file and looked at Haithem.

Every cord in his neck stood up, and his eyes were wide and blazing. I'd seen him angry but never like this. Because this wasn't anger or even pain. This was fear—the kind you feel when everything essential to you is about to be torn away.

I knew. I'd experienced this kind of fear before.

For Haithem to be afraid?

It had to be something worthy of terror.

And I was terrified.

Terrified my heart was about to experience failure after weeks of such ups and downs. Terrified that I'd

come to the limits of what I could take. Terrified that
the one thing I'd allowed to become essential to me was
about to be annihilated.

TWENTY-EIGHT

"TAKE IT," HE SAID.

I didn't want to take it any more than I'd want to pick up a live snake. But I did. I slid it to the edge of the table and opened the cover.

A disc rested on top of the pile. I pushed it aside, picked up the paper on top. It took me a moment to decipher the image. *Haithem*.

His profile, captured—although grainy—on some kind of security camera.

"I don't understand what this is."

He pressed a hand to the table. "You will."

I picked up the next paper. Another picture of Haithem, this one superimposed next to a different image.

I scanned the page and recognition hit. "This is me the day we met—after the elevator." I read the line of text at the top of the printout. "This is from a news site?"

He didn't answer.

"Why are there pictures of us on the news?" I looked back at the images. "Are you wanted by authorities?"

"I'm not the one the authorities are looking for—not really." He straightened.

My neck twitched.

I grabbed the next sheet in the pile.

This one was me.

So was the next.

All me.

Pictures of me.

"Why am I news?" I dropped the papers and rifled through the pile.

Headlines.

Missing girl—The Disappearance of Angelina Morrison—Mayor's Daughter Vanishes.

Articles.

Lines and lines of texts that I was shaking too much to read.

"Why do people think I'm missing?" I grabbed an article, pulling breath into my lungs. "You emailed my parents."

He rounded the table.

"You emailed my parents, and they emailed back."

He stood in front of me and lifted his jaw.

"Yes, you did—you did send it." A sob caught in my chest. "You told me all the horrible things my mother said." I shook the papers at him. "Why would you say that if it was a lie?"

I looked at the papers in my hands and cried.

"It wasn't safe to send anything that could lead back here." He stepped closer, his hand out. "Not when you'd already been reported missing."

I stepped away from his touch. "But you lied to me— why lie to me?" I stared at him. There was still a chance. Still a chance he could explain. Maybe I'd misunderstood. He wouldn't do this to me. "Why say all those things?"

"I couldn't let you go until I could make sure I'd be able to get the prototype to the manufacturing plant without being intercepted." He closed the space between us. "You had to be here for two more weeks. I wasn't sure who you were, and I didn't want to have to hold you prisoner. I didn't want you to fight every moment."

I barely heard his explanations.

"Do you have any idea what they must be thinking?" I wiped my face on my wrist. My gaze caught on another headline. A sob halted midway up my throat.

I picked up the news printout.

"Homicide detectives calling for…" I glanced up. "Homicide?"

Finally, his expression cracked.

Guilt—remorse.

Too little, too late.

"It's the common assumption in these cases…" he whispered.

My heart clenched as though a fist ripped through my chest and squeezed it.

"No, no, no—" I panted, dropping the papers. The room spun. "They can't think that. Not them. Not after everything…"

I slipped, and he grabbed me around the waist.

I cried. Cried so loud, it echoed. Cried so hard, my body shook. Cried words I didn't understand.

And I let him hold me. Damn him, no matter how much I hated him, I couldn't push him away. Didn't have the strength for it.

I only had the strength to purge.

I burned out quickly. Sobs drained to hiccups.

I pushed away from him and breathed. "I have to get home. I have to let them know—" I glanced at Haithem. "What time do I leave tomorrow?"

"Angel…" He shook his head, then bent down and sorted through the printouts, coming up with one. "Don't you know what this means?"

I looked at the image, the one of him and me next to each other.

"Don't you understand what it means to be publicly linked to me?"

I went numb.

I couldn't feel my hands. With numbness came clarity. I understood now, why he'd let his secrets free. Not because he trusted me, as my heart willed me to assume.

He planned to keep me.

Keep me locked up tighter than that treasure of his.

I couldn't tell any secrets, because there'd be no one to hear them.

"I won't be going home, will I?"

The way his features stiffened told me all I needed to know.

I didn't think I could hurt more.

But I could.

I wrapped my arms around my middle, my stomach a malignant mess of pain, and tore my gaze from him.

He'd lied to me.

Been lying to me this whole time.

Perhaps about everything.

Perhaps about his feelings for me.

Could he fake the way he looked at me? The way he held me? The way he fucked me?

He was a master player. Could I have been so willfully blind? There'd been signs. I'd feared this before. Maybe I'd never understood how all this worked. Maybe I couldn't recognize true devotion because I'd never really had it.

All my certainties shattered. I'd been certain. Now everything I believed, everything I knew, balanced on a pinpoint.

"Did you ever love me?" I whispered.

"Yes." He said it without pause. Without taking a breath.

Like someone telling the truth.

But then, I'd experienced his skillful deception.

"I don't believe you," I said, and reached behind me for the table, one arm still wrapped around my middle.

"I love you."

I shook my head. "This isn't love." Tears rolled again. "This isn't what love does."

"I know," he said. "I warned you I'm not good, that I wouldn't do the right things." His voice was like sandpaper on my soul. "I warned you not to cultivate my feelings."

He came closer, and I couldn't move away.

"I told you not to fall for me. I tried to stay away."

I held on to the table, staring at the surface. The heat of his body, so close yet not touching, warmed my side.

"But you wouldn't leave me be."

I shut my eyes. *Truth.* If only this much from him.

"You sought me out. You demanded my touch. You stole my heart."

Each new truth hit me with another stab to the guts. I had no words to deny any of it.

His shirt grazed my elbow.

"But this is all my fault—and you should hate me—because I never should have brought you here."

He touched me, finally, a hand on my arm.

A reassurance I hated and craved.

"But I saw you on the docks that day."

His words were a tug on my brain, yanking a thread of realization through the agony. He'd seen me? This entire time I'd been here because he'd suspected me of being after his secret.

"I couldn't take the chance you weren't who you appeared to be." He'd come after me not because I was irresistible but because he thought I was something I'm not.

My fists flew to my chest. I couldn't make the pain less. Couldn't hold my heart inside my body. "That's why you tracked me down. You never wanted me the way I wanted you."

He touched the hands I clasped. "You want proof I love you?"

I dragged my gaze back to him. Watched him speak.

"If I didn't care, I could have sent you home. Until today, you never had anything that could truly jeopardize me." His voice dropped an octave. "So I could have sent you on your way, and maybe, just maybe, no one would ever recognize that image of me. Maybe they'd never put it together."

I shivered, apprehension rolling across my skin.

"Maybe you *could* go home tomorrow. Your family gets you back. You slip right back into your life." His caress turned to a grip. "Maybe you'll be fine." Then he took my arms, made me face him. "But maybe you won't."

My heart beat like a death-metal band screamed and rattled in my chest.

"Maybe one night someone with questions breaks in your back door—like they broke in my parents' back door—and maybe no answers will satisfy them." He leaned toward me. "Then no one gets you back. Not ever again. Not your family. Not me." His features contorted, and his eyes shut for a pause. "That's why I told you that you don't want my love. Because I'm that self-ish. I won't give you the choice."

"What choice do I get then?" I waited for him to answer me. This man who'd given me the kind of freedom I'd never known. I waited for him to take it all away.

He pulled me in, looked down into my eyes. "You get to choose me."

My chest touched his. My skin flared to life. My body, soul and heart such hopeless traitors.

"Or not..." he said, and for the first time since knowing him, I saw him hesitate.

He led me to the window and pulled back the curtain.

I looked outside. I hadn't noticed the yacht had stopped moving.

A large land mass lay outside. Mountainous and vegetated. Not huge but not tiny, either. Not like the island he'd taken me to before.

The island where I'd first bared my soul and let him take it.

I stared at the beach. A large white building covered with vast expanses of windows rested a third of the way up the incline of a hill. "What is this?"

"This island is rented through one of my companies, untraceable to me."

I glanced from the window to him.

"You're free to stay here for the next five months, never having to look at me again." He stared at the island. "It's fully staffed. You'd have everything you need." His Adam's apple moved. "Once distribution begins, there will be no stopping me, and then it will be safe for you to go home."

He turned to me. "You can leave me," he said. "I'll still protect you. I always will."

The pain in my stomach exploded into my chest.

How was it possible that this could break my heart even more—that he'd let me leave. I should be grateful for this one healthy gift—but all I could think was *please don't let me go.*

His expression changed.

My old Haithem, the one who played to win, rose up through the pain to stake his claim. "Remember what you said to me, Angelina?"

His voice swam like satin over naked skin—tantalizing. "You said you knew me—that you'd take my good and my bad."

His words wrapped around me, and I did remember my vow.

"You swore you'd pay the price for our love…"

My head swam, and I felt those very words on my lips as clearly as the moment I'd said them. Fantasy and reality converged like flames hitting water, leaving me trapped in a boiling mist, where fantasy and reality were one and the same.

EPILOGUE

LONG FINGERS CLOSE around my throat. Not squeezing, not hurting, but commanding. I look at him. This man I love. This devil I adore. He's gorgeous—dark hair, darker eyes, olive skin, body and features all chiseled hardness. But that's not what makes my veins jump under his hand. That's not what makes my skin slick with sweat.

There's more to this man than meets the eye.

His thumb strokes my pulse, gleaning secrets right out of my blood. His mouth curls to the side, forming a smile that reveals he knows exactly what I'm thinking.

"Didn't I warn you, Angel," he says, and his thumb moves up to my chin, "that it's not a good idea to love me?"

My pulse leaps from erratic to chaotic. I can't answer, only listen in horrified fascination to what I know will come next.

He traces the groove below my bottom lip. "Didn't I warn you my love would be bad?"

Shivers run hot then cold over my skin.

"Didn't I tell you, you'd pay for my heart?" He touches my mouth, dragging my bottom lip down.

My body sings, my blood hums right down to my womb. I can't resist him. He did warn me. He truly did. But I was greedy. I wanted him anyway.

I didn't understand how bad he could be.

He's the devil. Tempting me with what I desire most.

Luring me to an irresistible destruction. A destruction I'm so close to I can smell it—taste it—touch it. Pain grips me, my insides bruise with it. My family believes I'm dead. The life I've left behind lies in tatters because of him. Because he keeps me.

He won't let me go.

He tilts my face, brushing his cheek against my ear. "I promise it will be worth it." His stubble chafes my earlobe, stinging and electrifying. I've felt those bristles scrape against my neck, my breasts, my thighs. There's not an inch of me that hasn't felt the sweet torture of their abrasion. "Can't you see it?" he asks. "The future where you're mine?"

My eyelids drift shut. I know it's only the hand cradling my face that's holding me up. I *can* see that future. I see it with fluorescent intensity. Life with the lights turned on. Life where living means more than existing. For everything he's taken from me, he's given me back more. He breathed a soul back into me. Without it, without him, I'd be a walking corpse.

I see our future. I ache for it, yearn for it, despise myself for it.

"Say it, Angel. Say, Haithem, I'm yours."

For all intents and purposes, I'm a prisoner—captive—perhaps even a slave. Because I have no choices but the ones he gives me. Yet, he gives me this choice—or at least the illusion of a choice—to choose him.

To love him.

As if making a choice had ever been an option. The moment I met him, I may as well have been branded.

The days and weeks since I've known him flow through my memory like a song. Each moment a lyric in time. Each word soldered into my heart. I see him for the first time with eyes wide-open.

Giver and taker.

A symphony of complexities—man of generosity and greed, cruelty and kindness.

The man I love.

Villain and hero.

The man who took me apart and put me together again—over and over.

I feel all the danger, all the fear, all the pain—pain sharp like a blade cutting right through my scar tissue. I feel it all. Sensations packed one on top of the other, cramming into me.

The hope, the joy, the need, the love.

It all flows in, and in, and in, filling me until my skin could tear.

I hope that it will.

That I'll burst and the skin will peel right off me. Then I'll be who I am. It all keeps coming, and it hurts. Hurts bad and good and I swallow every last drop of it like some obscene glutton.

Because under it all is one undeniable truth.

Haithem is mine.

I fought for him. I won him. I earned him.

All of him.

I knew it from the moment we first joined together, his body in mine, that there was no longer he or I, only us.

He hurt me to save me—and I'd hurt to save him.

He is mine, and I am his.

I press my hand over the one holding my cheek and raise my chin.

"Haithem," I say finally, "I'm yours."

* * * * *

*Haithem and Angelina's story concludes in
DIDN'T YOU PROMISE, available June 2016.*

*Turn the page for an excerpt from
DIDN'T YOU PROMISE by Amber Bardan,
available June 2016 at all participating e-retailers.*

*Available June 2016 from Carina Press
and Amber Bardan*

*He has only one choice. He's promised to protect her.
And Haithem always keeps his promises.*

*Read on for an excerpt from
DIDN'T YOU PROMISE*

ONE

February

I LOOKED ACROSS the bed to where he stood placing clothes into a brown leather bag. He glanced up, caught my gaze, and smiled. His lips rose on one side, and deep grooves buried into his cheek. My lungs burned. No matter how many times I saw that smile it stole my breath.

I grinned back.

Haithem smiled wider, crinkles fanning his eyes. The sun shone orange in the window behind him. Lit up the black of his hair with a warm undertone.

Click, click, click.

I captured the moment. Not only because he looked magnificent—like a scene torn from a magazine—for the first time since I'd met him wearing blue jeans, making casual look formal. Paired with a black T-shirt, he should've looked nondescript. That's what we were going for after all. I don't think he realized how impossible that would be—like asking water not to look wet. You can't disguise the essence of what something is, and everything about Haithem commanded attention. I captured the moment because in that one instant nothing had ever been so simple or so pure.

Haithem and I, and nothing but *us*.

No more secrets, no more lies and, no matter how

much it hurt, everything between us was honest—and with that honesty we were untouchable.

Except, in a few short hours we would leave the bubble of our secret little world, and I had no idea what waited for us outside.

He'd warned me it'd be dangerous.

I wasn't afraid of danger. I'd learned that everything worthwhile carried risk. I'd sacrificed enough already to prove that. Changing the world wouldn't be easy but we were about to do just that. Not with guns, weapons, or explosives. Not with words, or politics, or diplomacy.

With technology.

Technology capable of saving the planet. Technology people would kill to have, and kill *us* to destroy.

He went back to packing, laying the last of his clothes in the bag.

My man wasn't only beautiful, wasn't only strong, or powerful, or brave—he was brilliant.

Somehow he was mine.

That simple fact was more frightening than whatever came next. He was mine, and I held thunder in my hands, with no idea how to hold on to something so mighty.

He left the bedroom and went into his adjoining office, reappearing with a small stack of books. I tucked my toiletries case into the side of my own bag. Haithem set the books one next to the other on top of his clothes.

"Only the necessities, ha?"

He pushed on top of the books. "These are necessities."

I crawled across the bed, kneeled in front of his bag and picked up the thickest volume. "Aristotle?" I looked up. Don't know what I'd expected. *The Art of War*? *How to Conquer the World*, possibly?

"Philosophy?"

He met my eye, daring me to tease him.

"Didn't take you for a philosopher."

He pushed the bag aside and leaned his palm on the mattress beside me. "Then obviously you've never read Aristotle."

"Maybe I should." I stared at the book in my hand, and flipped open the pages, dog-eared with pencil marks in the margins, at odds with the meticulously neat Haithem I knew.

I stopped and read out a highlighted line. "Courage is the first of human qualities because it is the quality which guarantees the others." I smirked and looked up. "Now I think I see…"

"You think so, do you?"

I forgot the book in my hands for a heartbeat, lost in the tone of his voice and the way he watched me. He always watched me, but sometimes at times like this he made me believe there was text written across my soul that only he could read. That he had access to secrets I didn't even know I kept.

I took a breath and broke from his gaze, then flipped through the book, pausing at a tagged page. Pencil left a thick smudge under a line. "To the query 'What is a friend?' his reply was—" I cleared my throat, voice getting sticky. "—'A single soul dwelling in two bodies.'"

I stared at the page, and re-read the words.

He tugged the book from my hands, closed it and put it back in the bag. The zip slid closed with a slow whine, and the vibration seemed to echo up my spine.

"You told me once that we were friends." I looked at him. "Tell me again."

He tugged the bag off the bed and rested it on the floor, then turned and fixed his attention on me. My skin heated, warming around me. He leaned over me, hands resting either side of my hips.

I breathed deep. Breathed in him. His strong yet subtle scent. He didn't touch me, yet I felt touched.

"Angelina, you are my friend." He raised a hand. Finally he did touch me—his fingers resting on my cheek, his thumb brushing my lower lip. "You are my heart." The rough pad of his thumb dragged across my mouth then pressed against my chin. "And now you are my family too."

My chest tightened around my lungs, squeezed out air and made my head spin. I grabbed his T-shirt, curling my hands around cotton. "I love you."

His eyes flashed from warm to hot.

He kissed me, mouth open over mine, searing and claiming. I pressed my tongue into his mouth, tasted and took him. Desire woke in my abdomen, rising through me like a flame. A sleeping ember waiting for his breath to bring it to life.

I pulled him closer in attempts to drag him over me.

He broke our kiss, but rested his cheek on my cheek. "There's no time for me to love you the way I need to." His fingers clutched the back of my neck. "But hold on to this, because when I do I swear it will be worth the wait."

His promise seeped into my skin—settled anticipation into my bones I wouldn't be able to shake until he fulfilled it. Bless him, because now I had something else to occupy my mind outside of what we were about to do. Maybe he did that on purpose—knowing him, he did.

Didn't make me any less excited.

He pulled away. "It's time to go."

I swallowed, then rolled off the bed and did up my bag. Haithem passed behind me and took something from the wardrobe.

"You ready?"

I turned and nodded.

He held what looked like a small stocking out to me. I took it and walked into the bathroom and stared in the mirror. My hair had already been pinned back, but now I stretched the beige cap over my head and watched my old self disappear.

Disappear behind the tan that only weeks on a yacht had managed to achieve on skin that usually only came in two shades—pale or burned. Disappear behind expensive clothes I'd never have owned, and never have worn—a white belted dress with a high lace neckline.

Disappear behind eyes that weren't my own. Contacts bled the pale green of my eyes into hazel.

I leaned closer to the mirror and stuck two strips of tape to my hairline, then took the mop of dark brown hair off the foam head resting on the vanity and pulled the wig onto my scalp from the back to the front, then adjusted the hair, and pressed over the tape. I combed back the hair with a brush. The bangs settled into place around my face and shoulders, just as wonder settled into my bones. Someone else stared back from the mirror. Someone with my bone structure but little else.

Someone older, sexier, and sleeker.

My ears rang. My heart beat faster than it should.

I should be afraid, shouldn't I?

That I'd lost myself. Given myself up for someone else. That was wrong wasn't it? To sacrifice your identity? Maybe I should've been ashamed, or worried. Yet my heart raced not with fear—but with thrill.

I'd shed a skin that never actually fit.

The lid on my world had been lifted. I smiled at the woman in the mirror, then left the bathroom.

Haithem glanced up from the screen of his phone, then tucked it into his back pocket and walked to me. His gaze scanned me, but not as it usually did. Not with desire and hidden meanings to be untangled.

He analyzed me.

Looked me over, up and down, searching for flaws in our disguise.

"Do I pass?"

He moved closer. "I'd rather just keep you on this yacht."

I laughed softly.

"What?"

"I just felt the feminist part of me develop a tic."

His forehead wrinkled but the side of his mouth kicked up. "That's not what I meant."

"I know," I whispered, even if maybe there were a few scenarios in which being *kept* didn't sound so bad.

He touched my brow with his index finger. "I'm concerned."

I lay my palm on his chest and stroked over his heart through fabric. I was learning to speak Haithem. Knew what *concerned* translated to. Knew that words like *worried*, or *afraid*, were not ones he could wrap his tongue around.

"Don't worry about me. We have this."

He rubbed my eyebrow the wrong way. "These give you away."

"Too light?" I touched my other brow.

He smiled. "Too ginger."

"I am *not* ginger." I smacked his hand away. "It's chestnut—auburn at the most."

"If you say so." He held up his hand in surrender. Pity his eyes didn't say surrender. "But I happen to like ginger-chestnut-auburn no matter how you call it."

My cheeks warmed, but not in the way they usually did when people used to talk about my hair. He didn't know over time I'd darkened to this shade. That as a kid I'd been adequately ginger enough to suffer the classroom ribbing that comes along with being at all different. It didn't really matter anymore, and I hadn't really known it'd still been a sore spot. What I did know was that Haithem's compliment made me hot.

That despite all logic, I loved everything about him too.

"Do you have your makeup case?"

I nodded then went to the bathroom and collected the case of cosmetics not essential enough to make it into my travel bag, and set it on the table. Haithem opened the case and rummaged through the contents, coming up with a dark brown eyeliner.

"Come closer," he said.

I stepped in, drawn by the rumble of his voice more than what he'd said. As always the simplest things he did, the most casual words, turned me inside out. Made me read carnal implications into the most mundane things. I don't know where this part of me had hidden before I met him. This must be what people meant when they talked about soul-mates—someone you're so connected to that they affect you on a cellular level.

He popped the lid off the eyeliner.

I knew what he planned to do. Yet I still fought the urge to remove my clothes in the hopes this was some kinky new drawing game.

"Close your eyes."

My core burst with heat.

Close my eyes?

Now that was not fair.

Something dirty had better happen. I shut my eyes. He held my chin, his thumb and forefinger gentle, but firm enough to remind me he touched me.

I breathed in.

Big mistake.

His scent filled my mouth, close enough to taste his cologne. My head swirled; it hit me like speed, or acid. Quickening blood, pounding heart, and a wild electric energy zinging just under my surface. I had to wonder what they were putting in cologne these days.

The fingers on my chin squeezed.

I didn't need to open my eyes to know he saw it—my desire. Betrayed by my open lips and shaking breath. Something pointy touched my eyebrow.

He wasn't deterred. Wasn't distracted by my lust.

But he knew it was there, his grip betrayed *him*.

I tried not to smile.

The pencil brushed across my brow in small sweeps. He paused, and then the point pressed against my other brow.

He stopped and rotated my face from side to side.

I opened my eyes. He watched my brows, a look of concentration biting grooves into his forehead. He placed the pencil into the case and pulled out an eye shadow palette.

"I'm surprised you know your way around a makeup case so well."

His attention moved from the case and he met my gaze.

There was no saving these panties now. I flooded. He'd been focused not unaffected. Now he didn't conceal his desire. His expression a warning of the kind of fucking I had coming.

I gripped the edge of the table.

I remembered what happens when you make a man like Haithem wait. You'd think it'd be fast, rough punishment. When I'd first met him that's what I'd thought of him. That he was the kind of man that took what he wanted by *any* means. A man who punished those who didn't comply with his demands. Not so, well, kinda— he could be rough. He could be demanding. But the few times he'd had to wait?

Perhaps you could call it punishment.

Because anticipation made him all the more determined to enjoy every-single-pulsing-moment. Made him focused. Made him draw things out, take me apart over and over until I didn't know how I'd fit back together again. The man was a freak that way.

He was a freak in many ways. For one he'd just told me with a look more than most people could articulate in an entire conversation. More than most people would be bold enough to communicate to someone else. He opened the palette and swirled a thin brush in a matte brown shadow, then filled in my brows. I watched him. Watched the concentration he could muster play out in the tension on his jaw and the narrowing of his eyes.

He put the shadow and brush back in the case and stared at me again.

"Okay now?"

"Almost." His fingers moved to the back of my neck.

Oh, thank god.

I shut my eyes and let my head fall back.

Air fanned my brows, tickling and electrifying my skin. His warm breath blew against my eyelids. I gasped, and gripped his T-shirt.

"Tell me your name."

I blinked, the blunt beautiful features above me coming into focus. "Angel—"

"Not that one."

My skin prickled. I knew what he wanted. We'd been through this enough times.

"Lina Kyriakou."

He walked into me, his hips touching mine, forcing me backwards. "And who are you, Lina?"

My back brushed the wall, the surface cool through the light fabric on my back.

I moistened my lips, my pulse fluttering so fiercely in my throat I almost expected to start spitting out butterflies. He'd coaxed me to say it before—the details of this first scenario.

My favorite of all the scenarios and plans we'd memorized.

Still the words made my tongue stick. I looked at him. Looked right into his midnight irises.

"I'm your wife."

Don't miss
DIDN'T YOU PROMISE by Amber Bardan
Available June 2016 wherever
Carina Press ebooks are sold.

www.CarinaPress.com

ACKNOWLEDGMENTS

FIRSTLY, THANK YOU to my husband. Without your support there would be no books. Thank you for being an awesome, capable father to our children and making my dreams possible.

Thank you to our parents, the grandparents of our kids, for always helping out when deadlines are near—and generally always. I owe a very extra-special thanks to my sister Melissa, for being my first reader, first beta reader, first fan and for making me believe in this story. This will always be our special book and your enthusiasm and excitement are what brought it to life.

I'm very thankful for my dear friend Dani—you've been my guru and Yoda, and without your guidance there'd be no writerly force with me.

Thank you to my agent, Laura Bradford, for your tireless dedication and for being delightful.

To everyone at Harlequin Australia and Carina Press, thank you for being wonderful and for giving this series the perfect home. It has been a sheer privilege working with my editors, Angela, Annabel and Kate—thank you for your savvy insights and helping make this book the best it can be.

Thanks to all my lovely friends at Melbourne Romance Writers Guild and also Romance Writers of Australia for making this journey an even greater one. Especially thank you to the beautiful Melanie from

Sassy Mum Book Blog, not only for all your support with promotion but for being a terrific friend. Thank you to Kristy from Book Addict Mumma for your advice and support, which are always appreciated.

My dear critique partners Eden Summers and Tracey Alvarez, thank you for the many hours of critiquing and cheerleading. Your support has meant so much.

This writing gig can be lonely—thank you to all my virtual friends. Connecting with you keeps me sane and grounded. Thanks to everyone who has taken the time to leave messages, reviews, comments and tweets about my books. Your words mean everything.

**Also available from Amber Bardan
and Carina Press**

Didn't You Promise

ABOUT THE AUTHOR

AFTER SPENDING YEARS imagining fictional adventures, Amber finally found a way to turn daydreaming into a productive habit. She now spends her time in a coffee-fueled adrenaline haze writing thrillingly erotic romance.

She lives with her husband and children in semirural Australia, where if she peers outside at the right moment, she might just see a kangaroo bounce by.

Amber is an award-winning writer, Amazon best-selling author, and member of Romance Writers of Australia, Melbourne Romance Writers Guild and Writers Victoria.

You can find out more about Amber by visiting her website, *www.amberabardan.com*. Connect with Amber on Facebook at *Facebook.com/amberabardan* or Twitter at *Twitter.com/amberabardan*.